# The Ever After

Center Point
Large Print

Also by Sarah Pekkanen and available from Center Point Large Print:

*Catching Air*
*Things You Won't Say*
*The Perfect Neighbors*

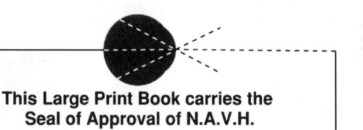

**This Large Print Book carries the
Seal of Approval of N.A.V.H.**

# The
# Ever After

a novel

## SARAH PEKKANEN

CENTER POINT LARGE PRINT
THORNDIKE, MAINE

This Center Point Large Print edition
is published in the year 2018 by arrangement with
Atria Books, a division of Simon & Schuster, Inc.

The text of this Large Print edition is unabridged.
In other aspects, this book may vary
from the original edition.
Printed in the United States of America
on permanent paper.
Set in 16-point Times New Roman type.

ISBN: 978-1-68324-905-4


Library of Congress Cataloging-in-Publication Data

Names: Pekkanen, Sarah, author.
Title: The ever after / Sarah Pekkanen.
Description: Center Point Large Print edition. | Thorndike, Maine :
    Center Point Large Print, 2016.
Identifiers: LCCN 2018023427 | ISBN 9781683249054
    (hardcover : alk. paper)
Subjects: LCSH: Domestic fiction. | Large type books. |
    BISAC: FICTION / Contemporary Women. | FICTION / Family Life. |
    FICTION / General.
Classification: LCC PS3616.E358 E94 2016 | DDC 813/.6—dc23
LC record available at https://lccn.loc.gov/2018023427

*For Sarah Cantin*

# Chapter One

So this is how you discover your husband is having an affair, Josie Moore thought.

She stared through the windshield of her Toyota Sienna, toward the glass door of their neighborhood Starbucks. Inside, her husband, Frank, was swirling two packets of sugar into his latte and a generous sprinkle of cinnamon into hers. In the backseat, their three-and-a-half-year-old daughter, Isabella, dozed with her head lolling sideways, and their seven-year-old, Zoe, played on a Nintendo DS.

Josie gripped Frank's iPhone more tightly in her hand.

If she were better organized, she might never have found out, Josie realized. But she was forever leaving something behind.

An hour or so ago, when they'd left to run errands and drop Zoe off at a birthday party, she'd been grateful that she'd remembered the wrapped gift and a packet of fruit gummies to bribe Izzy to stay contained in her seat.

What Josie had forgotten was her cell phone. It was probably on the kitchen counter; she remembered setting it there when she'd gone to grab the gummies. But even though they'd driven only a few blocks by the time she'd realized it was missing, she hadn't asked Frank to circle back. He'd masterfully wrangled Izzy into her seat as she'd arched her little back in protest—he'd sung "Mary Had a Little Lamb" but substituted in "rhinoceros," which had made her giggle and relax—and it didn't seem worth the effort.

Besides, Josie was with her husband and daughters, cocooned in the car they'd owned for six years, the one with Magic Tree House books tucked into the seat back pockets and Goldfish cracker crumbs wedged so deeply into seams that no vacuum cleaner could extract them. If an emergency occurred—if one of the people she loved most was hurt—she wouldn't need to be summoned by a phone call. She'd be right here.

Time was behaving strangely.

Josie felt as though she'd been suspended in this parking lot for hours, but surely only a few minutes had passed since Frank had dashed under that green awning and through the glass door.

Frank had been the one to suggest coffee. He'd asked what size latte she wanted as she dug through her purse, checking again even though she'd known it was futile. "Um, a Grande. No, just a Tall—I already had coffee this morning. Shoot, I forgot to order a refill on Izzy's EpiPen." They'd never needed to use the EpiPen, but after

Izzy had eaten a few almonds and developed hives, the pediatrician recommended they carry one. "Give me your phone, okay?"

Frank had already found a parking spot and had turned off the car engine by then. He'd paused, his hand on the door, one leg already out of the Sienna and planted on the pavement.

"My phone?" he'd repeated.

"Yeah. Her old EpiPen expired. I need to get her refill." She'd stretched out her palm.

Frank had frozen. Not for very long; just for the same amount of time as it had taken for her heart to contract in a single, powerful beat.

What happened next was curious: the day seemed to slam on its brakes, and Josie's senses grew acutely heightened, allowing her to notice and catalog minute details of everything that followed. Her skin prickled, and her heartbeat quickened.

She'd experienced this sensation a few times in the past, such as when a strange man had followed her onto an elevator and had stood too close, and another time when she'd found herself alone on a shadowy subway platform late at night.

Her brain was signaling a warning: *danger*.

She'd watched as Frank had begun to move again. He'd bent over his iPhone, shielding it from view. He tapped on the screen seven or eight times. Then he handed it to her.

"Here you go," he'd said, his words sounding rushed. "Venti, right?"

"Yeah . . . no . . . Tall," she'd said.

Frank's eyes had darted to the phone she was now holding. Zoe had sighed and rested her feet on the seat back in front of her. A crumpled brown napkin had teetered on the edge of the trash can next to the coffee shop entrance. Josie had taken it all in, feeling oddly numb.

She hadn't mentioned the sprinkle of cinnamon. After twelve years of marriage, he knew how she took her coffee.

"Want a cookie?" he'd asked. "Or, like . . . a, ah, a scone or anything?"

One of his legs was still out the door, but he'd seemed reluctant to leave.

"No," she'd said.

"You sure?" he'd asked. Then, without waiting for her reply, he'd climbed out and jogged into the shop.

The glass door she'd been staring at for the last five minutes pushed outward, but the person who emerged wasn't Frank. It was a woman holding a cardboard tray filled with drinks. She clicked a key fob at the Pathfinder nested next to their spot. Josie watched as the woman came closer, put her tray on her roof, then opened her vehicle's door. It clanked into the side of the Sienna.

The woman whipped around, her mouth making a little O of surprise. "I'm sorry!" she said, her

10

words carrying clearly through Josie's open window. "I hope I didn't dent it."

Josie waved her off. "No problem!" she said. "It's an old car!"

"Are you sure?" the woman asked.

"Absolutely," Josie said. She gave the woman a big smile, despite everything. Maybe because this was such an easy problem to solve.

She tried to think about what she should do next. When Frank returned, he'd want his iPhone. She wasn't going to give it back to him yet. But she didn't want to make a scene in front of the children.

What she should do is hide it, she decided. She started to tuck it in the console between their seats. But it would be too easy for Frank to find there. She bent down and pushed the phone beneath her seat, then drew in her legs, so that even if it began to slide out, her feet would block it.

"Why is Dad taking so long?" Zoe whined. "I'm going to miss the party."

"You're not going to miss the party," Josie said evenly. If this were any other day, she might have answered in a tone of reassurance, or perhaps one of annoyance, depending on how stressful the morning had been. But now she felt herself gathering inward. Her voice contained no inflection, because that was what required the least amount of energy.

11

She could see Frank so clearly in her mind's eye: At this very moment, he was wearing a long-sleeved, dark gray shirt and jeans. Not a dressy shirt; it was the thick, comfortable kind that was good for yard work or for lounging on the couch watching football. He was five foot ten and broad-shouldered, with a booming voice and a full head of light brown hair. He didn't have great teeth; they were a bit crooked, and frankly, they could use whitening. And his nose was beaky. But his eyes had sucked her in from the moment they'd met at a mutual friend's party a few years after she'd graduated from college. They were the warm, rich shade of root beer. When they'd first fixed on her, she'd thought they were the kindest eyes she had ever seen.

Would her husband look different when he finally emerged through that glass door?

Would she?

When you had children, you made rules not only for them but also for yourself.

One of Josie's steadfast rules was: No fighting in front of the kids.

Bickering, sure. She and Frank squabbled over his driving (too fast) and hers (he felt she was too timid when it came to changing lanes). Like every other couple she knew, they argued over the thermostat setting. They debated which movies to see (he loved Woody Allen; she hated him, and had even before the whole marrying-his-almost-stepdaughter situation). They never could agree on which restaurant to choose on their rare date nights, or when was the right time to leave a dinner party, or whose fault it was that Zoe's school permission slip hadn't been signed.

Come to think of it, they bickered quite a lot.

The glass door opened. Frank approached the car. *Interesting,* Josie noted in a detached sort of way: he looked exactly the same.

"One Venti latte," Frank said, handing it to her with his crooked-teeth smile.

She accepted it without comment. Without meeting his eyes.

She saw Frank look at the empty cup holders, where they usually stuck their phones while driving. She saw him look down at Josie's lap. She turned to stare straight ahead.

He didn't ask for his phone back. It was another detail she cataloged.

*He knows that I know,* Josie thought.

"So, to the birthday party?" Frank asked. Josie nodded.

"It's at Sky Zone, right?" he said. This Josie ignored. Frank knew exactly where the party was. They'd discussed it before pulling in to get lattes.

She didn't want to speak to him, not at the moment. Nor did she want a sip of her latte. It all required too much energy, and on some instinctual level, she was aware she needed to stockpile hers for what was coming.

"Zoe Boey Boom-Ba-Booey," Frank suddenly burst into song. He banged his palms against the steering wheel, like it was a drum. "How's my girl?"

"Good," Zoe said, still focusing on her Nintendo DS.

"Why don't you put that away?" Frank suggested. He glanced at Josie out of the corner of his eye. She remained silent.

"Tell you what, after the party, how about I make a fire and we do a cookout dinner?" Frank suggested. "Get some hot dogs and marshmallows and roast them in the fireplace?"

Frank was good about making dinnertime fun, Josie noted, as if she were a judge considering a felon, weighing his character references. He made breakfast for supper, he created living room cookout nights, he bought dough from Trader Joe's and stretched out crazy shapes for the kids to decorate with sauce and cheese. "Circle pizzas are so last year," he'd say. "Here's a sunflower for you to decorate, madam."

Frank kept sneaking glances at her. He still hadn't asked about his phone.

He opened his mouth, then shut it. His hands tightened on the wheel. Zoe continued her game on her device. Izzy made a kind of grunting noise in her sleep.

14

Josie pressed her feet harder back and imagined she could feel the phone against her heels.

The email she wasn't meant to see was directly beneath a promotion from their local bookstore, offering a 15 percent off coupon. There was a new Thomas the Tank Engine book Izzy wanted, mostly because it came with a little track and toy train.

Josie had touched the wrong line.

There were so many ifs that could have changed the course of this day, and of her life, Josie thought as she watched the pavement disappear under the car's spinning wheels.

If her index finger had landed a few millimeters higher, she would be blithely sipping her latte right now and asking Frank to swing by the bookstore on the way home.

If Frank had been quicker in Starbucks—say, if that woman who'd ordered four drinks hadn't been ahead of him—he might have made it out to the car before she'd finished calling the pharmacy. She never would have glanced down at his email in-box, which had popped up when she'd closed the phone screen.

If Izzy had woken up before she'd touched the wrong line, if the pharmacist had put her on hold, if Zoe hadn't been silently engrossed in her game and instead had distracted her with a question . . .

Frank braked at a red light. He glanced at Josie, then reached for the radio and rapidly flipped through a half dozen stations before shutting it off. His posture was rigid.

The bookstore had sent that coupon to their house by snail mail, too, as part of a bigger flyer advertising new releases.

Josie had gotten the flyer just last week. She'd flipped through it and had pulled out the little plastic coupon. She'd meant to put the card in her wallet, but she'd forgotten it in the stack of mail they kept in a basket on the dining room table.

Josie was forever leaving things behind.

If need be, she thought, she was capable of leaving her husband behind.

# Chapter Two

"Don't you dare lie to me" were the first words Josie uttered.

They stood on opposite sides of the living room, separated by the coffee table, the one Josie had chosen because its edges were soft and wouldn't hurt a child who tripped. In the kitchen, their golden retriever, Huck, lay on the linoleum floor in a patch of warm sunlight. Zoe would be bouncing on trampolines and eating cake at the party for the next two hours. Izzy was upstairs, flopped on Josie and Frank's bed, watching Nickelodeon. Josie had made sure to turn the volume a few notches higher than usual and close the door.

Frank spread out his hands. "It was only a few emails," he said. His eyes were wide and scared-looking. "Just flirting. That's all it was."

She practically spat her response: "Bullshit."

How was she so certain? Josie wondered. The email from a woman named Dana hadn't referenced any clandestine meeting. There were other, older emails from Dana—Josie had spotted them as she'd scrolled through Frank's messages. But she hadn't read those. Not yet.

"Okay, okay," Frank said. Frank's eyes suddenly darted up and to the right, then shot back down to fix on Josie. "It was only kissing. It happened twice. That's all it was."

"It was more than kissing," Josie said, this time feeling less certain.

"Only kissing," Frank repeated.

"Don't say 'only'!" Josie nearly shrieked.

A chink formed in the thick wall holding back her emotions—just a tiny hole for her burst of fury to escape through before the wall resealed itself.

"I'm sorry, I'm sorry," Frank blurted. He stared at her as if she were a wild animal he'd encountered on a hiking trail.

Josie folded her arms across her chest.

"Twice," she said.

Frank nodded vigorously. "Twice. Kissing. That's all—I'm sorry, baby. I was drunk and it just— I'm so sorry."

In the corner of the living room, Izzy and Zoe had left a pile of toys. The living room was the one part of the house Josie tried to keep tidy, since it was not only so small, but also the first room people entered. Frank had promised to clean up those toys earlier today while she'd taken the girls out to buy the birthday present. Had he been emailing with Dana instead? Another hot wave of anger pulsed through, but Josie pushed it back behind the wall.

"Who is she?" Josie asked. She didn't know anyone named Dana.

"No one," Frank said quickly. "Just someone I met on a business trip."

He was lying, she was fairly certain. But about which parts?

His phone was now in the zippered cosmetics bag in her purse. She'd slipped it there while Frank was helping Izzy out of her seat. Her purse was currently hidden in the back of her closet so Frank couldn't tamper with the evidence. Frank wasn't the only one who could be sneaky, Josie had thought as she'd knelt on the floor of her closet, hiding her bag behind a stack of clothes she'd earmarked for Goodwill.

"You didn't clean up the toys," Josie noted.

Frank's eyes widened, then he dropped to his knees, as abruptly as if he'd been shot, and began scooping Bratz dolls and their accessories into his arms.

"I don't want you to do it *now*," Josie snapped.

He dropped the toys and stood up again without a word.

Was his sudden eagerness to please a troubling sign, perhaps an indication that things with Dana were more serious than Frank had admitted? One of the things Josie and Frank repeatedly bickered about was what she called his selective memory. He never forgot the NCAA Tournament schedule or a poker night with the guys. His mind grew more slippery, however, when it came to chores that inconvenienced him. He never leapt to do tasks the first time she asked; there was always a sigh and an "In a sec, hon."

But Frank was so good with the girls, Josie thought as she folded her arms and considered him. He was a wonderful father. He let them put butterfly clips in his hair and paint blue polish on his toes. He wrestled with them, coached Zoe's baseball team, and bought them toy trucks as well as tutus.

*The girls.*

Josie nearly doubled over.

*No,* she thought. She could not think about Zoe, with her gap-toothed smile, or Izzy's soft, pudgy hands. Josie would not forecast the future or make any decisions now. She fought for, then found, her equilibrium. She would stay right here, in the middle of this strange, stretched-out taffy afternoon, and gather evidence. She would remain apart from what was happening; she would stay in the role of the judge.

This morning, she'd been consumed with thoughts about getting to the grocery store, taking poor neglected Huck for a long walk— which would double as her own poor neglected exercise routine—and weeding through the stack of mail that accumulated every few days, paying the bills and tossing the junk.

Her discovery was an axe, cleaving away everything extraneous. All that mattered were the nine words in the email she'd seen on Frank's iPhone.

Frank was waiting for whatever she would do next. His eyes beseeched her: *Please. Please let's stop this. Please let's make it go away.*

She could choose to believe him. If he could stop this, she could make it go away.

She had practice, after all. Josie had believed him during those other times when her stomach had clenched like a fist and the rising hairs on the tops of her forearms had tried to warn her that she needed to pay attention. But she hadn't had any evidence back then. And she was a worrier; everyone knew that. What mother of young children wasn't? It came with the territory; danger lurked everywhere in the form of uncovered wall sockets and open stairwells and cars that drove too quickly down their street. So Josie had pushed away those unsettling feelings. She had chosen to believe her husband in the past. To believe in their marriage.

Maybe she should do that now. Perhaps he wasn't lying.

Only kissing, he'd said. Only two times.

His phone waited in the back of her closet.

If she retrieved it and handed it to him, Frank would delete the messages. He'd put a halt to the flirtation; Dana would dissolve away. Josie would pay more attention in the future, perhaps deliberately spot-checking his phone, or popping by his office unexpectedly. He'd be on notice.

Or she could climb the stairs and read through every single email. She could determine when this had started, and how far it had already gone.

Josie still felt preternaturally calm, but her body began to shake, as if it were a separate entity in the throes of its own private, visceral reaction to her discovery.

She wanted to know. But she also didn't want to know. No, that wasn't quite it. What she truly wanted was for the truth to be exactly what Frank had said it was. A few kisses, a few flirty messages. Something forgivable after a handful of therapy sessions and a couple of weeks of sleeping apart. After all, hadn't she, Josie, harbored a huge crush on a stay-at-home dad named Steve whose kid was in Zoe's class? She'd acted like a schoolgirl, blushing whenever he'd spoken to her and texting her friends a photograph of him when he'd worn black running shorts that revealed his tanned, muscled legs.

Maybe Frank's flirtation wasn't much worse than hers had been.

Those nine words in the email: *Sighhhh . . . Thought of you this morning in the shower.*

The first word had been the giveaway. It was the fingerprint, the failed alibi, the murder weapon. The other eight were merely supporting evidence.

"Mommy!" Izzy yelled from upstairs, her voice slightly muffled. "I'm hungry!"

"Daddy will get you a snack," Josie shouted back, her eyes pinned on Frank.

"What does she want?" Frank asked. She regarded him silently.

"Ah, crackers, or maybe an apple?" Frank continued.

"Figure it out," Josie said. Frank was trying to distract her. He wanted to ease the conversation onto safer ground.

There was more on his phone. Of course there was more.

She had known this all along. She'd known it even before Frank had shifted his eyes up and to the right. Even before he'd frozen while getting out of the car. Even before they'd left the house that morning.

"I need to rest for a little while. Stay here," Josie said. She spoke to Frank in the same tone she used with Huck when the dog tore up the garbage. Frank responded the same way Huck did—with sad eyes and an innocent expression.

Josie turned and began to walk upstairs, her body leaden, as she headed to where the phone awaited.

*I would leave him.*

One of Josie's best friends, Karin, had made that declaration just a few months ago. They

23

were discussing the plight of another mom from the elementary school Zoe and Karin's twin daughters attended, whom they'd bumped into on the street right after morning drop-off.

Josie had immediately noticed that the woman had lost about fifteen pounds since the school's Halloween party only a few weeks earlier.

"Wow, you look amazing!" Josie had said a little enviously, wondering: *Atkins? Juice cleanse?*

The woman had responded by letting loose a torrent of words: Her husband had been having an affair. It had been going on for months and months, but she'd only recently discovered it. It was with a woman who was newly divorced—she was older than he, and she had kids who were already teenagers. The other woman was rich, too; a few years ago, she'd opened a clothing boutique that was doing very well. It specialized in high-end exercise clothes. Her breasts were almost certainly fake. He'd moved out. He was already living with her.

It was far too much information, far too raw and intimate a revelation, for a street-corner conversation with an acquaintance. Josie had reflexively taken a step back, away from what felt like an onslaught.

But Karin—calm, steady Karin, who never seemed to get flustered—had handled it beautifully. She'd put a hand on the woman's arm. "I am so sorry," she'd said. "You're going to be okay. I know it's hard, but you are better off without him."

The woman hadn't appeared to hear Karin. She'd just nodded robotically and had ricocheted off. Josie had the sense she needed to find someone else as soon as possible and tell her story again. It was as if she were a survivor of a natural disaster, trying to make sense of the tsunami that had swept through her life.

"I would leave him. I would kick that son of a bitch out of my house so fast," Karin had said as they'd watched the woman stride down the street.

"It sounds like he's the one who left, though," Josie had responded.

"Then I would take him for everything he had," Karin had declared, giving a little snort. Josie had no doubt that Karin would really do it.

Josie had thought of Karin's husband, Marcus, a busy partner in an accounting firm who managed to be the most hands-on father she'd ever seen. He took their six-year-old twins out for long hikes every Saturday morning, no matter what the weather, giving Karin some alone time while also tiring out the girls. At school functions, he kept an eye on the twins, saying he wanted to give Karin a break. Sometimes Josie wondered when Marcus got a break.

"As if Marcus would ever have an affair," Josie had said.

"Yeah, he knows I'd chop off his wiener," Karin had said, and they'd both laughed.

Josie hadn't considered it odd that they didn't discuss whether Frank might have an affair, or what Josie would do if she discovered it. To be honest, she hadn't even noticed the omission of that hypothetical dilemma from their conversation.

Now she wondered: Did Karin suspect what Frank was capable of?

And if Karin suspected, did other people? They lived just outside of Chicago, but their suburban neighborhood had a small-town feel. You couldn't go to the Kids Cuts barbershop or the local Irish pub without running into someone you knew. Maybe other people had seen Frank and Dana together.

Josie paused, her hand on the bedroom doorknob, until her wave of nausea passed.

"Sweetie?" Josie moved in front of the television, blocking Izzy's view to get her attention. "Daddy needs you downstairs!"

"Why?" Izzy asked.

"I think he has a surprise. Something fun he wants to do with you. Maybe go to the grocery store for marshmallows," Josie said. "Hurry!"

Frank was much better with electronics than she; Josie needed to keep him occupied in case he was capable of remotely erasing the messages from his phone. She didn't think he'd dare do that, even if it was possible, because it would be such an admission of guilt. But she was reevaluating what she thought she'd known about her husband.

The thought propelled her to move a little faster. Josie went into the closet, pushed aside the bag of Goodwill clothing, and retrieved her purse. She brought it to the center of the bed and took out Frank's phone.

She felt her chest grow tight. She wondered whether he'd changed the code since meeting Dana. Frank was good with names—he was a people person—but he had a terrible memory for numbers. His pass codes were always simple, and he rarely changed them. He'd asked her to keep a record of the last one, which was 2244.

"I think I can remember that," she'd said, laughing.

She tapped it in. The iPhone opened itself to her.

# Chapter Three

Josie began to scroll down through the messages, going backward in time. She'd already seen the first one, dated a week ago. There was another email exchange with Dana ten days ago.

Frank had written: *Birthday girl! See you at seven!*

Dana had replied: *Can't wait!*

Josie stared at the words until they blurred.

He'd taken Dana out on her birthday?

Josie thought back to her own forty-first birthday the previous month, just ten days before Dana's. Josie had bought herself a Fitbit, along with some running shoes, and had told Frank it was his gift to her, to get her motivated to run a 5K. He'd helped the girls make cards, which they decorated with stickers and filled with coupons for things like a hug and a promise to unload the dishwasher. They'd all gone to a Tex-Mex restaurant and she'd had a couple of frozen margaritas and pretended to be surprised when she'd reached into the gift bag. The girls had behaved beautifully. It had been a nice night.

Wait—had Frank been seeing Dana even then?

She scrolled down, trying to find the first message in their correspondence.

It had come in seven weeks ago. Seven weeks!

Josie checked the dates again and did the math twice, because the numbers felt slippery in her mind. Mid-November until now, early January. Yes. Seven weeks. It had been going on for seven weeks. Over her birthday, over Christmas!

Her pulse quickened, but the wall held.

She put down the phone and stared into space. She thought of how possessive Frank had been about his phone recently, how he'd seemed so attached to it. She'd opened the bathroom door last week, assuming he was in the shower because the water was running, and had seen him sitting on the toilet, staring at the screen. He'd given a surprised yell—a high-pitched, almost theatrically shocked shriek, which was ridiculous considering how many times she'd walked in on him in the bathroom through the years—and she'd rolled her eyes. "I need my hairbrush," she'd said, grabbing it off the edge of the sink and walking back out.

Maybe the odd shriek wasn't because she'd surprised him. Maybe it was because she'd surprised him while he'd been messaging with Dana.

She looked around her bedroom again, taking in the framed photographs of the girls on the walls, the clothes draped over the cheap elliptical machine she and Frank had bought two years earlier as a Christmas gift to each other, the basketball shoes he'd left a few inches away from the closet, rather than tucking them inside as she'd asked. ("In a sec, hon.") The room felt at once deeply familiar and utterly alien. She'd slept in this bed, next to Frank, on the soft jersey sheets she'd bought at Target. She'd performed her usual rituals, like rubbing coconut oil into her feet before covering them with socks, while chatting with Frank about his day. She'd flipped through TV channels while he'd stood a few feet away, slipping the silky tie from around his neck and unbuttoning his blue oxford shirt, revealing the dark, coarse hair covering his pale chest. She'd awoken at around three o'clock one morning last week to find Izzy sprawled across her chest and Huck snoring in the middle of the bed. While all of those things happened, Frank had been having an affair.

It seemed impossible.

She tried to think of what to do next. Confront Frank? But he'd been lying to her for so long. She couldn't trust anything he might say.

What she needed was the family calendar, the one hanging on a hook in the kitchen. She needed to see when he'd been out of town, when he'd supposedly been working late, when he'd said he was going to meet friends for a drink or to watch a game.

She needed facts.

She thought of the frantic woman she'd run

into with Karin near the school, and she suddenly understood the woman's compulsion to recite the narrative surrounding the implosion of her life, to include strange details like the name of the boutique owned by the other woman. When nothing made sense—when you found yourself abruptly transported into a new world because your old one was constructed on a crumbling foundation—you clung to what little truth you knew.

Her name was Dana. It had been going on for at least seven weeks. He'd taken her out for her birthday.

These were the only truths Josie knew.

She picked up Frank's phone and dialed Karin, who answered quickly.

"Hello? Frank?" Karin asked, sounding surprised.

"No, it's me," Josie said. "I'm using his phone."

"Oh, hey, how— No, we're not going to McDonald's. Stop asking."

"You're with the kids?" Josie asked.

"Yeah, in the car, but we're about to— Hang on, we're pulling into the mall. Can I call you later?"

"Sure," Josie said.

Karin paused. "Are you okay?"

Josie's throat closed up. She couldn't answer.

"Jos?"

"I'm okay," Josie managed to say, but it came

31

out as a squeak, like the noise a baby mouse would make.

"Marcus, take the kids inside," Karin said instantly. "I'll meet you at the food court."

Josie could hear Marcus's deep voice responding, but she couldn't make out the words. Then Karin: "I don't know. Go, girls, go. What? Hang on, Josie."

Then the background noise faded away and the only thing Josie could hear was Karin taking a deep breath. "What is it?" she asked. "The children?"

"No, God, no," Josie said. Her voice was suddenly working again. "The girls are fine, I'm fine, everyone is fine. Frank is having an affair."

"Frank is having an affair," Karin repeated, her tone low.

"I think it started seven weeks ago," Josie said. "Her name is Dana. Do you know anyone named Dana?"

"It started seven weeks ago," Karin repeated again. "Her name is Dana. No, I don't know anyone named Dana."

*Why do you keep repeating everything I say?* Josie nearly asked. Then she realized Marcus must be nearby, and that Karin was echoing for him, letting him know the details of the crisis.

The fizz of irritation she felt at this realization disappeared at Karin's next words: "Do you want me to come over?"

"No, he's downstairs with Izzy," Josie said.

"Frank is still in the *house?*" Karin's tone was incredulous.

"I found out about an hour ago, okay?" Josie's voice broke. "Don't yell at me!"

"Oh, sweetie, no—I'm sorry," Karin said. "Should I come get you? Do you want me to pick you up? Do you want to come stay with us?"

Josie looked around the bedroom again. Zoe's pink princess pajamas were splayed limply on the floor, a stack of Angelina the Ballerina books and a sippy cup sat on the nightstand, and Izzy's soccer trophy decorated the dresser. Some of the gold was flaking off the little player.

How could she leave her children, her home? If anyone left, it should be Frank.

*Oh my God. Had he brought Dana here?*

No, he couldn't have. Josie worked out of her home, selling a line of educational children's toys at trade shows and directly to preschools and organizations. She traveled to a few shows and festivals a year, but most of those only lasted a day or so, and the entire family always came along since the festivals were kid-friendly. And though Josie was out and about all the time, running errands and shepherding the girls to activities, her schedule was too erratic to be predictable. Frank could not have conducted his affair in their home.

33

"How did you find out?" Karin was asking. "Did he tell you?"

"I found emails from her," Josie said.

"That stupid—" Karin stopped herself.

"Do you think he loves her?" Josie's lips trembled and she pressed them tightly together. Maybe Frank *wanted* to leave.

"No, he doesn't, it's just a midlife-crisis fling," Karin said. Karin had very definite opinions about everything. She was almost always right.

"What am I going to do?" Josie asked.

"I'm coming to get you," Karin said. "I'll bring you to my house. Marcus will take the kids somewhere. We'll have wine and talk."

"Okay."

"Thirty minutes. Sit tight. Just hang on, sweetie. Pack a toothbrush and a nightgown just in case. Actually, forget that. Don't pack anything, I have extra. See you soon."

"But what if he loves her?" Josie tried to say, but her mouse voice was back, and besides, Karin had already hung up.

Despite Karin's instructions, Josie did end up packing a few things. But not a toothbrush or a nightgown. She went into the kitchen and took out a folded cloth grocery bag from under the sink. In it she put the hanging wall calendar they kept by the breakfast table, her laptop with its electronic calendar, her phone, and Frank's

34

phone. She held on to the bag while she went into the playroom, where Frank and Izzy were seated on the couch, watching *SpongeBob*.

"I'm going out for a while," Josie said.

"Are you okay?" Frank asked. She must have conveyed with her eyes that the question made her want to slap him, because he flinched.

"You stay here with Izzy," she said. "Pick up Zoe at four. Get them pizza or something for dinner. No, Zoe had pizza at the party—whatever. Get it again. I don't care. Put a pull-up on Izzy if I'm not home by bedtime."

"Can I ask where you're going?" Frank asked meekly.

"No." She couldn't bear to look at him, with his arm around Izzy, acting like the devoted family man. She hated him.

"Look," Frank said. He started to rise but she held up her palm.

"Don't."

Izzy looked up and began to suck her thumb, a habit she'd mostly given up. "Mama?"

Josie couldn't bear the fact that Izzy was picking up on the ugly new charge in the air. She wanted to go to Izzy, to pick her up and nuzzle her neck and feel her warm, sturdy body, but that would require moving closer to Frank.

Frank had caused this. He needed to deal with it.

"I'll be back soon," she told Izzy, backing up

as she spoke. "I love you! Daddy's here! See you soon!" She turned and ran out the door, then kept running all the way down the block.

While she waited on the corner for Karin, Josie thought about sex.

She and Frank had met just after she'd turned twenty-five. They'd dated for a couple of years, then moved in together. A month before her thirtieth birthday, they'd gotten married. Zoe came along when Josie was thirty-four, and Izzy was born shortly after Josie's thirty-seventh birthday.

They'd been together for sixteen years, nearly half of her life. Nearly half of his, as well; at forty, Frank was eight months younger than she. It wasn't surprising that the early heat had seeped out of their relationship long ago.

These days she and Frank made love about once a week, usually on Saturday nights, and occasionally they threw in a morning quickie while the kids watched TV. Sex was almost always at Frank's instigation, except for the time a few months ago after a party during which Josie drank an entire bottle of wine. Lately, Josie felt about sex with her husband the way she did about exercise: it wasn't something she particularly craved, but once she started, she realized it felt good and she vowed to do it more often.

Did other long-married couples feel that way about sex? She wondered.

She still found Frank attractive, or she had until her discovery cut off her access to her emotions. He annoyed her and occasionally repulsed her—he had a disgusting habit of blowing his nose in the shower—but she liked to feel his strong arms around her when he came home from work at night. She liked to slip her cold feet between his legs under the covers. She liked to flop on the couch next to him and watch *Homeland* or *Modern Family*.

If Frank had slept with Dana, it was definitely over. She would never be able to have sex with him again. She'd barely be able to be in the same room with him, to breathe the same air.

Karin's blue minivan crested the hill and came into view. Josie waved and Karin gave the horn a little toot. She pulled up to the curb and Josie climbed in.

"First, a hug," Karin instructed. She opened her arms and pulled Josie close to her generous curves. Josie laid her head on Karin's soft, wide shoulder. Unlike many of the mothers at the school, who wore spandex to drop-off and immediately rushed to spin class, Karin didn't obsess about her weight or hair. She ate what she felt like eating, let her long, dark curls dry in whatever direction they pleased, and she joked that she only reached her target heart rate when she watched a Brad Pitt move. Josie knew Marcus made good money, but Karin's home was as soft and unpretentious as she was: squishy couches with floral prints filled the living room, and the kitchen counters were covered with a hodgepodge of cookbooks and plants and spices and, often, a tray of cooling cupcakes or a slow cooker filled with chili.

"Let's get you back to the house," Karin said when Josie pulled away. She shifted the car out of park and began to drive. "Marcus took the twins to a movie, then he'll call us and if we need him to, he can keep them out until bedtime."

"Can you just pull into someone's driveway and turn around?" Josie asked. "I really don't want to drive past the house."

"Of course, sweetie," Karin said. They proceeded in silence for a few moments. Then Karin said: "You saw his emails?"

"Yeah, we were getting coffee, and I needed to make a call— Damn, I forgot to pick up a prescription. Izzy's EpiPen refill," Josie said.

"Do you want to ask Frank to do it?" Karin asked.

Josie shook her head. "Can we just— It's a few blocks away. The CVS."

"Heading there now," Karin said.

"He said he met her on a business trip," Josie said. "He said it was nothing. Only kissing, twice."

Josie saw Karin's jawline tighten.

"You don't believe him?" Josie asked.

"Do you?" Karin asked. Another thing about Karin: she never lied.

Josie looked down at the cloth bag by her feet. "I still have his phone. I haven't looked at all the messages. I thought I could go through them at your house. I've got my calendar, too. I have to figure it out, I need to know when he saw her and what they did. I was with the kids all those times—I was so fucking stupid, Karin, I was just puttering around and telling him to go to his dumb work happy hours as long as he did something with the girls on the weekend so I'd get a break, too, and all the while, the whole time—maybe not the whole time, but for the last couple of months—he was—he took her out for her birthday—"

Karin's arm was around Josie before Josie realized that Karin had pulled the minivan to the side of the road. Josie hadn't realized she was crying, either; her chest heaved and the tears dripped down her face, but she wasn't making a sound. She still felt numb. Why couldn't she feel?

A passing car honked at them—Karin's minivan was sticking out a bit into the lane—but Karin just lifted a hand and gave the driver the finger.

"It's going to be okay," she told Josie. "You can stay with me. The girls, too. You can do whatever you want. What do you want to do?"

Josie reached for her purse and pulled out a napkin. She blew her nose.

She said the only thing that came to mind, because life went on, just like the traffic streaming past their stopped vehicle, no matter how still and frozen you felt inside.

"I want to go to CVS."

After they'd completed the errand and driven back to Karin's house, Karin put on the teakettle while Josie huddled on the couch under a crocheted blanket. But she didn't want to be alone in the living room, even though she had a clear view of Karin in the open kitchen, so she wrapped the blanket around her shoulders like a shawl and went to sit on a stool at the counter.

"Chamomile or mint?" Karin asked.

"Chamomile, I guess." It didn't matter. She couldn't believe she'd ever had a strong opinion on anything as irrelevant as the flavor of her tea.

"Are you sure you don't want wine, too?" Karin asked, but Josie shook her head. She didn't need to unfeel any more deeply.

Karin settled the teapot and mugs and spoons between them, and put a jar of honey next to Josie. Then she took the stool next to Josie's. "Here?" she asked. "Or the couch? The couch is cozier."

Josie nodded and picked up her mug and followed Karin.

Karin blew on her steaming tea, then asked gently, "What did the emails say?"

So Josie stood up again and retrieved the cloth bag from the bench by the front door—she had been overly aware of it there, next to a basket of shoes and coats hanging on hooks, like it was just another household object—and she brought it back to the couch.

She tapped in the code to Frank's phone and pulled up his messages. She covered her mouth with her hand.

"Are you okay?" Karin asked.

Josie nodded. "I just— I just felt sick for a second there."

"When was the last time you ate?" Karin asked.

"I had a yogurt and banana this morning," Josie said.

"You missed lunch. What can I get you? I've got lasagna, or potato salad, and there's tons of ice cream in the fridge . . ." Karin loved feeding people and often brought buckets of Dunkin' Donuts Munchkins to school meetings. *It terrorizes the Barbie moms,* she'd whisper to Josie before popping a donut hole into her mouth.

"I don't think I can eat," Josie said. She tried a sip of tea and the mug clanged against her front teeth. Her hand was shaking, she realized.

"Would you rather I go through them?" Karin asked, gesturing to the phone.

41

Josie shook her head. "I need to do it. I just want to take it slowly."

But once she'd scrolled down and opened the first email she could find from Dana—subject line *What is with this weather?!*—she found herself racing through them all, greedily consuming the sentences, bingeing on the words.

When she finished, she leaned back against the couch, unable to decide if the news was good or bad.

The email referencing the shower was by far the most incriminating. The others were flirty and friendly, but not overtly sexual. If Frank had deleted that first email, the others would have made her suspicious. Perhaps even more suspicious than she'd been in the past. But she might have convinced herself the notes were only that—a flirtation.

The problem was, Frank deleted lots of emails rather than leaving them clogging his in-box. He'd always had that habit because he got agitated when the number on the envelope icon passed one hundred, which Josie attributed to the mild case of ADHD she'd long ago diagnosed him with. Frank had saved some messages from Dana. Had he deleted others?

Josie was suddenly certain the seven or eight rapid movements she'd seen him execute just before he'd handed her the phone were evidence that he had. She checked his trashed mail. It was empty.

Now that she'd made the decision to want to know, those expunged emails gnawed at her. They would tell the story Frank had tried to conceal.

She tilted the phone toward Karin.

"What is with this weather," Karin read without intonation.

"Hang on." Josie looked at the cloth bag.

How did she have the presence of mind to assemble the clues she'd need to untangle Frank's lies? Josie wondered. Her body felt frozen; yet her brain was sharp and supple, guiding her almost of its own accord.

Josie pulled the wall calendar out of her brown bag and flipped back to the previous month. There! Frank had gone to Atlantic City on a business trip seven weeks ago. He'd stayed for two nights. The message from Dana had come in on his final day of the trip. So perhaps that was where they'd met. Maybe she, like he, was a pharmaceutical sales rep.

It would jibe with his story that he'd met Dana on a business trip. Perhaps that piece was true. Josie told this to Karin.

"We could try to find out who she is," Karin said. "If you want to know, I mean. Google her name and 'pharma rep' and see what comes up. Or we could try to do a reverse email search. I saw something about that on a talk show once—you can get the person's name and home address if you have their email."

Josie nodded slowly, considering it. Dana used only her first name followed by a string of numbers for her email address. But Karin was right; her first name was unique enough to winnow her down.

Josie could try to find out whether she was married. How old she was. Whether she was pretty.

Josie tried to swallow, but her mouth was so dry that her throat simply constricted ineffectually.

"Karin?" Josie said. "I'm ready for that glass of wine now."

# Chapter Four

Here was the thing about the hot stay-at-home dad named Steve: Josie's interactions with him weren't simply limited to the exchange of nods or smiles in the school hallways and that one sneaky photograph.

This past summer, during the week before school began—and several months before Frank had begun his affair with Dana—Steve had invited Josie and the girls over to his house on an afternoon when his wife was away.

Zoe and Steve's daughter, Penny, were on the same soccer team. They didn't know each other well, since they'd never been in the same class. But on one September afternoon right before Labor Day, the coach had paired them up for drills. They'd left the field giggling, and Penny had grabbed her father's arm.

"Can Zoe come over to play? Please? Please?" she'd asked.

Steve, who'd been juggling a water bottle, Penny's soccer ball, and a book (a historical biography, judging from the cover, which made him even sexier), had glanced at Penny, then at Zoe, then at Josie.

"We've met," Steve said. "Haven't we?"

Josie nodded, even though they never had, at least not officially. "I'm Josie," she said. "Zoe was in Mrs. Marshall's class last year. Your daughter had Mr. Kapp, right?"

"Right," Steve said. His eyes were very blue against his tanned skin, and smile lines radiated out from them. "So, does your daughter want to come over? She's more than welcome to."

"We have to swim or we'll die!" Penny shouted. Both girls were red-faced and so sweaty their jerseys were clinging to them; it was three o'clock, which always seemed to be the hottest time of the day. Josie bet it was more than a hundred degrees out. Josie and Izzy had sought refuge under the shade during practice, but it hadn't helped much: sweat dampened Josie's hair at the roots, and her T-shirt clung to her back.

"We need to swim!" Zoe echoed.

"Me too!" Izzy hollered.

"Oh, that's so nice," Josie said. "I don't have her suit or anything, so . . ."

Then she remembered that she did. The pool bag containing suits for all of them was in the trunk of the Sienna. She'd packed it in case they'd decided to swing by the community center on the way home.

The girls were all chanting "Swim, swim, swim!" and jumping up and down, even Izzy.

Steve looked at them and laughed. He was sweating, too, but on him it looked good.

"Looks like we're outnumbered," he said. "Tell you what, why don't all three of you come over?"

He lived only a half mile away from Josie's house, in a part of town where the lawns were wider and the houses more stately. She'd driven by his place a dozen times and had admired the stone front porch and old-fashioned gas lamp at the end of the front walk.

When Steve opened the door and welcomed them in, Josie noticed a few signs of his wife—a bracelet on the kitchen counter, a pair of black pumps under the bench in the foyer—but no evidence she was on the premises. She assumed Steve's wife was traveling. She often seemed to be. Josie wasn't quite sure what she did, but she went to Europe and Asia frequently and wore expensive-looking suits when she came to school functions.

Coincidentally, Frank was also traveling this week.

Steve showed them to the large, main-floor bathroom, offering it for their use in case they needed to change. But Josie had already done so at home. She'd pretended to the girls that she'd forgotten their suits so she could dash up into her own bathroom and shave her legs and pick up her more flattering bathing suit, the emerald-green tankini, rather than the black one-piece she usually wore to the Y.

The girls immediately ran outside and splashed into the pool. Zoe was already a fairly strong swimmer. And Izzy wore a suit with a built-in flotation device around the middle, which meant Josie could ease herself into the water at her own pace.

Steve stripped off his T-shirt and walked over to the diving board. "Cannonball!" he called before he propelled himself into the air as the girls shrieked. He surfaced, shaking his hair out of his face and smiling.

Then he did an easy freestyle to the shallow end of the pool, where Josie was leaning against the wall.

"This feels great," she said. "Thanks for inviting us."

"Anytime," Steve said.

They were close enough that Josie could see silver droplets of water glistening on his tanned shoulder. The thought occurred to her that she'd like to lick one off. She looked away, hoping that if Steve saw her blush, he'd mistake it for a sunburn.

"Daddy!" his daughter summoned him. Steve slipped under the water and swam away, sleek as a seal.

The kids grew hungry, so Steve ordered a pizza around five thirty. "How about a beer?" he'd asked her after he'd passed lemonade juice boxes to the kids.

By then the girls were wrapped in towels and sprawled in front of the television. Josie had put her shorts and T-shirt back on, but Steve was still wearing just his suit trunks as he padded barefoot into the kitchen.

"A beer sounds great," Josie said. She'd let Huck out in the backyard when she'd gone home to change, so she wasn't in any rush.

Steve popped the cap off a Sierra Nevada and handed it to her and she joined the girls on the couch, pretending to watch the Disney movie. She felt surprisingly relaxed, given the situation. But maybe it was because Steve was being so nonchalant. He'd probably had plenty of moms over to his house before, Josie realized. It was an atypical situation for her, but not for him.

The pizza arrived just as she was finishing her drink, and Steve brought her another beer, which she sipped as she nibbled a slice of pepperoni. Then the movie ended and the girls ran back outside. Josie joined them in the pool, but as soon as she slipped into the water, they raced back into the house, with Penny yelling that they wanted Popsicles.

"Fickle little beasts," Steve said. He was sitting on the edge of the pool, dangling his feet into the shallow end. Josie laughed and started to pull herself out, but Steve showed no signs of wanting to move. So she stayed in the pool, the water lapping gently around her waist.

The sun had sunk low in the sky, and dusk began to gather around them. A few underwater lights illuminated the deep end of the pool, but the shallow section, where Josie stood, was inky. She couldn't see her knees or feet below the surface.

"This is the first time today I haven't felt hot," Steve said as he lowered himself into the water with a sigh. He was maybe three feet away from her now.

She could see the girls in the living room through the sliding glass doors. They were eating Popsicles, and their attention was fixed on the screen. Normally Josie would have rushed inside to make sure they weren't dripping on the floor. But she didn't move.

"This summer has been brutal, right?" Josie said.

A lone cricket began to chirp nearby. The shadows stretched longer across the lawn. The moist, thick air had cooled significantly and now it seemed almost exactly the same temperature as the water.

"I'm ready for school to start," Steve said. "It'll give me more time for photography."

Josie blinked, thinking of the stretched-canvas photos she'd admired in the living room. They were all nature scenes: hiking trails winding up a mountain; a lone, prickly cactus standing tall against the blazing sun, a squirrel carrying its baby in its mouth. "Were those your photos inside?"

"Yeah," he said. "It's a hobby."

"I thought they were professional. Wow, you're really good."

"Thanks." He tilted his head back and took another sip of beer. Josie watched his Adam's apple rise and fall as he drank. He was one of the sexiest men she'd ever seen.

Steve set down his bottle and ducked down lower in the pool until only his head was above the water.

"What about you?" he asked. "What do you do when you're off duty as a mom?"

"I'm never off duty," Josie said with a laugh, meaning it. But then she wished she could snatch back the words. They made her sound dull.

"Dancing," she blurted. "That was what I loved most before I had kids."

"Like, ballet, or . . . ?" Steve asked.

Josie shook her head. "Just dancing," she said. "I mean, I studied a little as a kid—some modern dance and tap—but my favorite thing to do was always to just go to a club and dance." She probably sounded like a party girl now, she realized.

"Cool," Steve said, nodding.

Had he moved closer? Perhaps by an inch or two.

Their surroundings suddenly seemed almost

51

unbearably intimate: all that exposed skin and darkness and languid water. She looked at Steve. It was impossible to discern his expression; he was facing away from the house, so he was backlit. But she thought he was looking at her, too.

Josie felt her body tighten. Goose bumps formed on her arms and she shivered. She held her breath.

She was backed up against the edge of the pool, the concrete lip pressing into her shoulder blades. She imagined Steve taking a slow, silent step closer to her. Her heart pounded in her chest.

"I should check on the kids," she said, her voice louder than it had been a moment earlier. She jumped out of the pool and hurried inside.

When she recounted the story to Karin the next day, she exaggerated a couple of details. In her retelling, Steve was just a foot away from her, and it was completely dark outside.

"He looks so good in a bathing suit," Josie had said, sighing.

"Take a picture next time," Karin had cracked, and Josie had laughed.

"Do you think he would've made a move?" Karin had asked. "If you hadn't skittered away?"

"I mean, I got a flirty vibe from him, but maybe he's one of those guys who flirts with everyone," Josie said. "I honestly don't know."

"So what happened after you jumped out of the pool?" Karin had asked.

Josie had shrugged. "We stayed another half hour and then I took the kids home. It was getting late."

She'd also poured herself a glass of chardonnay and had sat in the living room, listening to a John Legend CD, feeling a smile play on her lips as she relived every detail of the afternoon and evening.

It was more fun to remember the encounter than it had been to experience it, Josie realized. She hadn't revealed to Karin that the overarching emotion she'd felt during that electric pause—right before she'd jumped out of the pool—wasn't lust or excitement or longing.

It was fear.

Having a crush on Steve from afar was thrilling. Imagining he desired her was delicious. The possibility of taking it any further was unthinkable. It would be like lighting the fuse to a bomb.

But that was exactly what her husband had done.

How could he?

When Josie was certain the girls would be asleep, she asked Karin to take her home. Karin wanted to walk her inside, but Josie asked to be dropped at the curb. She didn't want Karin glaring at

Frank and making pointed remarks about how Josie and the girls could come stay with her anytime. Karin had many strengths, but subtlety wasn't among them.

By now, Josie had obtained a little more information: Dana was married. She also worked as a pharma rep. She lived maybe twenty minutes away.

She wasn't beautiful, but she was pretty enough—at least in the photographs Google had turned up. Like Josie, she had pale skin and shoulder-length, dark blond hair. So Frank apparently had a type.

But Dana's eyes were set a shade too close together, making her look a bit intense. Frank had always told Josie he loved her big, wide-spaced eyes. What did he compliment Dana about?

She appeared to be fairly short. But she was very slender, which infuriated Josie, who'd carried an extra ten pounds since Izzy's birth.

Josie had thought seeing the other woman's face would conjure intense feelings of rage or jealousy. But that hadn't happened—at least not yet. Dana looked like an ordinary woman, the kind Josie saw every day in the grocery store or at PTA meetings.

Josie had also cross-referenced Frank's emails with her calendars. She was desperate for more facts. More truth.

She was certain she had pinpointed the date

of one of Frank's encounters with Dana because Dana had written a message referencing the "killer" margaritas she'd drunk the previous evening. The message was carefully phrased—it wasn't incriminating—but if you parsed the words, its lack of context indicated Frank already knew about the margaritas. Which Josie suspected meant he'd been there.

Her own calendar had revealed Josie's schedule that evening: *Movie with Tamara,* she'd written. When Josie thought back to that night, she found the details formed surprisingly quickly in her mind, like colors and shapes lifting up from a developing photograph.

She'd been looking forward to seeing *La La Land* all week. She'd missed it when it had first come out, but their local theater showed older releases every Wednesday night.

Josie had phoned Frank that afternoon at work to remind him she had plans. He'd seemed flustered.

"Agh—forgot, I've got this work thing tonight. What time is the movie?" he'd asked. (She could remember their conversation word for word! It was incredible, really.)

"Eight thirty," she'd said.

"I'll be home by eight," he'd promised. He'd been a few minutes late, but the theater was just a five-minute drive away, so Josie hadn't been stressed. Tamara had already texted that she was planning to arrive early to get tickets and secure seats.

It had seemed like any other evening.

But now Josie realized she'd tucked away certain moments in her mind, as if carefully wrapping them in a packing box for future excavation. The ones that stood out the most sharply had been warning signs; perhaps that was why she'd cataloged them, then buried them beneath a layer of distracting, everyday busyness.

That night, when she heard Frank's car pull into the driveway at ten after eight, she'd risen from the couch and had gone to the landing at the bottom of the stairs, where a small closet held their coats. She was putting on her black leather jacket—a night out without the kids meant her puffy down North Face coat stayed behind—when Frank came in.

"Hi," she'd said, stretching out her arms for a hug, feeling happy. The kids were asleep, the house was tidy, and she had a fun night ahead of her. Frank had walked over and embraced her briefly. Because the landing was up a step, they were nearly the exact same height. (She somehow remembered *all* of these details!)

Frank had responded to her gesture, but he'd pulled away quickly. Away from the kiss she gave him, and out of her arms.

"Don't you have to hurry to make it to the movies?" he'd asked.

"Right," she'd said, ignoring the little frizzle of hurt she'd felt. She'd smelled beer on Frank's breath, but he said he was going out for a work thing. No big deal.

She'd been unsure whether the movie had left her feeling happy or sad, but she'd enjoyed it. She couldn't remember what had happened when she'd returned home—whether Frank was already asleep or in bed watching TV. She'd probably changed into a nightshirt and brushed her teeth and climbed under the covers and fallen asleep quickly. It was late for her, especially for a school night. Other than that, the evening had seemed completely unremarkable.

Still, when she thought back, these were the details that rose like cream to the surface of her mind: Frank had seemed flustered when they'd spoken about their evening plans on the phone, he'd arrived a few minutes late, he'd smelled like beer. And he'd pulled away from her kiss.

Now, as Josie walked up the steps toward her front door, she wondered why she hadn't put the pieces together sooner. Maybe it was because she hadn't wanted to believe it could be true.

Josie inserted her key into the lock and pushed the door open. She turned and waved to Karin, who was idling in the driveway. Then she stepped inside.

Frank was seated in the living room, on the

couch, with the newspaper by his side. He looked up at her warily.

"You're reading the paper?" she asked incredulously.

"No, I was just— I was waiting for you," he said.

"Well, here I am," she said.

He leaned forward and steepled his hands and stared into her eyes. Clearly he'd been rehearsing. "Jos, I'm so sorry. I never should have done it—"

"How did it happen?" Josie interrupted.

Frank frowned at her, looking puzzled.

"How did it *start?*" Josie clarified. "Where? Who flirted first?"

"In Atlantic City," Frank said.

"And?" Josie prompted when he hesitated.

"I went to a dinner. A ton of people were there. There were drinks first . . . One of the companies sponsored the whole thing, so . . . Anyway, I went to the bar and she was there. And . . . Do you really want to hear this?"

*No,* Josie thought. But she nodded.

Frank cleared his throat. His eyes were red-rimmed. Had he been crying, too?

"She came up to me and said, 'Hi, Frank Moore.' "

"And?" Josie prodded.

"And I just said hi, because I had no idea who she was."

Dana could not have come up with a more effective opening line if she'd practiced for weeks, Josie realized. Dana had inflated Frank's ego. She'd made him feel memorable. Important. Her words seemed . . . predatory.

She looked at Frank sitting on the couch, staring up at her beseechingly. He'd cleaned up the girls' toys but he'd missed a tiny pink shoe for one of their dolls.

"I thought I should sleep here tonight." Frank gestured to the couch. "I can shower in the basement tomorrow morning."

As if that gesture would make everything okay. As if it would offset those emails, the birthday date, the pushing away.

Josie also knew these facts about Dana: Dana was a year younger than Josie, and she was married. Josie had even read her wedding announcement. Dana had a husband named Ron who was probably as stupidly unaware as Josie had been just this morning.

"You disgust me," Josie said. She felt a piece of the wall crumble, allowing some of her rage to steam through. She blinked back tears that felt as sharp as diamonds.

"I know," Frank said.

"I hate you!" she said, her voice raw and loud. She wanted to hit Frank, to hurt him, to throw everything in the room at him. But he looked so sincerely miserable that despite everything, she felt a softening toward him, and that only made her angrier. "You need to move out!"

"Josie, no, please." Frank collapsed to his knees. "I fucked up. I'm so sorry, I'll never talk to her again—"

She'd been playing Candy Land with the girls and cleaning the bathroom and schlepping in food from the grocery store while he'd been conducting an affair. One encounter would have been bad enough. Maybe she could've chalked it up to drunkenness. But he'd woken up the day after he'd cheated, presumably talked to his family—because Josie and the girls spoke to Frank every day when he traveled—and then he'd gone back to Dana for more.

"Please," Frank was saying, but Josie turned and walked upstairs, leaving him kneeling on the carpet, just as he'd done when he'd proposed to her all those years ago.

# Chapter Five

Josie knew she wouldn't be able to fall asleep that night. Ten hours had elapsed since her discovery, but it seemed as if a lifetime had passed—or, more accurate, as if her entire life had unspooled.

She had tucked her purse and cloth grocery bag in the back of her closet again, behind her Goodwill bag, even though she had forwarded the emails to her own account so she could have an independent record of them. That had been Karin's suggestion. Karin had also given Josie the name and phone number of a divorce lawyer. "I'm not saying you have to decide now if you want to go down that route," Karin had said. "But call her anyway. You've got to protect yourself."

Josie wondered if Karin had asked Marcus for the referral, and what the two of them had said about the affair. *If you ever . . .* she could imagine Karin saying. Then Marcus would have given a little laugh and responded, *Never, my love.* Josie could see them hugging, feeling more appreciative of each other, the way people always do when a catastrophe touches down close to home.

Josie shut the door to her closet, then slipped

off her shoes and lay down in bed still wearing her jeans and sweater. It was cold in the house—Frank always set the thermostat too low—so she reached down and grabbed the edge of the extra comforter that was folded at the bottom of the bed. She pulled it up over herself and closed her eyes and somehow dozed off almost instantly. It was as if her battered brain had flicked a switch and shut itself off.

She awoke abruptly to a silent house. The clock on the nightstand revealed it was nearly three in the morning. She got up and padded quietly into Zoe's room, then into Izzy's. She could see their faces in the glow of the night-lights they both used. Her girls were sleeping peacefully. Their worlds were still intact. She stared at each of them for a few moments, then went into the bathroom and brushed her teeth, but she didn't bother to wash her face. She opened the medicine cabinet and took out a Benadryl and swallowed it, knowing it would help her doze off again. She climbed back into bed and ran through the events of the day in her mind repeatedly, her thoughts on a continual loop.

She imagined Frank and Dana close together on barstools, sipping margaritas, their bodies turned toward each other. She thought of them kissing, of Frank's hands roaming over Dana's body. The physical betrayal was bad enough. Even worse was the knowledge that her husband and another woman had shared this intimate secret. That they'd been linked together so strongly, in their own private world, while Frank pretended to live a normal life with Josie.

*Seven weeks* was the last thing she could remember thinking.

When she opened her eyes again, the brightness in the room told her she'd slept later than she had in months. She rubbed her eyes, then checked the clock. It was nearly eight o'clock. Frank must have intercepted the girls, because it was their habit to run into the master bedroom as soon as they awoke, and Zoe and Izzy rarely slept later than seven—and naturally, they never did so on the same mornings.

Josie went into the bathroom and took a long, hot shower, trying to clear away the lingering fog from the Benadryl. She turbaned her hair into a towel and wrapped herself in her robe and walked to the closet. She pulled her softest turtleneck sweater and her most broken-in jeans off the shelf, craving a comforting buffer around her body. Then she towel-dried her hair and got dressed.

When she went downstairs, she saw Frank had the girls doing art projects at the kitchen table. He'd made pancakes, as he did every Sunday morning. He'd also washed the frying pan unprompted, which he almost never did.

"There's coffee," Frank told her. "And I can make more pancakes . . ."

Josie shook her head and reached for the box of tea bags. She didn't want anything from Frank, not even his leftover coffee.

"My babies," she said, walking over to the table and kissing the tops of their heads.

"I'm not a baby," Zoe said.

"Me neither," Izzy added.

"Yes you are."

"I am not! You're a baby!" Izzy's face turned red. She was two seconds away from screaming, or throwing her Play-Doh at her sister.

"Hey, guess who the baby is?" Frank chimed in. "It's me. Waah. Waah. I want a bottle."

Both girls laughed. Frank looked at Josie, hope in his eyes.

*What, you think I'm going to forgive you because you stopped the girls from fighting?* she thought.

"What would you like to do today?" Frank asked. Josie raised her eyebrows and he looked down.

She was taking a savage satisfaction in showing him how ridiculous his comments were, in making him feel stupid. Maybe because she had been foolishly unaware for so long.

"I mean, I saw on the calendar that Zoe has a Girl Scouts meeting, so . . ." Frank continued.

"They're having that little carnival," Josie said.

64

Every family had brought along a simple game for the kids to play; for weeks, she had been collecting thin-necked bottles to arrange in a cardboard box for a ring toss. "We need prizes for the winners. Lollipops or something."

"Do you want me to take them?" Frank asked. "Or all of us . . . ?"

"I don't know yet," Josie said.

She realized Zoe was watching her, and she made an effort to soften her tone.

"Excuse me," she said to Frank. He looked confused.

She gestured to the cabinet behind him, where they kept their mugs.

Yesterday morning, she would've put a hand on his arm to nudge him aside, or she would have simply reached behind him, brushing her body against his, while they chatted.

Frank stepped aside, giving her a wide berth, and she took down a chunky blue mug. She hadn't eaten anything since breakfast yesterday, but food held absolutely no appeal.

*All I needed was the adultery diet,* she thought. She bit back a harsh laugh.

The house was too quiet. Frank kept looking at her as he moved around the kitchen, scooping up bits of Play-Doh the moment they hit the floor and putting the milk back in the refrigerator after Josie added a splash to her tea. *Forgive me,* his every gesture seemed to beg.

She reached for Huck's leash in the basket by the back door.

"I'm going to take him for a walk," she said as Huck leapt to his feet eagerly.

"Okay," Frank said. "Sure."

She attached the leash to Huck's collar, then put on a coat and gloves and went outside, still holding her mug of tea. Its warmth was welcome through the fabric of her gloves.

The Sunday paper was still on the front walk. Tomorrow was a school holiday and Frank had planned to take the day off, which meant they were halfway through the long weekend.

As Josie walked around the block, she stared at the houses she passed. Their neighborhood was a pretty one, with wide sidewalks lined by mature trees. Most of the homes were simple, two-story brick ramblers, but residents had added personal touches—wooden decks, curving flower beds, and wide front porches. Basketball hoops stood in more than a few driveways, inviting neighborhood kids to come play after school. Stop signs marked nearly every corner, easing the minds of parents.

*What a great place to raise a family.* Josie was certain she and Frank had said nearly those exact words to each other the day they'd signed the mortgage papers to buy their house.

As she and Huck turned the corner toward home, Josie passed by a neighbor named Maggie whose children were older—all but one were already in college.

"Good morning!" Maggie called cheerfully as she bent down to pick up her newspaper off the front walk.

"Morning!" Josie said. Instead of turning back to the warmth of her home, Maggie walked toward Josie, even though she was only wearing yoga pants and a thin sweatshirt. Josie's first thought was that she somehow knew, that word had already traveled through the neighborhood and Maggie was coming to offer her condolences.

"I loved having the girls visit yesterday," Maggie said. "Tell Frank to drop them off any-time!"

"Oh?" Josie said. She struggled to wrap her mind around this new piece of information. "I was out so I didn't know . . . When did he bring them?"

"Around four," Maggie said. "Just for a bit. They were delightful!"

At four o'clock, Josie had been at Karin's house.

"I'm glad," Josie said. "Thank you." She continued on her way.

Why had Frank done it?

Had he met with Dana during that time? Josie felt as though her skin were burning; if she opened her mouth, she would spew fire. But no, she couldn't believe he would have done that; if

67

Frank wanted to leave her for Dana, she would have sensed it by now. He seemed desperate to fix things between them.

She returned home and unclipped Huck's leash. Before she could enter the kitchen, Frank approached her in the hallway.

"Where were you yesterday?" she hissed. "When you left the girls with Maggie?"

"I was looking for you!" Frank blurted. "I thought you were out walking somewhere because you didn't have your car and I was worried."

She nodded. "Okay," she said. That seemed plausible. She hadn't told him she was going to Karin's. She exhaled, and her body unclenched.

But, as she would discover later, it was just another lie.

By lunchtime, Josie knew she needed to get away. Her initial shock was yielding to a deep, crimson fury. If she had to be around Frank much longer, she knew she'd explode. And she wasn't ready for that confrontation, not yet. She gave Frank curt instructions about where to take the girls that afternoon for the carnival. He listened, then followed her upstairs and watched as she threw things into an overnight bag: a pair of pajamas, clean underwear, a book from her nightstand, a sports bra in case she felt like exercising (but no running shoes; she wasn't thinking clearly

68

enough to plan out the full outfit), her favorite old frayed-collar sweatshirt.

"Can I ask where you're going?" Frank said timidly.

"I don't know. Maybe a hotel," Josie said, realizing as she said it that that was exactly where she wanted to go. Everyone else had clear ideas about what she should do: Frank wanted her to forgive him; Karin wanted her to leave. Josie knew what her mother—who was in a miserable marriage with Josie's father—would say: *Marriage requires sacrifice,* with the implication being that swallowing this episode and moving on with Frank was a sacrifice Josie should make, no matter what the cost to her. Maintaining appearances was the supreme goal in Josie's family.

Josie needed to be alone, to think, without the sound of everyone else's voices arguing in her head.

"Are you sure?" Frank asked. "Can we talk first?" She shook her head.

Then she paused.

"Unless there's something else you need to tell me," she said.

Frank looked startled. "No," he said. "I've told you everything."

Frank was standing too close to her; he hadn't showered yet today and she could smell his body odor. She felt as if she might gag.

She grabbed her bag and ran downstairs. The girls were in front of cartoons now, and Josie swept them into a hug.

"You guys!" she said, making her voice bright. "I have to go away just for a night, but you are going to have so much fun with Daddy! He's taking you to the Girl Scouts carnival!"

She was prepared for protests, but the mention of the carnival distracted the girls, as she'd hoped it might. They gave her kisses and she promised to call at bedtime and then she ran out the door, feeling the pressure inside her build to an almost unbearable level.

She reversed the car down the driveway, then flung the gearshift into drive. Before she could press on the gas, the front door opened and Frank came running down the walk in his bare feet.

"Wait!" he called, waving. She rolled down her window. If he asked for his phone back she'd run him over.

"Do you want me to go instead?" he asked.

"I want you to have not cheated!" she hissed.

She peeled away, anger making her foot slam down on the gas, her tires giving a squeal.

Frank yelled something else that she couldn't hear clearly. It might have been "Be careful!"

Josie made two decisions as she pulled out of the neighborhood and onto a larger traffic artery: One, she would treat herself to a decent hotel, rather than a motel off the highway. And two, she wanted to hear the voice of the woman whom Frank had kissed.

Frank's phone was still in her purse. She was going to use it to call Dana.

Josie found the Courtyard Marriott that Frank's parents had stayed in the last time they'd come to visit, and she pulled into the wide, circular drive. A bellman hurried to open the door for her and she thanked him, wondering whether he assumed she was a traveling businesswoman, someone weary of being on the road, someone independent and unencumbered.

But of course, she was still wearing her wedding and engagement rings. She'd removed them only twice, during the last few months of each of her pregnancies, when her fingers swelled painfully. As she approached the reception desk, her thumb fingered the cool metal of the rings, trying to gauge how easily they would slip off.

"Reservation?" the clerk asked.

She shook her head. "Is that a problem?"

The hotel was probably busy during the week, with business travelers coming into Chicago, but today, the leather sofas and oversized chairs clustered in the lobby were empty. An old Carole King song—"You've Got a Friend"—played over the speakers. It had always been one of Josie's favorites.

"Not at all," the clerk said, tapping away on her computer. "For how many nights?"

"Just one." Josie could always extend it.

"I can give you a corner room for two twenty-nine," the woman said. "It's an upgrade for the price."

"A corner room sounds great," Josie said. She, who bought most of her clothes at Old Navy and always put the cheapest gas into her car, would have taken it at twice the cost. She wondered how much Frank had spent on Dana during the course of their affair. Had he paid for those killer margaritas? Frank was always picking up the check; Josie liked his generous spirit at times, but it also annoyed her, such as when they went out with his colleague Barton and his pretentious wife, who always waited until Frank had grabbed the check before trying—not very hard—to take it away. Frank had paid the last three times they'd had dinner together, and Josie had told him she wouldn't agree to another one unless Barton picked up the bill.

"Even if you have to outwait him," she'd said. "Just go to the bathroom or something."

Frank had agreed, but Josie had known that if Barton delayed more than a few minutes, Frank wouldn't be able to control his compulsion. She'd been dreading the idea of another dinner.

Maybe she would never need to go to one now.

Dana could go instead, she thought. She'd

intended it to be a sarcastic, throwaway notion. But she felt as if something hard had rammed her in the stomach.

"May I have a credit card?" the clerk asked.

Josie slid her Visa across the divider, and a moment later, the clerk returned it along with two keys in a little paper folder. "The tenth floor," she said, smiling as she indicated the room number written on the folder. "Enjoy your stay."

"I will," Josie said, smiling back. Surely something in her eyes or her face had changed during the past twenty-four hours, Josie thought. Evidence of what was happening must be written on her in some way. But neither the clerk nor Maggie had seemed to notice anything amiss.

Maybe, though, Maggie had tucked away a few details in her subconscious that would only emerge down the line if she learned Josie and Frank were divorcing. Weeks or months from now, Maggie might think back to the cold morning when Josie had been out walking Huck, and suddenly remember with remarkable clarity how surprised Josie had been to learn Frank had dropped off the girls.

Josie stepped onto the glass-walled elevator, realizing she hadn't been alone in a hotel in at least ten years. It rose swiftly, making Josie's stomach drop. The girls would have loved it. Izzy probably would have asked to ride up and down a dozen times.

She missed her daughters, and she hated Frank more for that.

The doors opened with the sound of a chime, and Josie pulled her wheeled overnight bag behind her as she walked down the hallway, staring at the numbers on the doors she passed.

She found her room and slipped her key into the slot, then pushed through the doorway. She stood in the deep quiet, taking in a long, slow breath. The room was pristine. It contained thick carpeting, a bed with fluffy white linens, a desk and straight-backed chair, and twin nightstands in blond wood with matching lamps. Atop the desk rested a phone, a complimentary bottle of water, and a small notepad with a pen placed diagonally on top.

Coming here had been the right decision. Josie needed the distracting clutter and chaos of her life to be stripped away in order to do what she had to next.

She tucked her suitcase in the closet and shut the door, then slipped off her shoes and placed them by the foot of the bed. She removed Frank's iPhone from her purse, then sat down at the desk. She found Dana's phone number in Frank's contact information, under her real name. As if he had nothing to hide.

Josie tapped the screen to dial the number, then quickly hung up. She didn't want to call from Frank's phone. If he'd managed to tell Dana they'd been discovered and that Josie had his phone, Dana would know it was Josie calling. And Josie wanted the element of surprise on her side.

Even as she reached for the hotel phone, Josie marveled at her ability to try to outmaneuver her husband at a time like this. If someone had asked her about her capacity for subterfuge a few weeks ago, she would have said that she was an open book.

She thought about the stories she'd heard of mothers who exhibited superhuman strength when their children were in danger—like a mom who'd lifted the back end of a car when her toddler was trapped beneath its wheel. Perhaps now, in the middle of the biggest crisis of her life, Josie was finally learning what she was truly capable of.

Frank never would have believed this side of her existed. He'd become a stranger to her, in some ways, this man whom Josie could have sworn she had pegged. But perhaps they'd both shielded parts of themselves from the other.

Josie dialed Dana's number again. She was aware her posture was rigid and her abs were clenched. Despite her lack of nourishment, the anger glowing within her gave her strength and a purity of purpose.

The phone rang a second time.

"Hello?"

It was a woman's voice, lower and more

gravelly than Josie would have expected, especially given Dana's slight stature.

"This is Frank's wife," Josie began. She hadn't planned what she was going to say, but as soon as she uttered the words, she knew they were the right ones.

Silence. She could hear Dana's quick inhalation, though. Dana hadn't hung up.

"How long have you been having an affair with my husband?" Josie asked.

Dana gasped. Josie felt a surge of satisfaction. Some of the power she'd lost during the weeks when she'd been foolishly unaware of the affair shifted back into her hands.

Then Dana whispered, "Hang on—please just hang on a second . . ." She sounded scared.

Josie could hear a rustle of movement, then a door closing. She wondered whether Frank had found Dana's deep, almost androgynous voice sexy.

"I'm here," Dana said. Her tone was a bit louder, but still relatively hushed.

Her husband—Ron—must be nearby, Josie thought. Perhaps he was watching TV on the couch, thinking his biggest worry was whether the Bulls made their next basket. If he was anything like Frank, he probably hadn't even noticed Dana had left the room, because he was so engrossed in the game. Did he think he had a happy marriage, too?

Josie felt a surge of pity for Dana's hapless husband. He and Josie were on the same side now.

"How many times did you sleep with my husband?" Josie demanded.

"I didn't—we just . . . No, I didn't sleep with him," Dana protested.

"How many times?" Josie repeated. Her voice was steely and unwavering. "I've got all of your emails. Maybe I should forward them to your husband?"

"No, no," Dana said. It sounded as if she had begun to cry. "Oh my God, please don't."

She, Josie, who shied away from confrontation, and who never thought of a comeback quickly enough when someone was rude to her, somehow knew exactly what to say.

"How many times?" Josie repeated. "Last chance."

Dana took in a long, shuddering breath, then continued. "I only saw him three times."

Three times. Not twice, as Frank had sworn.

Josie fell back into the chair, squeezing her eyes shut, feeling as if she'd been punched.

She'd wanted to know this information. She'd used a threat to extract it from Dana. She'd thought she'd been prepared for the worst, that she could handle whatever she learned. But each newly exposed lie seemed to tear away another strip of the protective, numbing layer around her body.

He must not have talked to Dana since Josie's discovery, Josie realized. Whatever he was doing yesterday when he dropped the girls at Maggie's, at least he wasn't meeting her. Because otherwise, they would have corroborated their stories. Dana would have insisted they'd met just twice.

"But we didn't sleep together," Dana said. "It didn't go that far."

So that meshed. But what else had Frank lied about?

Josie's mind spun back to exactly what Frank had said. *It was only kissing.* Dana contended they hadn't slept together.

But there was a pretty big gray area between those two assertions.

"Hello?" Dana said.

"Hold on," Josie snapped.

She didn't have much time. Dana could hang up at any second and refuse to speak to her. And Frank would be going back to work on Tuesday. Josie couldn't keep his phone much longer; he needed it for his job. Once he had it back and he talked to Dana, they'd be able to compare notes and conspire on a story, one that minimized what they'd done. Josie might never know the truth.

She had already made the choice to dive off this cliff. She had to use this time to find out whatever she could.

She stood up and paced the room.

"Frank said it was more than three times," Josie

said. It was a gamble; if she was wrong, Dana would know how little information Josie actually had. But Josie's instincts told her to take it. There were a lot of open nights during a seven-week period.

Dana's voice broke. "It wasn't . . . It was five. Okay. We got together five times. I'm sorry, I forgot . . ."

Her words ripped away another swath of padding, leaving Josie feeling raw and exposed. But she managed to press on, to keep talking. Her brain stayed clear and fiery even as her body reeled from the blows it was taking.

"You expect me to believe you just forgot?" Josie asked.

Dana was silent.

"Are you still married?" Josie asked.

"Yes," Dana whispered.

"Good luck with that." Scorn rippled through Josie's tone. "I have a feeling your husband is going to find out about everything."

She ended the call and slammed down the phone.

Five times, she thought. *Five.*

She wanted to curl up on the bed and sob like a child. *It hurts,* she thought. Had anything ever hurt her this much before?

She wanted to punch Frank, to hit him as hard as she could. To make him feel the same sort of agony that was tearing through her body. *How could you?* she thought. *How could you do this to me?*

In her wallet was a little piece of paper containing the number of the divorce lawyer. The lawyer, a woman, would be a shark if Karin had recommended her. Maybe Josie would phone her.

But she needed to make a different call first.

As she walked toward Frank's iPhone to pick it up off the desk, it began to buzz.

Josie looked down at the name flashing on the screen: *Dana.*

She scooped it up and pressed accept. "Hi," Josie said, a brittle edge lacing her tone. "Were you looking for my husband? Trying to set up date number six?"

Dana hung up without a word.

Josie couldn't help it. She laughed.

Then something in her body snapped and the tension she'd been holding broke. She began to cry. Not the deep, wrenching sobs she'd felt herself suppressing all day. Tears slid down her cheeks as silently and steadily as drips from a faucet.

Josie had heard somewhere that an emergency room surgeon confronted with daily horrors always allowed himself thirty seconds to steel himself for what lay ahead before he approached a patient on a gurney.

She began to count: "Five, six, seven . . ."

When she reached thirty, she went into the

bathroom, splashed cold water on her face with her cupped hand, and then looked down at Frank's cell phone, which she was still holding in her other hand.

This was the only chance she would have to learn everything, she reminded herself. After tomorrow it would be too late.

She dialed their home number. Frank and the girls probably hadn't left for the carnival yet.

He answered right after the first ring. "Josie?" He sounded hopeful.

"I need to see you," she said. "I'll come by the house after the carnival tonight. I'll call you right before I show up so you can come outside."

"Okay, sure," he said. Maybe he thought any contact was a positive thing, moving them past this crisis and toward a resolution. He needed to be punished for that.

"Oh, and Frank?" she said.

"Yes?" he asked eagerly.

"Your girlfriend has a weird voice," Josie said. "It's so deep and creepy."

She hung up before he could respond. She stared down at her hands—hands that had rubbed Frank's back after he'd thrown it out while cleaning the gutters; hands that had wiped the bottoms of their children and picked low-sugar cereal off the grocery store shelves and written checks for their mortgage—as if she had never before seen them.

· · ·

Josie passed the hours until it was time to meet Frank by taking a long, brisk walk outside. She was too restless to stay in her room. She managed to eat a croissant she bought at the café in the hotel's lobby but couldn't stomach anything else.

"Would you like a latte with that?" the woman at the café counter had asked.

Josie had shaken her head. "No thanks," she'd said. She didn't know whether she would ever be able to drink a latte again, or even hear the word, without remembering.

She went back to her hotel room and walked over to the desk. Beneath it was the refrigerated minibar. Josie pulled its door open. Inside were little bottles of vodka and rum, along with orange juice and Coke for mixers. She shut the door, erasing the vision.

She needed to remain clearheaded. And she had to press on, even though it felt counterintuitive to dig into the source of her pain. Wounds needed to be covered up; they demanded time and medicine to heal. But Josie couldn't pause. She had a narrow window of time to reestablish a true foundation on which to balance herself.

At any minute now, Frank could chance a call to Dana's home. Even if he didn't have the number, he could find a way to get it. It was probably listed. Frank was a smart guy who thought quickly on his feet. If Dana's husband answered, Frank could simply pretend to be a telemarketer and hang up.

*Phone calls,* Josie thought. She looked at Frank's cell phone again. Had Dana left Frank any voice mail messages that could provide more information?

Josie fought the sense of trepidation as she looked through Frank's call history. But there wasn't a single one to Dana listed. She then checked his voice mail messages. The few messages he'd saved all had *Home* as the source. Josie listened to them just in case. They were simply funny messages from the girls; Josie had several of those saved on her phone as well.

Josie checked all of Frank's texts, even the ones from male names, but they revealed nothing suspicious. Perhaps Frank and Dana had only communicated by email. Or maybe he had simply erased the records of their phone calls and texts.

The thought of such subterfuge made everything worse. It seemed so calculated.

Josie checked Frank's email again, even though she knew he wouldn't risk sending one to Dana now that Josie had access to his accounts.

What else?

She went over to the bed and lay down, folding her arms behind her head as she tried to think.

She'd already made one mistake, Josie realized as she stared up at the ceiling. She should have let Dana's call go to voice mail. Then she could

83

have texted Dana, pretending to be Frank. She could have tried to obtain more information that way.

But maybe she wouldn't have changed anything, given how satisfying it had felt to answer Dana's call. To have Dana be the one feeling upset and frantic.

Had the two of them laughed at her? Josie wondered. Maybe Frank had discussed Josie and their marriage with Dana.

An image thrust itself into her brain: Frank and Dana together in Atlantic City, in a hotel room much like this one, sharing breakfast in bed amid the rumpled sheets. Dana sitting up and handing Frank his mug of coffee, Frank's hand resting on Dana's bare back.

*Did you sleep with her?* she wondered, feeling her hands clench. She leapt up off the bed, trying to expel the image from her brain.

And then, as horror rose within her, Josie wondered: *Were there others?*

# Chapter Six

*Four years earlier*

Josie had never been angrier with Frank. Where was he?

She was almost six months pregnant with Izzy—an ultrasound had already revealed the baby's gender—and she needed to pee so desperately it was painful.

Josie and Frank had gone to the mall to look at infant car seats, even though Zoe's old one was still perfectly good. But Josie had learned from wretched experience that lifting a sleeping baby out of that soft, padded contraption and trying to carry her into the house and transfer her into a crib without waking her guaranteed a disastrous ending.

BabyFace, the store that anchored one end of their local mall, sold car seats that could be detached from a base that remained in the vehicle, then popped into the frame of a stroller. Which meant Josie could simply carry Izzy, car seat and all, into the house or wheel her along on errands if the baby dozed off during a drive. That contraption would be worth any amount of money.

Where *was* Frank? Josie wanted to lean on the horn in frustration. They were supposed to have lunch after their trip to the mall; Josie was craving Mexican food with such an intensity that she'd actually dreamt about eating a burrito last night. Zoe was at home, being watched by Josie's mother. Given that the baby was due soon, this would likely be one of their last days together as a couple for quite a while. And now Frank was ruining everything.

He'd asked her to go on ahead to the car and drive around to the curb in front of the store while he carried out the big, heavy boxes.

"See you in five," he'd said. She'd been waiting for more than fifteen minutes.

She should have used the restroom before leaving. BabyFace had the roomiest and cleanest bathrooms in the mall; they catered to the needs of their clientele.

If Frank didn't show up in another sixty seconds, she was going to abandon the car here and go inside again, even though signs clearly warned patrons that this lane was simply for loading purchases. He was probably chatting with the cashier or the customer behind him in line. Conversation was his stock in trade as a salesman; Josie used to admire his ability to connect with people. Now she wanted to strangle him for it.

She crossed her legs, but that made her even

more uncomfortable. *Stop blabbing, Frank, and get out here!* She mentally willed him the message.

Oh, here came her loquacious husband now. He was strolling—strolling, like he had all the time in the world—out of the store, accompanied by a young guy wearing a blue polo with the BabyFace logo. The young employee was pushing a flat cart loaded up with Frank's boxes.

"Hey, Jos!" Frank broke into a grin. "Can you pop the trunk? This is Dave. He's going to help me load up the car."

Josie smiled at Dave, shot Frank a death glare when Dave bent down to deal with the first box, then climbed out of the car and waddled furiously into the store. "Bathroom!" she called back over her shoulder at Frank. She wasn't even sure he'd heard her; he was too busy laughing at something Dave had just said.

Her irritation at Frank lingered after she exited the stall and washed her hands. She recalled how just last month they'd gone to a neighbor's house for the unveiling of the neighbor's new two-level renovation. "How long are we gonna have to stay?" Frank had asked. "I was going to try to hit the gym tonight."

"Just an hour," Josie had responded. She wanted to soak in a bubble bath and watch *The Voice* after Zoe fell asleep.

After they'd toured the home and admired

the walk-in closets and sparkling kitchen, Josie found Frank and asked whether he was ready to go. He'd looked at her in surprise. He was flopped on the sectional sofa in the basement with a few other guys. "Oh, I'm staying here to watch the game," he'd said, gesturing to the huge TV affixed to the wall.

"Really?" she'd responded.

"What?" Frank had asked. "Isn't that okay?"

He'd stayed for four hours, arriving home long after Josie and Zoe had both fallen asleep. She hadn't bothered to bring up the incident the next day—it wasn't worth an argument—but now her grievances formed a hard, rocky stockpile.

It was selfish, when you thought about it. Frank was so busy trying to charm everybody, wanting to make friends, that he sacrificed the needs of his own family. She was going to have a serious talk with him about this, because once the baby came along, she would be far less patient about this sort of thing.

She strode out of the store. Frank was in the driver's seat now, his aviator sunglasses on, bobbing his head to John Coltrane. The man did have good taste in music; she'd give him that.

She opened her door and looked down at her seat. A box wrapped in shiny silver paper and tied with a big gauzy bow rested there.

"What's this?" Josie asked.

Frank smiled at her. "It's for you. That's what

took me so long. Sorry to keep you waiting, baby. I had to run to the other end of the mall and pick it up."

Anger slid out of her, like air out of a balloon.

She picked up the box and settled into her seat. "Can I open it?" she asked. Josie adored getting presents, which Frank knew. He also knew that as a child, Josie's parents had adhered to the rule that children should only receive one gift apiece on their birthday and at Christmastime, stocking stuffers excluded.

She'd told him about that family rule shortly after they'd begun to date. "Plenty of kids don't get *any* presents, though," she'd said, shrugging. "I was a little spoiled, I guess, because I was always jealous of my friends who got more."

On her next birthday, Frank had shown up with an armload of gifts for her, including not only a bottle of her favorite perfume and the cowboy boots she'd admired in a store window, but also the retro Easy-Bake Oven she'd told him she'd deeply coveted in the third grade.

Now Frank put a hand on her knee. She felt his warmth through the fabric of her skirt. "You can't open it until lunch," Frank said teasingly. She turned the box over in her hands. It was about the size of a hardcover book, but it felt so light that she knew that wasn't what it contained.

"Aren't we going to the Blue Taco?" she asked when he turned the wrong way out of the mall.

Frank just smiled and turned up the music.

He drove ten miles away, to the nicest Mexican restaurant in the area, one with stone walls and cozy leather booths and waiters who wheeled around carts containing avocados and limes to make fresh guacamole table side.

"A virgin margarita?" Frank suggested, and when Josie nodded, he ordered two. "And a double order of guacamole, please," Frank told the waiter.

Then he grinned at Josie and slid out of the booth to sit next to her.

"Go ahead," he said.

She tore into the wrapping paper—her parents had always made Josie and her sister open their celebratory gifts slowly and carefully, which sucked some of the joy out of the moment—and opened the lid of the box. Inside was a single sheet of paper. When Josie unfolded it, she saw flight and hotel information filling the page.

"We're going to Cancún," Frank said. "You and me and Zoe, but we're staying at a resort that has child care so we'll have some time alone. They do prenatal massages and there are cabanas lining the beach. You're going to love it, baby. Both of my babies are going to love it."

He reached down and rested his palm on the curve of her belly.

She flung her arms around his neck, thinking of massages to ease her swollen ankles and achy back, and a sandy beach filled with the sound of soothing waves, and child care so she could put on a sundress and have an evening out with Frank.

It was the best gift she could imagine receiving.

"I just love you," she whispered in Frank's ear. She blinked back tears. How could she ever have been angry with this man? "I love you so much."

She let go of Frank and the waiter delivered their margaritas. Frank raised his. Their glasses clinked together.

"I love you, too," he said.

Those four days in Cancún were close to perfect. They stayed on the ground floor of a beachfront hotel, in a room with creamy tile floors and bright teal accents. They slept in a king-sized bed that faced the blue-green waters of the Gulf. Every morning, the three of them took the elevator to the rooftop restaurant, where smiling waiters twisted cloth napkins into animal shapes for Zoe and offered flutes of fresh-squeezed orange juice. Josie devoured huevos rancheros—eggs smothered with salsa on corn tortillas—for breakfast, napped along with Zoe under the shade of a thatched bamboo umbrella, and made love with Frank on a comforter spread out over the sand just beyond their room's sliding glass doors.

"Happy, Jos?" he asked her afterward, smoothing her hair back from her face. They were huddled under a blanket for extra privacy, even though an awning overhead and thick hedges on either side shielded them from view. Over Frank's shoulder, she could see a crescent moon.

"So happy," she responded.

"It's not as fun as our honeymoon, though," he said, and she laughed. They'd gone to Aruba, and it had started raining an hour after they'd stepped off the plane. *I wasn't going to let you out of the room today anyway,* Frank had said. The next day, he'd come down with a terrible stomach flu. Josie had gone to the beach alone one afternoon while he lay curled in bed, after making sure he had crackers and water at hand, and she'd stepped on the jagged edge of a broken shell, cutting the insole of her foot so deeply that the resort doctor had to give her two stitches.

"Worst honeymoon ever," Frank said.

"We made up for it with this trip." Josie shifted onto her side and Frank spooned her from behind.

"What do you think the baby is going to be like?" she asked, then she said, "Oh!" and grabbed Frank's hand, moving it lower on her abdomen.

"With a kick like that?" Frank kissed her shoulder. "Probably a holy terror. Or an NFL punter."

"Do you think Zoe's going to be good with her?" Josie asked. Zoe had shaken her head when they'd told her she was going to be a big sister. *No, thanks,* she'd told them, like she was rejecting the offer of an apple.

"Sometimes," Frank said.

"Yeah, and sometimes she'll be awful," Josie said. "That's the law of sisterhood."

They'd crawled back into bed around midnight, and the next morning, they'd awoken to hear Zoe's high little voice asking why there was so much sand on the floor.

Eleven weeks later, Izzy was born.

Josie thought she was prepared for the birth—even though Zoe, who had taken eighteen hours to emerge, had taught her that no one could be truly ready.

But her bag was packed, her mother was on standby to care for Zoe, and Josie was poised to demand an epidural the moment she entered the hospital.

Her contractions began around three o'clock on a Thursday afternoon, which was the absolute perfect time. She didn't have to wake up her mother in the middle of the night, Zoe was already home from preschool, and Frank was able to leave the office ahead of rush hour. Josie was even able to place an online Peapod grocery delivery, so the house would be stocked with food when she came home from the hospital.

Frank was flustered when he came through the

door. "You okay?" he almost shouted at Josie. She was sitting next to Zoe on the couch, watching *The Little Mermaid*—or, more accurately, watching Zoe and stroking her hair and soaking in these last moments when her daughter was her only child. As excited as she was about Izzy's arrival, it felt bittersweet.

"I'm fine, sweetie," she said.

"Your bag!" Frank said. He bolted upstairs, then thundered back down a moment later, empty-handed.

"I already took it to the car," she said, feeling the corners of her mouth curve into a smile.

"You're not supposed to lift anything!" he protested.

"Frank, I lift up Zoe every day," Josie said. "And she's a lot heavier than that bag."

Zoe nodded in agreement but didn't move her eyes from the screen.

"Okay, so . . . I guess I should go change and then we can go," Frank said. "Oh, no, Jos, what's happening?"

Her eyes were closed and her teeth gritted. She'd been about to tell Frank to calm down, that they had plenty of time and that they couldn't leave because her mother wasn't even there yet.

But she couldn't talk. She could barely even breathe. Her entire focus channeled into enduring the pain. Her earlier contractions, the ones that had started around three o'clock, had made her feel as though a pair of giant hands were gently squeezing her abdomen, stealing away her breath. They were perhaps a two and a half on the pain scale that went up to ten.

This contraction was easily a seven.

Then, just as quickly as it had come on, it disappeared.

Josie lifted a shaky hand to her brow and wiped away beads of sweat, then she noted the time on her iPhone.

"Contraction." She panted the word, but managed to keep her voice even so she didn't alarm Zoe.

"Where's your mom?" Frank asked, his eyes darting around the room, as if he might have overlooked her presence.

"She won't be here for another hour or two," Josie said. "I didn't think there was any need for her to rush."

"I'll call her." He ran to the kitchen. She could hear the rapid cadence of his voice, then he hurried back into the living room, just as another contraction hit.

This one was even worse, the pain spiraling deep inside Josie, as if someone were twisting her insides with a corkscrew. She gripped a throw pillow, her fingernails digging into the fabric, as her body clenched. When it passed, she checked the clock. Just three minutes since her last one.

They were supposed to go to the hospital when her contractions were ten minutes apart.

She'd imagined taking a warm bath and going for a family walk before kissing Zoe good night and leaving for the hospital. But now she knew she had to get there fast.

"I need to get to the car," Josie said as she struggled to her feet.

Frank looked at her face. Then he transformed.

He scooped up Zoe in one hand. He grabbed Josie's purse with the other. He opened the front door and held it with his foot until Josie passed through.

"Wait here," he told her as she paused on the front step. "Do not try to climb down those without me."

She watched as he ran to the car, strapped Zoe in, tossed in Josie's purse, and hurried back with a look on his face she'd only seen during the other times he'd transformed.

It had happened three or four times before, always in a crisis. Her laughing, overly social husband became a grim-faced man of singular focus. Once, it occurred when a young boy had come down the sidewalk on a wobbling bicycle that was seemingly out of control, heading directly toward Zoe, who was coloring with chalk.

Josie had been kneeling in the garden about ten yards away, planting purple and yellow pansies, and she'd looked up at the sound of the boy's approach. "Zoe!" she'd yelled, knowing she couldn't get to her daughter in time. "Look out!"

She'd seen a blur of movement out of the corner of her eye. It was Frank, who'd been pushing the lawn mower around to the front yard. He'd abandoned the machine and was sprinting diagonally across the yard, faster than Josie had ever seen him move. Then he'd hurdled the hedge—actually hurdled it, like a high school athlete at a track meet. Josie expected him to scoop up Zoe, or shield her body with his own, even though she knew he wouldn't be able to avoid impact. Instead, Frank planted himself in front of the onrushing bicycle, reached out, and grabbed the handlebars. The bike jerked to a stop. The boy fell off and tumbled sideways onto the grass.

Josie watched, openmouthed, her trowel still in hand. By the time she reached Zoe, their daughter was already in Frank's arms, and Frank was extending a free hand to help up the boy.

"Too bad you didn't catch that on video," Frank said, but he was breathing hard, and his eyes were wide.

"How did you— Frank, you saved her!" Josie cried. She reached out and wrapped her arms around both of them. The boy had already climbed aboard his bike and was wobbling down the sidewalk again.

Frank winced. "Pretty sure I pulled a hamstring," he joked, reaching down to rub his thigh.

Josie put a hand over her rapidly beating heart. "You are the best father in the entire world," she said.

Now, as Frank ran toward her as she stood on the front stoop, she saw that intent look on his face again. And as another contraction spiraled deep within her, stealing her breath and nearly sweeping out her legs from beneath her, she felt sure of one thing: Frank would keep her safe, too.

"Stay with me," she pleaded with him as they pulled into the hospital's emergency entrance. The ride had been torture, seemingly filled with potholes and stop signs and clueless drivers who were moving well below the speed limit. She'd been vaguely aware of Frank calling her mother again, instructing her to meet them at the hospital, and of Zoe asking from the backseat whether Mommy was all right.

"I will," Frank promised as he put the car into park. "I just gotta run in and get someone to help us."

He disappeared through the automatic doors, and a moment later, an orderly bearing a wheelchair came out.

"Ma'am?" the orderly said as he opened Josie's

door. "Can you come sit here?" He reached for her arm.

"No—don't touch me," Josie gasped. She felt her eyes starting to roll back into her head. She was in agony, gripped in the force of a contraction that made her want to thrash in pain. But she instinctively knew movement would make it worse, so she gripped the armrest and waited it out.

"Okay," she panted a moment later, blinking back tears. "Okay."

She eased herself into the wheelchair. "Zoe," she said.

"She's right here," Frank said. "C'mon, Zoe, you're going to see Grandma and then tomorrow you'll get to meet your baby sister. I've got your bag, too, Josie. Your music and everything."

She lost track of time, but she clung to his voice. It threaded through everything that followed. She knew her mother must have arrived, and Frank must have handed Josie off to her. She was aware of someone trying to insert an IV into her arm—those needle jabs were almost laughably insignificant on the pain scale—then a ridiculously young doctor was examining her.

"Where's Dr. Barr?" she gasped during a lull in her contractions. Now they were about one minute apart. She'd forgotten to call her doctor; she'd been waiting for the mythical ten-minute contractions.

"On her way," Frank said. "Look at me, Josie. We got this."

*We?* she thought.

"Epidural," she panted. "Why is it taking so long?"

She saw the doctor look at Frank. "She's already nine centimeters," the doctor said.

"Nononono," Josie moaned. She knew what that meant; she'd heard stories about women who arrived at the hospital too late to receive painkillers.

"We can't give her an epidural at this point," the doctor said.

"Are you sure?" Frank asked. "Look at her! She's in pain. Can't you do something?"

"The anesthesiologist is with another patient," the doctor said. "He probably wouldn't be able to get here until she's ready to push anyway."

Then he shrugged. The ridiculously young doctor shrugged.

Josie wanted to rise up off the table and attack him.

"God, Jos, I'm so sorry," Frank said. "Do you want, um, an ice chip?"

She gripped his hand as another contraction overtook her.

"Okay, we're going to do this," Frank said. "We're going to breathe through it. I'll breathe if you can't. Ready? One, two, three . . ."

It was agonizing and endless and grueling; the

violence gripping her body felt otherworldly. But an hour later—Frank would later tell her that's how long it took, since she had no concept of time—she heard Izzy's hoarse little cry. The doctor laid the warm, wet bundle that was her daughter on her chest, and suddenly, the pain was almost all gone.

"You did it," Frank said. His hair was rumpled, and he was still in the dress shirt he'd worn to the office, though he'd discarded his suit coat and tie somewhere.

He leaned down to kiss Josie.

She was too weak and drained to speak. She couldn't even nod.

"She's perfect," Frank whispered.

"Would Daddy like to come and watch her get her first bath?" a nurse asked.

Josie found her voice. "Not yet." She looked at her husband's face. He had one hand on Izzy's tiny back, and he was crying. She covered Frank's hand with her own. "Can we stay like this a little longer?"

They couldn't, of course. Things changed with two children; life grew busier, harder, messier. Izzy wasn't a great sleeper, and Josie sometimes felt as stretched out as the old Gumby doll she'd purchased for Zoe at a yard sale. She never left the house without a diaper bag and drinks and snacks for the girls, but more than once, she'd arrived at the park and realized she'd forgotten to brush her hair. She snapped at Frank more often, too, but it felt justified, especially when he sauntered in the door after work, went upstairs to change, and flopped on the bed and channel surfed until she came to find him.

"I just need a few minutes' break, okay?" he'd say to her.

"What about me?" she'd respond, stress making her voice brittle. "I haven't had a break either!"

One of the worst fights of their marriage came when Zoe was three and a half, and Izzy was just six months old. Josie had staggered to bed around nine o'clock following a day in which she'd done nothing but wipe up spills, change diapers, soothe, clean, pacify, fix, repair, and cook.

Frank was downstairs on the couch, watching a game, of course. She was the more sleep-deprived of the two of them, because Izzy refused to take a bottle. "Princess and the Pea syndrome, huh?" Frank had said.

"Sure, joke about it," Josie had said, aiming for a funny tone but landing more in passive-aggressive territory. Izzy's particularities meant that Frank could no longer do nighttime feedings. He could sleep through the night while she alone tended to the baby. She felt hollow-eyed from exhaustion.

"I'll be up in a minute," Frank said.

She'd crawled into bed and had fallen asleep almost instantly, as though she were falling into a dark tunnel.

Then she awoke to feel someone tugging at her. She rolled over, expecting to see Zoe. But it was Frank.

"Hey," he said. "Sorry, you were using my pillow."

She blinked. *"What?"*

"I bought this new pillow yesterday, remember?" he said. "It's one of those memory-foam ones."

She vaguely recalled him mentioning he'd passed by a store and picked one up at lunchtime, but that wasn't the point. She wasn't asking for clarification about Frank's preferred brand of sleep support.

"You were pulling a pillow out from under my head?" she said. "While I was asleep?"

"I didn't know you were asleep," he protested.

"What, my closed eyes weren't a clue?" She was wide-awake now, seething with the injustice of it all. Izzy would be crying in another hour or two for a feeding, and Frank would just roll over and nestle more comfortably into his memory-foam pillow while she, Josie, got up and took care of their daughter.

And when was the last time she got a lunch hour? When did she ever get to go to a restaurant for a salad someone else had made, or to browse through interesting shops on her way back to an office?

Her anger was so close to the surface that she knew it must have been brewing there for a while. "You are so inconsiderate!" she shouted. She sat up and brushed away hot tears. "I can't believe you woke me up so you could be more comfortable!"

"Jos, come on," Frank said. "You were only in bed for a minute. I didn't think you were really asleep."

"A minute of actual time, or a minute of Frank-watching-a-game time? Because those are two very different things."

"Seriously?" he said. "Are we going to start this argument again? Jos—what are you doing?"

She stalked across the room and yanked open the closet door, searching for her overnight bag. "I'm going to a hotel!" she yelled.

"What? Fine, take the pillow."

"I don't want the pillow! I want to sleep!" she wailed. She climbed back into bed.

"So sleep," Frank said.

"Just—just—shut up!" she snapped. She flipped to her side, putting her back to him. Prolonging the battle would eat into her precious rest time.

She hated her husband sometimes, she thought.

She rolled over to see him lying flat on his back, staring up at the ceiling.

"Don't ever wake me up again!" she hissed. Then she flipped away again.

"Don't worry, I won't," she heard Frank mutter in a tone that felt like an insult. She edged farther away from him on the mattress, resenting him more with every one of his exhales. And when Izzy cried in the night, Josie made sure she let the baby wail an extra minute before she rose, so that Frank would have time to become fully awake, too.

They didn't speak to each other the next day. They never resolved the fight, either. But as time passed, it seemed to dissolve.

There were also moments of grace during those hard years, like flashes of sunlight glinting on the surface of a dark ocean.

One sunny Saturday in early October, shortly after Izzy had turned nine months old, they drove to a Halloween festival and clambered into a wagon for a hayride. Zoe curled up on Frank's lap, while Josie cradled Izzy. Josie's leg pressed against Frank's every time the wagon went over a bump or made a turn. When they went around a particularly sharp curve and the hayride driver shouted, with mock fear in his voice, that everyone needed to hold on because they might flip, Frank wrapped an arm around Josie. The four of them were so close together, every one of them touching another, linked into a single unit.

*We're a family,* she had thought, and happiness enclosed her, so deep and profound it nearly made her dizzy.

# Chapter Seven

*Present day*

Josie pulled up in front of their home and turned off the car engine. Stillness settled around her as abruptly as a slap.

The sun had slipped below the skyline, but the house was well lit and she could glimpse movement inside. The girls should have had dinner by now. Josie wondered whether Frank had done anything to make it special. Perhaps he'd cooked hot dogs and macaroni and cheese and had plated the meal to look like silly button faces with wild orange hair.

She exhaled and leaned back in her seat. She didn't want to get out of the car for this conversation. She'd keep the keys in the ignition and her foot on the gas so she could drive away at any time.

The front door opened and Frank came out. He wore jeans and a plain gray T-shirt. He already looked thinner, somehow, even though Josie knew that was impossible.

Or maybe he had lost a few pounds recently, and Josie simply hadn't noticed because Frank was so familiar to her—his body, his habits, his voice—that she'd stopped actually seeing him long ago. It was possible. Frank was better about such things than she; he always commented when she got her hair cut or wore something new.

Perhaps he'd lost a few pounds for Dana.

She flung open her car door and got out then, riding on a surge of anger-infused adrenaline. She folded her arms and watched as Frank drew closer.

She had to stay clearheaded, to the extent that it was possible. She'd already selected her opening words on the drive over.

"You lied to me," she said.

Frank's brow creased.

"On top of the obvious lies," Josie said. "Dana and I had a nice little chat today."

Frank's eyes closed and something swept across his face, tugging his features downward.

"Five times, Frank?" Josie said. She drummed her fingernails against her forearms. "*Five* fucking times?"

"I'm sorry," he said, his voice low. "I'm so scared. I didn't know what to do."

"You haven't shown me a lot of respect, Frank," Josie said. "Why don't you start now by telling me the truth."

"It was five times," Frank said.

"Are you sure?"

His head snapped up and he looked her in the eye.

"Maybe I just told you that to trick you," Josie said. "You don't know what I know. How much I've learned."

"It was only"—he backpedaled—"I mean, it was five times. I swear. I swear on my life."

"Did you two have fun on her birthday?" Josie asked.

Frank's eyes widened. Josie's lips curved into a cold, hard smile. There was something intensely satisfying about watching him twist after what he'd done to her.

"How did you—" Frank began.

She could see him mentally scrambling to try to recall exactly how many emails might have been on his phone, and what he and Dana had written. In another thirty-six hours, he'd be able to find out. Frank had used his work email account to message with Dana. So when he went into his office, he could use his work computer to access the account. Maybe he'd even try to go in tomorrow, on the holiday. She'd have to seal off that avenue now. She needed to stay a step ahead of him.

They were locked in a chess game.

"I didn't sleep with her," Frank said. "I'm telling you the truth, Josie. I couldn't do that to you."

A cold pebble of a laugh shot out of Josie's mouth. "What integrity you have."

Frank looked down and scuffed the toe of his sneaker against the pavement. "Do you want me to leave? I can go to the hotel."

"Sure, why not. Invite your girlfriend to join you."

He didn't respond.

She looked at the house. "What are the girls doing now?"

"Watching a movie," Frank said. "They had dinner."

"Don't let them watch too much TV," Josie said. "Get them outside tomorrow. And do not leave them with a neighbor again. You need to watch them. I don't want them out of your sight. Do not take them into the office so you can talk to your girlfriend, either."

"No, Jos, I wouldn't." Frank looked wounded.

"Who paid when the two of you went out?" Josie asked.

"Um, the first two, it wasn't— I mean, I think I did. Just for a few drinks."

"That was *our* money! Not yours to spend on dates with other women!"

It was such a minor transgression, considering. And yet it burned a hole in Josie's gut as she thought about how she'd bought cheap T-shirts and selected a minivan with cloth seats instead of the far-easier-to-clean leather.

She turned away from Frank and caught sight of someone approaching. It was a woman Josie didn't recognize, dressed in jeans with rolled-up cuffs and a long red coat.

*Dana?* Josie thought wildly. Her pulse quickened.

But as the woman drew closer, Josie realized she was too young; she was probably only twenty or so.

"Hi," the woman said as she drew closer.

Incredibly, Josie found herself smiling. "Hi," she and Frank said in unison.

"Nice night," the woman said. She had a slight accent. She offered her hand. "I'm Nicola. I'm here as an au pair for the Robertsons."

"Nice to meet you." Josie shook Nicola's hand, then watched as Frank did the same. The sight of his large hand closing over the delicate, paler one shot a spear of jealousy into Josie.

Frank had touched another woman like this. And he'd done so much more.

"I was trying to find the park with the swings," Nicola said.

"It's down another two blocks," Josie said. "Make a left on Beech Avenue and you'll see it."

Nicola thanked them and moved on.

"Josie," Frank began, but Josie held up a hand. When Nicola was out of hearing range, she indicated to Frank to go on.

"I know this has done tremendous damage to you. To us," Frank said. She saw his throat move as she swallowed. "Can we go to counseling? I can find someone. I'll do anything I can to fix this. I swear, I want to kill myself for hurting you."

"You're a good salesman. But I'm not buying it." The venom coming out of Josie's mouth stunned even her. She had never spoken to anyone like this before, with such cutting contempt. "If you had any kind of decency, any shred of respect for our marriage, you would have stopped it after one time and confessed. But you just kept going. You'd still be having an affair if I hadn't caught you!"

Frank's eyes were red-rimmed. "I am so sorry. I will say that to you until the day I die."

She couldn't let him hijack this conversation; she needed to control the chessboard.

"Is she married?" Josie asked. It was a test.

Frank passed: "Yes."

"Kids?"

"She has a son." Frank scratched a spot above his ear. "I don't know much—she never talked about him."

"Do you have any idea of what the two of you did?" Josie asked. "Two families, destroyed. Hope it was worth it."

Frank didn't answer, but he seemed to crumple into himself.

*Good,* Josie thought.

"You say you didn't sleep with her," Josie said. "But you kissed her. There's a lot of room between those two places. What else did you do, Frank?"

She held her breath. Her pulse pounded wildly in her ears. She grew dizzy. She felt as if she were stretching out her hand toward a downed electrical wire that might still be live.

Frank cleared his throat. When he spoke again his voice was so low she could barely make out the words. "We— I mean, there was a little more than kissing."

The probing was too dangerous now. She recoiled from the explosive shock it delivered, even though there were other questions she desperately needed to ask: *How far, exactly, did things go physically? Do you care about her?* And: *What about that night last year when you said you went to a work dinner and I couldn't reach you?*

But Josie found herself retreating, first walking and then running to her car. Her chest heaved with shallow, panicked breaths. She climbed in and pulled away from the curb, leaving Frank standing on the sidewalk, staring after her but making no move to stop her.

# Chapter Eight

The world had grown wild and uncertain; it reminded Josie of a book she'd read to her children about a boy named Max, who was transported to an island where nothing was familiar, where monsters roamed and turbulent waves thrashed in the sea.

Josie exited her hotel room and took the elevator down to the parking garage. After fleeing from her conversation with Frank, she'd spent all of ten minutes back in her room before realizing the uneasy energy pulsing through her body made it impossible to stay. She had to get out again.

She still wasn't hungry, but she knew she needed to eat something to keep up her strength. She'd thought about having dinner in the hotel restaurant, but one glance inside convinced her it was too dimly lit and empty. Plus the eager smile and beckoning gesture from a passing waitress indicated that the service would be overly attentive. She didn't want to be alone with her thoughts, nor did she want to make polite conversation with a stranger. She needed the sounds and movement of other people to not only distract her but camouflage her.

Josie unlocked her Sienna and climbed in, noting how strange it felt to suddenly have so much unstructured time alone. In her other life, the one that no longer existed, she'd be collecting laundry and making a grocery list and answering emails, all the while tending to the needs of the kids.

Josie nearly slammed on the car brakes as she caught sight of the time on the dashboard clock. She and Frank were supposed to have a date tonight. They'd talked about trying a new Peruvian restaurant. A neighborhood teenager was scheduled to show up at seven o'clock, which was almost the precise hour now.

If she hadn't found out about the affair, she'd be dabbing perfume behind her ears and slipping into heels. Trying to look pretty for her husband. The thought was an ember in her chest.

She thought about texting Frank before she remembered she had his phone. He'd have to deal with it, make up an excuse for the sitter. Frank might need to learn how to manage on his own from now on, she thought.

Josie wound through the streets surrounding the Marriott, passing a Chipotle and then a Starbucks—the green awning another electric shock of a reminder—before settling on a tapas restaurant. It looked expensive. Josie hoped her bill totaled more than all of Frank's dates with Dana.

She found a parking spot near the entrance, shut

off her engine, and opened her door. Then she closed it again. She adjusted the rearview mirror and considered her reflection. Her skin was clear, but her lips were chapped and the lines spreading out from her eyes seemed more pronounced than before. She opened her purse and removed her makeup bag. She took some time to apply dark sable eyeliner, a little blush, and some lip gloss. She finger-combed her hair, smoothing the flyaways, then exited the car.

Maybe she'd flirt with a handsome man sitting alone at the bar. It would serve Frank right. She had a free pass to kiss anyone she wanted. Perhaps if she had an affair of her own, the score would feel more even.

The thought sent an unexpected thrill through her. She still had the number for Steve, the hot stay-at-home dad, in her phone contact list.

She pulled open the heavy wooden door to the restaurant and stepped inside. She immediately realized she'd made the correct choice in coming here. Small tables were nestled throughout the floor space, ringed by cushioned booths covered in plush red leather. Against the back wall, flames danced in a giant fireplace. The bar was crowded, and the buzz of voices and laughter filled the room, mingling with John Legend's voice pouring out of the speakers.

"One?" the hostess asked as Josie approached the stand.

"Yes." Josie had never minded eating alone. Especially these days, when Izzy's possible almond allergy often complicated their family trips to restaurants.

Josie followed the hostess to a table that was nestled against the wall, turning one side of it into a booth. Josie slid onto the soft red leather and accepted the menu that the hostess opened like a book.

She perused the offerings before settling on a trio of small plates: a romaine leaf salad with goat cheese and slices of mandarin oranges, spinach sautéed with garlic, and spicy shrimp.

"And a glass of pinot noir," she told the waiter.

"Very good." He gave a nod. He was an attractive man, muscular and dark-haired with a slight accent. Perhaps in his late twenties. No wedding ring.

What would it be like to kiss him? Josie wondered, watching him walk to another table and noticing his black pants were a touch too tight.

She'd had boyfriends before Frank, of course. A serious one during her senior year in high school, and two more in college. Plus there had been a handful of other guys she'd made out with after meeting them at frat parties or bars. But her other physical encounters were so distant in her mind that recalling them was like remembering a scene from a movie. She could visualize the setting, but she couldn't access the sensations.

The waiter brought her wine along with a small dish of mixed black and green olives. "On the house," he said as he laid them down in front of her. She smiled as she thanked him.

"How is the wine?" he asked.

Josie took a sip. "Delicious."

It wasn't her imagination. The waiter was lingering at her table. Had he noticed her awareness of him? Perhaps she was giving off pheromones announcing her availability.

She'd stopped looking at men as possibilities many years ago. That part of her had felt closed off. If she kissed the waiter—or anyone—would she think of Frank?

Josie felt certain she would, even now. Especially now.

Another diner gestured for the waiter, and he moved on. Josie selected a plump green olive and leaned back. Nearby, a family—father, mother, and teenaged daughter—were eating together. Josie studied them, noticing how the mother carried the conversation. The father's head was bent low as he focused on his dinner, and the daughter's phone was partially hidden under her napkin.

Josie couldn't hear her words but could sense the effort the mother was putting into trying to engage her family. The mother lifted the breadbasket, offering it to the others, then served her husband a bit of her entrée. He barely looked at her.

*Jerk,* Josie thought. Perhaps he was having an affair, too.

She wondered how she and Frank and the girls had appeared to others in public. Not a perfect family—Izzy had a tendency to throw tantrums—but a good enough one. Frank was an expert at cajoling Izzy back into a good mood. He was a touchy-feely guy, too; he often reached for Josie's hand or wrapped an arm around her.

They probably looked happy, Josie thought. If she had been able to step outside of her body and regard the four of them objectively, she was sure that would have been her conclusion: a happy family.

They had probably appeared that way the entire time Frank was conducting his affair.

A loud ding sounded from within her purse. Josie reached for her phone, but the only texts on it were ones she'd already seen earlier that day: a few from Karin, asking whether she was okay (I'll call you soon, Josie had replied), and one from the room mother in Zoe's class, reminding parents to check the lost-and-found basket because it was nearly full.

This sound had originated from Frank's iPhone.

As she pulled it out of her purse, Josie noticed her hand was shaking, which angered her. *Your fault, Frank,* she thought. He was the one who'd thrust her onto this dangerous island, where lattes and hotel rooms and iPhones had become monsters.

The text was from a neighbor named Ryan, a guy they'd known for years: **Bro, you on for poker at my place Thurs?**

Josie felt some of the tension leave her body as she slipped the phone back in her purse. Before she gave it back to Frank, she'd need to scroll through his contact lists, taking note of any women's names.

But not tonight. She'd taken in all she could endure for one day.

Josie's eyes flitted around the restaurant, alighting on the romantic young couple leaning toward each other over the votive candle in the center of the table; the laughing, rowdy group of five women; and the older man alone near the corner. He was the other single diner. His head was bent over a newspaper, but he looked up with a smile when a waitress delivered his dessert.

How many people in this restaurant had cheated, or were cheaters? Josie wondered. There must be statistics somewhere; she was certain she'd read them. The number was shockingly high, as she recalled—maybe 50 percent, or even 70. So most of the people in this restaurant probably had been affected by an affair.

It was one of the most depressing things Josie had ever contemplated.

The flirtatious waiter swung by her table. "Another glass of wine?" Josie looked down, not realizing she'd finished it.

"Sure," she said.

The waiter probably had a girlfriend, too. Perhaps he gave free olives to all the women who dined alone in his section.

She had known the odds. Why had she ever thought she could be immune from this epidemic?

*Stupid,* she chastised herself. She hadn't wanted to believe it. She'd been like a little kid playing hide-and-seek, covering only her head, leaving herself completely exposed.

When the waiter brought her a fresh glass of wine along with her salad, she avoided his eyes.

A moment later her cell phone vibrated on the table. Her home number showed on the display.

She let the call go to voice mail, then immediately checked the message in case Frank was calling to say something was wrong with the kids.

*Mommy?*

It was Zoe.

*I just wanted to say good night . . . and that I love you.*

Josie stared down at her phone, feeling tears well up in her eyes.

She had always tried to put her kids first—

what mother didn't? She'd bought them organic baby food and she'd covered the sharp-edged slate around the fireplace with soft padding, she'd soothed her girls through nightmares, she'd talked to the teachers when a mean girl had made fun of Zoe's hair and tried to get other kids to join in.

Her central purpose was to be the protector of her children. To be there for them.

Right now Zoe needed her.

But Josie couldn't call back her daughter to wish her good night because she worried that when she heard Zoe's sweet, high voice she'd break down in tears.

She stuck the phone back in her purse, tallying this fresh wound with the others Frank had caused.

As she picked up her fork and toyed with a lettuce leaf, an image came to her, of the last time Zoe had been upset. The same mean girl who had made fun of her hair, telling Zoe the short cut made her look like a boy, had excluded Zoe from a birthday party. Only five kids were invited, so it wasn't a big deal—except to Zoe. She'd cried when she'd come home from school that day.

And Frank had left work a little early after Zoe had called him to report the slight. He'd taken Zoe out for frozen yogurt, letting her pile on so many sugary toppings that Zoe had trouble remembering them all when she recounted the evening to Josie. Then he'd bought her a Wii and a dance party game to go along with it.

"A *Wii?*" Josie had been torn between anger and understanding when Zoe came in, her cheeks flushed with excitement, carrying the box. They'd planned to buy the girls one for Christmas— which was two months away.

"I know, I know." Frank had turned those root beer eyes on Josie. "My girl was so sad. I couldn't stand it."

Josie had shaken her head, half exasperated at Frank. And half enamored with him.

Frank was a fixer.

Josie realized she was fidgeting with her wedding and engagement rings, rubbing her left thumb along the hard metal.

She speared the piece of lettuce and forced herself to chew and swallow it even though she felt nauseous. Her girls needed her to be strong for them. And Josie needed to be strong for herself, so she could resist Frank.

Because she knew he would do everything in his power to fix them.

# Chapter Nine

Today was the last day of discovery, Josie thought. Tomorrow Frank would return to work. He'd talk to Dana. Whatever else was going to come out would emerge today.

She'd managed to get a little sleep last night, even though she had been dreading the darkness, certain her mind would torment her once she finally stilled her body. When she'd returned from the restaurant, she'd watched a silly game show on TV in which contestants ran around a supermarket, filling up carts with the most expensive items possible. At one point during the show, she'd glanced at the nightstand, where her iPhone rested next to Frank's. She'd reached over and pushed Frank's onto the carpet, where she couldn't see its glowing blue screen. Then, around eleven thirty, she'd rolled onto her side and drifted off. She'd slept straight through until four thirty, awakening in the exact same position, as if she hadn't moved at all during the night.

Yet she still felt exhausted, so depleted she wondered whether she was coming down with the flu. Her limbs ached heavily and her sinuses were stuffy. She'd taken a hot shower around five, then she'd put on the hotel robe and had curled back up in bed.

She knew she needed to get organized, to make a plan. She imagined Frank closing the door to his office tomorrow morning and cupping his hand around the phone receiver as he whispered to Dana. They'd compare notes as they crafted a story to minimize the repercussions of their affair. Josie needed to squeeze every bit of truth possible out of him before that happened tomorrow.

But her body refused to cooperate. It kept her tethered to the bed, where she spent the morning listlessly watching a Jennifer Aniston comedy. At around ten, she ordered room service, selecting eggs Benedict, which she adored but rarely had the chance to enjoy. She hadn't been able to eat much last night, and she told herself she'd feel better when she had something in her stomach.

Immediately after she placed the order, a thought sizzled through her mind like a lightning streak: if Frank and Dana had spent the night together on their business trip in Atlantic City, then woken up and shared breakfast in bed, there might be evidence.

The realization galvanized her, sweeping away her lethargy. She bolted out of bed, her breath coming quickly, scrambling to grab her purse from where it hung on the knob of the closet door. Frank had a credit card he used for business travel, one that his company had given him. Presumably his room was billed to that account. But Frank might not have charged a breakfast for two on it, since anyone in the office who reviewed that expense would presumably have flagged it.

*Who paid?* she'd asked Frank.

*I did.*

Maybe he'd charged breakfast in bed with Dana to his personal credit card—to their credit card. He might have felt safe doing so, because he was the one who saw the statements.

Josie and Frank had fallen into an unspoken routine when it came to household chores. He cooked dinner on nights when he arrived home early; she shopped for groceries and made the other meals. She did all of the laundry and took on far more than half of the household cleaning—they'd bickered about that countless times, with Frank claiming he did at least 40 percent (another lie)—yet nothing ever seemed to change.

But Frank handled the bills.

He collected them from the pile of mail in the dining room every week or so and took them into the office, where he kept a checkbook and stamps. He'd told Josie that occasionally, during long conference calls, he pressed the mute button and knocked off that chore.

Josie dug her hard gray card out of her wallet,

then flipped it over and located the customer service number.

She dialed it and was eventually connected to a customer service representative whose voice contained a bright smile.

"So, I just—" Josie's voice was husky. She realized she hadn't spoken to anyone since the waiter the previous night, more than twelve hours ago. Normally, by this time, she would've cajoled the girls to get dressed, negotiated with them about what to eat for breakfast, and hustled them out the door to the park or the free play hour at the local gymnastics center. She cleared her throat and began again.

"I need to double-check a charge," Josie began. She sat down on the bed and pulled her knees to her chest, wrapping her free arm around them.

"Certainly, I can help you with that. Can you give me your name?"

"Josie Moore." If they divorced, she'd have to go back to her maiden name, Shaw. She'd have a different last name than her children.

"Wonderful. And can you just first verify the primary cardholder's social security number?"

Frank was the primary cardholder. He'd opened the account before they'd gotten married, then he'd added Josie to it. But Josie had committed Frank's social to memory long ago because he was so terrible with numbers.

She heard the woman's computer keys clicking, then: "And which charge would you like to verify, Mrs. Moore?"

Josie hesitated. "I'm not sure exactly . . . It would be in Atlantic City. Can you just let me know about any charges that were made to this card about two months ago in Atlantic City?"

"Certainly," the woman said again. "Let's see . . . I'm finding an eight dollar and forty-six cents charge at an Arby's. Then I see a bigger charge here—"

"Yes," Josie interrupted. "What was that one for?"

"Just a moment, please . . ." The woman's voice was a shade less bright, perhaps because of the tension in Josie's.

Josie's abdomen clenched.

"It was a four-hundred-dollar cash advance."

"Cash?" Josie echoed. "Why would he do that? Why wouldn't he just use an ATM if he needed cash?"

The customer service representative remained silent.

"Are those the only charges?" Josie asked. She became aware that she was tapping the fingers of her left hand against her thigh and she stilled the motion.

"They're the only ones I see originating in Atlantic City." By now the smile had completely vanished from the woman's voice.

Josie thanked her and hung up. She dropped her head into her hands. Had Frank needed money to wine and dine Dana? Perhaps he'd been wary of removing the money from an ATM, knowing she might see a sudden dip in their joint checking account balance.

Four hundred dollars would have paid for a few very nice meals.

She'd ask him about it. But she'd hold the information close until the right moment.

Her head jerked up at the sound of a knock on the door.

She uncurled her legs and stood up, the carpet soft beneath her bare feet. She slowly walked across the room and looked out the peephole.

It was only room service.

"Just a second," Josie called. She grabbed the bathrobe from the closet, wrapped it around herself, and opened the door.

The delivery woman wheeled a cart into the room. "Here?" She gestured to a small table by the window.

"Perfect," Josie said. She watched as the woman made a production of removing a tray from the cart, centering it on the table, and whisking off the silver cover from her entrée.

"Your eggs Benedict. Sugar and cream for your coffee, and a glass of filtered water . . ." The woman pointed to each item as she named it.

"Great, great," Josie said.

"Is there anything else you need?"

"No. Thanks."

"Are you here on business, or on pleasure?" the woman asked as she handed Josie the leather folder containing the bill.

"I— A vacation."

"How nice. And where are you from?"

"Ahh, Ann Arbor," Josie said. She'd never been to Michigan, but it was the first thing that had popped into her mind. She gave up scanning the small print to see whether a service charge was included, added four dollars to the total, and quickly handed back the bill.

"Enjoy your visit." Josie hurried to the door and held it open as the woman wheeled the cart back out. The woman was older, and beneath her black skirt, her ankles looked swollen and tired. Josie felt a flash of guilt, not for the lie but for answering so abruptly. The woman had only been trying to be nice.

Perhaps the room service attendant was divorced. Maybe she needed this job to make ends meet. Josie recalled the total on the bill: her breakfast had cost twenty-one dollars, twenty-five with the tip. It was almost certainly more than her server made in an hour.

If she and Frank divorced, Josie might need to get a better-paying job. She would insist upon staying in the house, of course. She was the primary caregiver, and the girls would need consistency. But they could barely afford one mortgage, let alone two.

Josie sat down heavily in the chair next to her tray of food. Then she picked up her fork and pierced a poached egg, watching the yolk run down the side of the English muffin.

All she had to do right now was eat breakfast, she told herself. She could deal with the rest of her life later.

# Chapter Ten

When Josie walked through her front door with her suitcase, the house felt unnaturally still.

"Izzy?" she called. "Zoe?"

In the kitchen, a note rested on the counter: *We went to the mall. Be back soon.* It was Frank's handwriting, but Izzy had decorated the paper with fat pink crayoned hearts. Josie stared down at them while she stroked Huck's soft ears, then she gave the dog a scoop of food, just in case Frank had forgotten this morning. It was one of Josie's usual chores.

Josie let Huck out the back, then thumped her suitcase upstairs and stared at the bed. The bedding was rumpled, which meant Frank had slept in it last night. There was still a dent in the center of his pillow. The television remote rested on his nightstand.

Had it been there the previous day? Josie couldn't remember.

Perhaps Frank had enjoyed a little television while she'd tried to force down a dinner that had been a disaster because of what he'd done. She felt a thrum of rage—how could he be watching sports? Frank shouldn't be allowed to sing along to his favorite song on the radio, or savor a hot, gooey piece of pizza, or linger in a warm shower.

She grabbed the remote and turned on the television. It was tuned to ESPN. She navigated to the screen showing the programs recorded on the DVR. She knew Frank loved *Game of Thrones*, so she deleted the episodes he hadn't yet watched. She didn't feel any better when she watched them evaporate from the screen, though.

She lifted her suitcase onto the bed and began to unzip it. Then she glanced at their closet again.

They'd divided it down the middle—Josie's things were on the left, and Frank's on the right, which happened to correspond to the sides of the bed they slept on. Josie walked over and pulled the closet door open wider. Frank's side was filled with suits on hangers, and more casual clothes—jeans and T-shirts—stuffed into drawers and bins. A few were crumpled on the floor, too. Although Frank was careful with his suits, he was terrible about taking care of his more casual clothes. The man was incapable of folding, so his things were always wrinkled.

She stepped into the closet. He'd probably worn suits when he'd gone out with Dana, since their dates were likely all after work. But Josie couldn't assume anything. Perhaps he'd also snuck out to see her on a weekend under the guise of going to the gym or getting a haircut.

She'd take advantage of the unexpected gap

in the day by investigating Frank's belongings, even though she suspected Frank would have thrown out anything incriminating by now. But he might have overlooked an item. She ran her hands through the pockets of his suits but turned up only a ChapStick, a few crumpled tissues, and a parking ticket dated the previous week. She searched his drawers and his jeans pockets, but nothing of interest turned up. She smoothed the crumpled bits of paper he'd left in the bowl of change on his dresser, but they weren't illuminating: he'd ordered coffee and a bagel at Au Bon Pain and had gotten his car washed a few days ago.

She wasn't sure what she was looking for. A receipt from another hotel that Frank and Dana had used as a daytime love nest. Or a tube of lipstick. Josie was hungry for more information about Dana, and even the brand of makeup she used could've told Josie something about her.

Her brain, which had felt almost aggressively sharp following her discovery, was growing muddy. She knew she was missing something. What was it?

The clue was the credit card receipt for Au Bon Pain, Josie finally realized. She'd only checked their card charges for Atlantic City. But it would be easy enough to review all of their Visa charges for the past two months. She could trace Frank's movements. If he and Dana had met for a lunchtime tryst at a hotel, he would have had to put it on their credit card. If he'd bought her a birthday gift, or a Christmas present, the name of the store and amount would be identified.

The thought of what she might learn made her feel as if she were teetering on the edge of a precipice. Maybe that was why her brain was slowing down. It could be a form of self-preservation, to keep her from learning too much, too soon, and falling into the void.

The front door opened and Josie heard the girls burst inside, arguing about who'd pushed whom and sounding, as they always did, as if they were a much bigger collection of people.

"Mommy?" Zoe called over the sound of Huck barking.

"I'm here." Josie walked downstairs. She swept past Frank without a glance and gathered her daughters into her arms. She could feel Frank's presence looming over her. Watching to see what she'd do next.

"Hey, how about we go out for dinner and then ice cream?" Josie suggested. "Just the three of us. We'll let Daddy get some work done here."

She kept her gaze lowered so Frank couldn't catch her eye. She scooped up her purse from where it hung at the bottom of the staircase banister, then shepherded Zoe and Izzy back through the door.

"When will you be back?" Frank asked.

"Later!" Josie closed the door in his face. She couldn't be around him.

It didn't matter that he could also seize the unexpected gap in the day to get a head start on damage control. She'd found out enough. She didn't need to talk to Frank again before he returned to the office, after all. What did it matter anymore?

Five times. More than just kissing.

She could never trust him again.

Today would be a turning point, Josie thought the next morning as she pulled on her jeans. Its contours were familiar, at least superficially: Frank would go into the office. Josie had emails to return and work to do around the house. The girls would go to school, Zoe carrying her Transformers backpack and Izzy with her Little Mermaid one.

Tonight, though . . . Josie had no idea what would happen when Frank returned from the office.

She stayed upstairs until she smelled coffee.

Frank always filled a to-go cup moments before he left the house. He had three that he rotated among. All were the kind that could be decorated and personalized with special markers, and Josie had helped the girls write their names as well as messages to Frank on them before wrapping them up.

Frank was stirring sugar into the insulated cup—*World's Greatest Daddy* was written on it—when Josie walked into the kitchen. He always added two heaping spoonfuls to his brew, despite the fact that she'd told him agave tasted just as good and was much healthier.

"Morning," Frank said. Josie just nodded.

He grabbed a sponge and began wiping down the counters, erasing his coffee dribbles. Somehow this felt like an insult, too: it had taken the discovery of his affair to get him to do his share around the house.

Josie reached into her pocket and pulled out his iPhone. Frank's sponge stopped moving mid-arc. She set the phone down on the counter. Frank stared at it, then jerked his eyes to Josie.

He'd shaved this morning and had nicked himself. A tiny red cut that looked like a little piece of thread was near his jawline.

She spun around and walked out of the room.

She imagined Frank driving down the block and pulling over once he was out of eyesight. He'd scroll through the emails, wincing when he got to the shower message.

Now he'd know exactly what he and Dana had written to each other. He would know what Josie knew.

Not everything, though. She was still holding some evidence close. The four-hundred-dollar advance on their credit card. The possibility of other charges that would tell more of the story. And the potential loose threads on Frank's phone—unfamiliar names and phone numbers—that she hadn't yet investigated.

"Kisses for Daddy!" Frank called upstairs. Zoe and Izzy thundered down for the morning routine: Frank gave them each ten butterfly kisses, then ten Eskimo kisses, and one giant "platypus kiss" in which Frank blew raspberries against the girls' cheeks. It always made them laugh, although Zoe made a production of wiping off her cheek and claiming it was gross.

"I love you all!" Frank called. There was a beat of silence. Then Josie heard the door close.

It wasn't even eight o'clock yet. Frank was eager to rush into the office.

"Breakfast, girls!" Josie said. She was aware that her voice was artificially bright. Suddenly she needed to hustle the kids outside, away from the charade she and Frank were putting on. Did Zoe and Izzy sense anything? The experts said kids took in a lot, even little ones, so maybe they did.

"Mommy, you're hugging me too tight," Zoe said, squirming away.

"I'm sorry, sweetie." Josie turned away, so that Zoe didn't see her wipe her eyes.

She had thirty minutes to fill before she could put the girls in the car and drive them to school.

It seemed like a very long stretch of time.

"Guess what? We're leaving now and we're all going to get a treat for breakfast. How about hot chocolate and croissants?" Josie suggested.

"Chocolate croissants?" Izzy always seized an opportunity to negotiate a better deal.

"Sure!" Josie said. "But only if we leave right now."

"Where are we going?" Zoe asked.

"I don't know." Josie rummaged through her purse to find her keys. "Panera."

She said it even though she knew that the girls might want hot chocolate from their favorite treat place, because it was rich and delicious and always topped with whipped cream.

*Please don't,* she mentally pleaded with them. She didn't want to drive into the same parking lot where her life had shattered.

Zoe was putting on her shoes and Izzy was checking her lunch box, to make sure the contents met with her approval. They were both distracted. Josie played a little game with herself: Maybe if neither of the girls mentioned it, it was a good omen. Maybe it would mean that Frank hadn't slept with Dana, that he'd only ever flirted with other women but hadn't crossed the line, and that there were no more surprises lurking ahead. It could mean the pain Josie was experiencing had already crescendoed.

Or would the good news be that Frank had had

dozens of affairs, that he was so evil and slimy that it would be easy to walk away from him?

Zoe finished tying her shoe and looked directly up at Josie.

"Why can't we go to Starbucks?" she asked.

# Chapter Eleven

"I only want to tell you this once, then not talk about it again," Karin said. "Okay?"

The day was unexpectedly balmy—at least, balmy for winter in the Chicago suburbs, which meant it was in the thirties but sunny with no wind—so they were walking outside, in Karin's neighborhood. Karin had offered to come to Josie, but as soon as Josie left the girls at school, the restless agitation swept over her again.

She felt as if her skin no longer fit; as if she were itchy everywhere but unable to scratch. She craved activity, but her usual routine—tidying the house, throwing in a load of laundry, returning work emails—seemed overwhelming. She'd slept fitfully last night, awaking every hour or two, but she wasn't the slightest bit tired. She was glad for the extra few minutes' distraction of driving to Karin's.

Before they'd gone ten steps, Karin said it: "I cheated on Marcus once." Just like that, her tone flat and unapologetic.

Josie's feet stuttered and she almost tripped. She glanced at Karin, her most solid, together friend, the woman with the happiest marriage around. The woman who said she'd kick Marcus out if *he* ever had an affair. "Why?" was the only thing she could think to say.

"We went away for the weekend with another couple," Karin began.

"Who?" Josie interrupted.

"You don't know them. We don't talk to them anymore. For obvious reasons," Karin continued. "This was before the twins were born."

Josie picked up her pace to match Karin's, which had quickened.

"It was this couple Marcus knew from work," Karin said. "The woman was in his office, and they became friendly when they worked on a project, so we met them out for dinner. It was one of those things, where you just hit it off as a foursome. Everyone liked everyone. But Marcus and the woman—Jane—had more in common, and I always seemed to end up talking to Brad."

Karin glanced at Josie. "Are you mad at me?"

Josie shook her head. "More shocked."

Was everyone having affairs? Apparently the answer was yes. Even the last people you expected.

"We all went away for a weekend," Karin continued. "It was a work retreat, at a resort where there were conference meetings during the day and dinners at night. A spa and golf course to entertain the spouses. Brad and I ended up hanging out the first day while Marcus and Jane were at some boring seminar. We had a couple of mimosas at brunch, then went to the driving range. It started to rain and there was an indoor theater so we caught a movie. It was totally innocent, but it wasn't, you know? Something changed that day. I can't even describe it. We hadn't touched or anything, but we were laughing a lot."

Josie's stomach tightened. It began at a work conference. This was hitting too close to home. But she didn't interrupt.

"We all went to dinner together that night. I was sitting next to Marcus. Brad was across the table from me, by Jane. And then during appetizers, during the middle of a speech by one of the partners, I felt my phone vibrate. I looked down and saw a text from Brad."

"What did it say?"

" 'Throw a roll at me if I fall asleep.' So I texted back, 'Why don't we throw them at the guy at the podium instead?' " Karin hesitated. "It sort of felt like that was when we crossed the line. If Marcus and I had spoken those words so everyone could hear it would be one thing, but . . ." Karin shook her head. "Anyway, later that night Jane went to bed early and Marcus was busy talking to colleagues. I was stuck in a conversation with the managing partner of Marcus's firm, this guy who always reminds me of a hyperactive rat terrier. I excused myself and told Marcus I was going back to the room. I could tell he wanted to stay;

he was having a fine time. So Brad offered to walk me back. He said he wanted to head in for the night, too."

Josie touched Karin's arm. "Wait, Marcus didn't pick up on anything?"

He must have felt so foolish, too.

Karin shook her head. "He just gave me a kiss on the cheek and turned back to the group. Anyway, the cocktails were on an outdoor patio that was set a bit away from the entrance of the hotel. You took a little path through some trees to get back to the rooms. The path was lit with these little round footlights, but it was still pretty dim. I told myself Brad was just being gentlemanly, that he needed a reason to escape all the work chatter. I told myself that up until the moment when he pulled me behind a tree and kissed me."

Josie sucked in her breath. She wanted to know more, but she also didn't.

"What was it like?" she finally blurted. She asked the hard questions quickly, before she lost her nerve. "Better than with Marcus? More exciting?"

Karin shook her head. "Just . . . different. I kissed him back. It was a long kiss."

"How long?" Josie asked.

"A few minutes," Karin said.

"Jeez," Josie said. "Weren't you afraid someone would see you?"

"Not during but right after, yeah. It was crazy.

Marcus couldn't see us from the patio, but he could've walked up along the path at any second. Or one of his colleagues."

It was hard to believe the kiss hadn't been more exciting than with Marcus, Josie thought, feeling a jab of jealousy. Otherwise why would Karin have risked so much?

"But then we broke apart and I don't know . . . I just wanted to get away. I went right to my room. Brad kept texting me, asking what was wrong . . . It was awful. I didn't respond. I told Marcus I was coming down with something. I stayed in our room the next day, and we left early."

Karin moved aside to let a woman walking a golden retriever pass.

"Does Marcus know?" Josie asked.

Karin nodded. "I told him pretty quickly. Right after we got home. I just couldn't keep it from him. He was so angry. I've never seen him like that."

"What did he do?" Josie asked.

"It was the way he looked at me," Karin said. She shrugged but her voice grew ragged. "Like he'd stopped loving me—like he didn't even know who I was anymore."

Josie nodded. She could see how Marcus would feel that way. "Did he confront Brad?"

"No," Karin said. "I don't know if Brad's wife knows, but I don't think so. She tried to get together with us a few times after that, but we always made excuses. She probably thinks I hate her or something. I feel awful about that. But the truth would be worse for her."

Would the not knowing be easier? In a way, yes. Josie hadn't known about Frank's affair for seven whole weeks. She'd been happy during that time. Perhaps if she hadn't borrowed his phone, the affair would have run its course, and she might have lived her entire life without ever discovering it. But she would have been existing within the bubble of a lie; she would have been living with a man who wasn't truly in their marriage.

"So Marcus just . . . forgave you?" Josie asked.

"Yeah," Karin said. "He did. He didn't talk to me for two days. Then we went to therapy. I suggested it. I told him everything, every last detail. He punched a wall when we got home. I've never seen him like that."

Josie couldn't imagine it. Easygoing, soft-spoken Marcus, who seemed always to be trying to woo Karin, even after all their years together.

"For him it wasn't just the physical act of the kiss," Karin said. "It was the betrayal. He kept going over the times the four of us had spent together, obsessing about things. Like whether I'd been flirting with Brad when I'd told him I liked his shirt this one time. Marcus said the two of us had turned him into a fool. His pride was wounded."

It was just one kiss, on one night. It seemed so minor compared to what Frank had done. Plus Karin had confessed. That detail was crucial. She had chosen to put Brad on the outside, and to let Marcus in.

If Frank had come to her and confessed, rather than let Josie discover his affair, would she feel any differently? The hurt and anger would still be there, but at least she'd know he felt guilt and remorse. It would probably still be unforgivable, though.

"Was it really an affair, though?" Josie asked. "I mean, I know it wasn't right, but you barely did anything."

Karin nodded firmly. "I have to take responsibility for this. I can't ever minimize what I did. It became an affair the moment I answered his text. The moment we created a secret."

The hurt fell over her again, heavy and gray as a dentist's X-ray apron. After Josie left Karin, she picked up Izzy at preschool and brought her home. She still had work calls to return, laundry to throw in, groceries to buy. But she couldn't do any of those things.

She parked Izzy in front of the television, and she crawled into bed. Visions invaded her head, memories that were shifting shape now that she was assimilating new information.

Like Frank gesturing for the waiter and ordering

Josie a second margarita on her birthday. She'd laughed, protesting that it was a weekday night, but Frank had just cupped a hand over his ear: *Did you say something? I didn't hear you, babe.* The girls had been playing with tortilla dough— the waitstaff at this place always brought kids hunks of it—and Josie had reached over and pulled off a piece, twirling it into a mustache and sticking it to Frank's upper lip. *Such a good look for you, handsome!* She'd laughed. The girls had wanted mustaches, too, so Josie made them for the whole family.

Frank's hand, warm and comfortably familiar, on her thigh, on the drive home. His reaching for her under the covers, sliding up her nightgown as he positioned himself over her.

Had he been thinking of Dana?

She thought of the time last summer when they'd gone to the pool and stood in line at the snack bar behind a woman who was wearing a white crocheted bikini. Josie had been aware of Frank's awareness of the woman. She'd felt a slight hitch in his energy as they'd stood behind the gloriously tanned, fit woman.

Josie had noticed the woman also. She'd taken in her sculpted shoulders and the curve in her lower back, wondering how someone her age could have the body of a twenty-year-old dancer.

The woman had gotten a bottle of water from the snack bar and sauntered away. Josie and Frank had moved up to place their order for hamburgers and fries for the girls, and within minutes, Josie completely forgot about the stranger in the white bikini.

Had Frank? she wondered. Or did Frank's eyes roam around the pool as he sought her out again?

Josie curled on her side, facing away from Frank's half of the bed. She felt so empty. Her entire marriage had been a sham.

She lay like that for two hours, until it was time to pull herself up and retrieve Zoe from school. She felt as though she were seeing everything through a foggy lens, as if the sun had fallen out of the sky. She ached down to her bones.

She put Zoe in front of the TV alongside Izzy and microwaved a bag of popcorn for them. She tore open the top of the bag and allowed the hot steam to escape before handing it to them, not even bothering to pour it into a bowl.

She wished she could ask someone to come stay in the house and care for the children, so that she could remain in bed. Her parents wouldn't be of any help, though. Her mother could run the kids to school and make them dinner, but she'd demand to know what was going on with Josie, and anything she said would undoubtedly make Josie feel worse. Josie would feel the weight of her mother's judgment in every impatient gesture she made: her mother would shut the dishwasher door a little too firmly, or run the vacuum in whatever room Josie was in. *Snap out of it,* her mother would be silently saying. As long as things looked good on the outside—if Josie's hair was brushed and her children were in tidy outfits—her mother would assume the complexities of Josie's life were also under control.

Josie couldn't ask Frank's parents, or either of his older brothers, even though they were all great with kids. They'd pick up on the tension running through the household. Josie wasn't ready to confide in any of them yet. Besides, they shared Frank's blood. They might take her side in this particular instance, but their long-term loyalty would be with Frank.

Josie thought back to the last time she'd been sick. It was two winters ago, when Izzy was still pretty small. Josie had come down with a fever that was quickly followed by chills. Her throat felt as if it were on fire. She dragged herself into the doctor's office, where she was diagnosed with strep. *Are you sure it isn't the bubonic plague?* she'd joked, then she'd coughed profusely into her elbow.

The doctor had given her a prescription for antibiotics and recommended lots of rest and fluids. Josie had stayed in bed for thirty-six hours straight, napping and sipping herbal tea with honey, the comforting low hum on the television filling the background. It was exactly what she wanted to do now.

But the person who had stepped in then, who had taken time off work and had organized the kids' meals and kept them entertained, was Frank.

When Frank arrived home from work that night, he walked directly into the kitchen, where Josie was stirring spaghetti in a pot.

"Ah, hey, can we talk for a minute?"

She looked at his face. Then she turned off the burner and followed him back outside. The spaghetti would absorb too much water and be ruined, but it didn't matter.

Frank was going to tell her something important. Perhaps he was going to ask for a divorce.

A sharp wind cut through her sweater and she shivered. Frank clicked the fob on his key chain to unlock his Honda Civic and Josie climbed into the passenger seat. *Had Dana sat here?* Josie found her eyes skittering around as she searched for something. A strand of hair. An earring that had fallen into the crevice between the seat and the center console. But there was nothing.

Frank pulled open his door and sat next to her. They were so close now; barely a foot separated them.

Josie moved as close as possible to her door and waited. By now Frank must have talked to Dana. If he wasn't going to tell her he wanted a divorce, then he would still be in damage-control mode. Whatever he was going to say would likely be a lie.

"Dana's husband called me today."

"What?" Josie heard the shock in her own voice. "What did he say?"

"He left a message. I didn't answer," Frank said. "Here."

He reached for his phone and navigated to the voice mail section. Josie felt an intense curiosity gripping her: How had Ron found out about the affair? Had Ron threatened Frank?

Ron's message began to play: *This is Ron Hallman. I don't want you to ever call my wife again. I don't want your wife to call my wife. You need to stay away from us. Got it?*

The message ended.

Josie stared at Frank's phone, feeling betrayed. Ron was mad at her for calling Dana? But she and Ron were in this together; they were an unwitting pair. Shouldn't they be aligned against their partners?

She glanced up at Frank. His face was expressionless.

"I know I've said this before, but there was no intercourse, Josie. I swear to you."

His voice was confident and assured. It was the kind of tone he used to convince Izzy that there were no monsters hiding under her bed.

Obviously that confidence came from his

knowledge that Dana was sticking to the same script. Josie felt fury ripping through her lethargy, so quickly that she knew it had been close to the surface all along, like lava boiling inside a volcano.

"Well, thanks, Bill Clinton." She spit out the words. "I guess that makes it all better."

He flinched. "I'm sorry, Josie. I'm so sorry."

She looked at him, really and truly looked into his eyes, for the first time since her discovery. She'd always assumed she'd be able to tell whether he was lying. She knew Frank's moods: She knew he liked being around his mother, but chafed when she reminded Frank that he was her "baby." She knew he felt a little competitive with his two older brothers, who'd been football jocks in high school. She knew he was self-conscious about his thickening waistline, and that he thought he was a better singer than he actually was.

He hadn't expressly told her any of those things. Through the years, she'd simply learned how to read him.

But now she couldn't glimpse what he might be concealing.

A wild thought seized her: What if Frank was lying about the voice mail, too? Maybe he and Dana had cooked up this plan and gotten someone to leave the message so that Josie and Dana's husband wouldn't compare notes?

It was a crazy notion. But Josie couldn't discount anything. She'd ignored her suspicions before. She wouldn't be that naive again.

"Can you play that message again?" she asked. She leaned her head back against the seat and closed her eyes, so that she didn't give Frank any clues about what she might be thinking.

"Sure," he said, sounding a little puzzled.

Josie kept her eyes closed until she heard Ron's voice. Then she snuck a glance at the phone, which Frank was holding out between them. She saw the nine-digit number displayed on the screen. She repeated it to herself over and over as she opened the car door, hurried back into the house, and reached into a kitchen drawer for a pencil and Post-it note.

# Chapter Twelve

*Five years earlier*

"You're going out for drinks with your ex-girlfriend?" Josie asked Frank.

"Yeah." He looked at her more closely. His forehead creased. "What?" Frank asked.

Josie knew these things about Frank's ex, whom he'd dated for all of his senior year in college: Monica was from Nebraska, she'd been an economics major, and she was drop-dead gorgeous. She had long red hair and pale, pale skin and blue eyes, but she didn't look like a fragile china doll. Her cheekbones were strong and her teeth were perfect. The first time Josie had seen a picture of Monica, she'd thought: *Jessica Chastain.*

Monica and Frank were Facebook friends. She always posted a message for Frank on his birthday, but didn't seem to interact with him often otherwise. She and Josie weren't online friends. They'd never met.

"Why is she coming to town?" Josie asked.

"A cousin's wedding," Frank said.

Josie nodded. "Is she married?"

"Divorced. They were just together for, like, less than a year."

There wasn't anything wrong with Frank wanting to catch up with an old girlfriend, Josie told herself. They'd reminisce about college days; they'd briefly resurrect their twenty-year-old selves as they dived into old memories. They'd probably have two drinks—three, tops—and Frank would be home within a few hours.

"Why don't you invite her here instead, honey?" she suggested.

The following night, at precisely eight o'clock, their doorbell rang. Josie had been trying to put Zoe, who was then two years old, to bed. But Zoe wasn't having any of it. She shot out of her toddler bed and ran to the top of the stairs, eager to meet their visitor.

Josie sighed, scooped Zoe up onto her hip, and headed to open the door. But Frank beat her there.

"M!" he boomed as he hugged their guest.

Josie walked up behind them as Frank released Monica. She held out her hand and smiled. "Hi. I'm Josie."

Josie had done her best to make a good impression: she'd applied sheer foundation and mascara, she'd worn a flattering new top, and she'd thoroughly cleaned the house, shoving shoes and toys into closets and setting a platter of cheese and grapes on the dining room table, out of Huck's reach.

"It's nice to meet you," Monica said.

Frank ushered Monica inside and Huck barked and everyone started talking all at once, including Zoe.

"It's always a little chaotic here, sorry." Josie laughed.

"Madhouse," Frank agreed. But he didn't laugh.

Frank reached for Monica's coat, helping her shrug out of it. They all moved into the living room and Frank took drink orders, then grabbed the still-barking Huck by the collar to drag him into the kitchen.

"Give him a treat and he'll quiet down," Josie called after Frank.

"Your daughter is just beautiful," Monica said in the ensuing quiet.

*So are you,* Josie thought. Monica wore a belted, silky black jumpsuit. It was an outfit very few women could pull off.

"Thank you," Josie said. "So! Have you been to Chicago before?"

Monica shook her head. "It's my first time. I thought it would be colder."

"You came during the right week," Josie said. "We're having a warm spell."

Monica's cheekbones were truly spectacular, Josie thought. She was every bit as beautiful in person as she was in her Facebook pictures, but there was also a remote quality about her. She didn't smile easily. She held herself somewhat rigidly. Josie couldn't tell whether she was aloof, shy, or simply uncomfortable about being here.

"Please come sit down," Josie said, gesturing to the couch. She remained standing, since she still had Zoe on her hip.

"Chardonnay," Frank said, coming back into the room and handing a glass to Monica. He'd used their wedding crystal instead of their everyday wineglasses. Josie hoped he'd rinsed it out first; it was probably dusty. He set the second glass, for Josie, on the coffee table, out of Josie's reach.

"Sweetie, were you going to put Zoe to bed?" Frank asked. The question felt abrupt.

"Oh." Josie blinked. "Of course. She just wanted to say hi to our guest."

"Don't want bed!" Zoe said.

"Off you go, pumpkin," Frank said.

"Want Daddy!"

"You can give Daddy a kiss," Josie said. "Then it's bedtime."

Predictably, Zoe didn't like that. She was overtired by now, along with being upset about missing whatever action was taking place in the living room. She wailed as Josie carried her up the stairs, screamed when Josie put her in bed, and wouldn't be consoled even when Josie climbed into the toddler bed next to her.

Frank's shadow appeared in the doorway a

158

moment before he did: "Jeez, Jos! Can you at least shut her door?"

"I—" Josie started to say, but Frank closed the door on her words.

"I did," Josie said anyway, into the darkness. "But it didn't catch and it swung open again."

Zoe's screams trailed off into whines and then the occasional mutter before she fell asleep. Her entire performance lasted for less than five minutes.

Josie took a moment to freshen her lip gloss and fluff her hair in the bathroom before she went back downstairs.

"Sorry about that," she said as she entered the living room. She took the spot on the couch next to Monica. Frank was seated across, in his favorite leather armchair.

"Oh, no worries at all," Monica said.

"She's a handful, but we kind of like her," Josie said.

"Zoe usually doesn't do that," Frank said. "I don't know what got into her tonight."

Josie took a sip of wine to hide her confusion. *Usually doesn't do that?* If there was one consistent thing about their daughter, it was her passionate hatred of bedtime.

"So, Charlie met her at a poker tournament?" Frank asked, turning to Monica. "I like her already. I'm giving the marriage good odds."

Monica smiled and nodded.

"Charlie's the cousin getting married?" Josie asked.

"Yeah," Frank said. "I met him once. Good guy."

There was a little pause.

"Josie, Frank, you have a lovely home," Monica said.

Aloof, Josie decided, and overly formal. Monica was pleasant but not warm. Josie wouldn't have thought she was Frank's type—and vice versa—but maybe the old adage that opposites attract had held true for them.

Frank had also taken care with his appearance tonight, Josie suddenly realized. His hair was gelled, he'd shaved since work—she knew because he always sported a heavy five o'clock shadow by the end of the day—and he was wearing a black sweater that Josie always complimented him on.

"Cheese? Crackers?" Frank offered. He brought in the platter from the dining room and set it down on the coffee table.

"Huck! No!" Josie jumped up. "Hang on, I'll put him out back."

She grabbed a rawhide bone from the box in a kitchen cabinet, opened the sliding glass door, and tossed it into the backyard. Huck ran after it.

"That'll buy us twenty minutes of quiet, at least if Zoe doesn't wake up," Josie joked when she returned to the living room. She pushed the platter closer to Monica. "Help yourself, please."

"Thank you." Monica took a cube of cheddar and nibbled it. Normally Josie would've dived into the Brie but in the face of Monica's restraint, she held back.

They all chatted for a while longer, then Monica declined Frank's offer of a second glass of wine. "I'm driving," she said with a smile.

"Ice water?" Frank suggested.

"Sure," Monica said. "That sounds good. I'm a little dehydrated from the flight."

"Where do you live again?" Josie asked, as if she hadn't creeped Monica's Facebook page just that morning.

"San Francisco." Monica accepted the glass of water from Frank—he'd selected an actual glass, not the plastic stuff they usually used because Huck's wagging tail was a threat to anything resting on the coffee table.

Most people would've added a detail or two, something that would inspire further conversation—"I love it there" or "I just moved three years ago"—but Monica let her responses lie flat.

And just like that, Josie could suddenly see how the dynamic between Monica and Frank must have worked. He was a people pleaser, and she didn't seem like someone who was easily pleased. She would have been a constant challenge to Frank, who was always driven to win others over, to make friends with everyone in the room.

"San Fran is gorgeous," Frank said. "That bridge, the piers . . . One of the world's great cities."

"Beautiful," Josie agreed. "The restaurants are amazing, too. And your work, Monica? What do you do?"

The conversation went on like that, with Josie and Frank peppering Monica with questions, then supplementing her answers with their own commentary. Josie wasn't exactly sure how it had happened, nor was she sure she liked it. It felt a little bit like Monica was a queen, and they were her subjects.

"Sweetie?" she said, and her husband turned to her. "I'm going to get more wine. Would you like another beer?"

"Yeah, sure," Frank said.

Monica still had more than half of her glass of water left, and Josie didn't offer to refresh it, as she might have with another guest. Josie was aware of what she was doing: She was trying to show that she and Frank were equals. That he might have served her the first glass of wine, but she was returning the gesture. It was a message she wanted to send not only to Monica but also to Frank.

It made her feel as if she and her husband were

a team, at least until Monica left at a little after nine. Josie had been surprised to see how early it was; she'd thought a good two hours had elapsed since Monica's arrival.

After they shut the door behind Monica, Josie turned to Frank, ready to rehash the evening. She was going to be careful about criticizing Monica—she'd suppress the term "ice queen" that yearned to spring to her lips—but she wanted to be honest. *What did you see in her, beyond her looks?* she planned to ask Frank.

But Frank spoke first. "Jeez, Jos, why'd you think it was a good idea to have drinks here? With Zoe and Huck and everything, it was a disaster."

Josie felt as if she'd been slapped. *It wasn't a disaster,* she thought. *It's our life.*

She thought of how she'd spent a long time cleaning the house, and how she'd asked Monica a dozen questions about herself but fielded only a couple in return. Frank hadn't appreciated any of that. All he'd cared about was impressing Monica.

She blinked back tears. But Frank didn't notice. He was already walking upstairs.

The next morning, Josie tried to continue their conversation.

"I worked really hard to make everything welcoming for her," she said. "I bought expensive cheeses and good wine, not the stuff I usually get . . ."

Frank was making coffee at the kitchen counter. He turned around and dropped a kiss on Josie's forehead. He'd already moved past his irritation. "I know, babe. Look, all I'm saying is it would have been easier if we'd gone out somewhere."

Josie felt deflated; that wasn't the point, even though Frank was right. He'd wanted to meet Monica at a restaurant, and Josie was the one who'd changed the plan. But the overtures Josie had made weren't exclusively for Monica's benefit. They were for Frank, too.

"It just would have been nice if you'd said thank you, that's all."

"Thank you," Frank said, so reflexively it defeated the purpose.

Things still didn't feel right to Josie, even though Frank kissed her again when he left for work and said he'd be home early. But then the dishwasher flooded the kitchen and Huck simultaneously became violently ill—the vet suspected he'd chased and eaten the frothy bubbles spewing all over the floor—and they never did have a longer conversation about the night. It seemed easier to let it go.

Monica still posted a message on Frank's page every year, the same simple "Happy Birthday Frank!" But she never came to town again.

Early in their marriage, Josie and Frank fell into the habit of divvying up the holidays like a pie.

Her parents lived less than an hour away, and his lived closer to two, which meant it was possible to celebrate with everyone. Josie always viewed this as a mixed blessing.

They traditionally spent Thanksgiving Day with Josie's family. Josie's mother's table could've graced the cover of a magazine, and her sister's twin daughters always wore pretty matching dresses. They drove to spend the following Friday night with Frank's parents and brothers, for an "Un-Thanksgiving" that included a touch football game, turkey and cranberry sauce sandwiches, and an Adam Sandler movie—usually *Happy Gilmore*.

They spent Christmas Eve with Josie's parents, then went home after dinner so the girls could wake up in their own home and open presents (at least, that was the excuse Josie used with her mother; she still harbored clear memories of those single-present Christmases). Early in the afternoon on Christmas Day, they drove to Frank's parents' again.

"Merry, merry!" Frank's mother shouted when she opened the door of her big colonial-style home to them. Zoe was six that year, and Izzy was almost three. "Doc, the kids are here!"

Frank's mother, Susie, always called her husband Doc, as did everyone in the family. Frank's father looked as if he could be the kindly neighborhood pediatrician, but he was a respected oncologist.

"Get out of the cold!" Doc urged as they stamped their snowy boots on the front mat. "Come on, we've got towels down on the floor for that."

"How was traffic?" Susie asked, as she always did.

"God-awful, Mom," Frank said, kissing her on the cheek. He and his father gave each other a handshake that turned into a hug.

"I've got hot buttered rum on the stove, shall I get you each one? And warm cider for the girls," Susie said, already moving toward the kitchen. "I'll put it in big mugs, you need to warm up." Susie always narrated her actions. Josie found it comforting.

"Hey, hey, look who's here!" Frank's oldest brother, Stu, came into the hallway. Frank was standing on one leg, trying to wrestle off his boot, and Stu gave him a shove, nearly toppling Frank over before Frank caught himself on the wall.

"Funny guy," Frank said, shoving Stu back, before they hugged and slapped each other on the back.

"Have you gotten shorter?" Frank asked.

"Just handsomer," Stu said.

Stu bent down and picked up Izzy and swung her around. "Wow, she's light. Not like my thugs." Stu had three sons, all two years apart.

166

"Aren't you feeding my little niece? Come on, let's get you some cookies. Uncle Stu's got you covered."

They headed into the family room, where there was a huge sectional couch. The rest of the family was already ensconced there. "World War Two, you moron!" Bob—Frank's middle brother—shouted as Josie and Frank walked into the room.

"You're the moron. It's the Korean War," Frank said as he glanced at the TV screen.

Watching *Jeopardy!* was another family tradition.

Josie sat down next to Lena, who was married to Stu. Lena passed her a bowl of popcorn. "Drive okay?" she asked as Josie dug in.

"Oh, the usual holiday traffic and whining kids. Delightful," Josie said.

Lena laughed and patted her hand. Lena, who was born in Bombay and had studied at Oxford and then Yale for grad school, might have been intimidating if she weren't so thoroughly lovely.

"Ha! World War Two! Wrong again, punk," Bob said, picking up a piece of popcorn and throwing it at Frank, who caught it in his mouth.

Izzy and Zoe were beelining toward the sugar cookies Frank's mom had baked—the same ones she made every year and always set out on a giant Santa platter—and two of Stu's sons were wrestling on the floor. Bob had a boy and a girl who were already tweens. His son was asleep by the fireplace—someone had draped a purple ruffled boa around his neck—and his daughter was helping Izzy pick out a cookie.

An hour later, as Josie sat at the card table with two rum punches warming her stomach, watching Bob teach Zoe how to play poker, she thought for the hundredth time how much she wished Bob and Stu and their families lived closer so that they could all be together more often. But Bob had moved to Northern Virginia directly after college, where he'd begun to work for a computer technology company that specialized in database software. Through the years, he'd risen in the ranks quickly, and he was now a senior vice president. Stu was on the opposite coast, in Seattle, where he had his own real estate firm. He was also quite successful, and his brothers loved teasing him about the fact that Stu personally appeared in local ads for his firm. Once, they'd blown up a newspaper ad and made a Flat Stanley figure that they'd slipped into Stu's seat when he briefly left the room.

"This kid is a shark," Bob said now, helping Zoe scoop up a pile of chips. "You must get that from your mom."

"I've been teaching her to count cards since she was six months old," Josie said. She picked up Lena and Stu's youngest, a deliciously chubby toddler named Sam, and settled him on her lap.

She always had a wonderful time when they

were with Frank's family. And she'd always assumed Frank did, too.

"This is what's at stake," Stu said the next day, holding aloft a trophy made of tinfoil. It was shaped like a baked potato, and Izzy had decorated it with a Cinderella sticker.

Stu gestured to the two checkers games set up on the dining room table. "I've made a spreadsheet. And I've got a timer. If you take longer than thirty seconds to make a move, you forfeit your turn."

"Anal," Frank muttered, at the same moment Bob said, "OCD."

"We start with our youngest and oldest pairs of contestants. Izzy and Stu Jr. will face off at one end of the table. At the other end, Doc and Susie will be locked together in combat for marital bragging rights."

"Is that your radio announcer voice?" Bob asked.

"Can you not say 'locked together' and 'marital' when you talk about our parents?" Frank asked. "It's traumatizing."

"Winners will advance to the next round," Stu said. He held up a stopwatch. "Players, take your seats."

Frank went over to stand behind Izzy—Stu had explained parental assistance was allowed for kids younger than six—while Stu took a spot behind his son.

"And . . . go!" Stu shouted.

"Men are so competitive," Lena whispered to Josie. "Too much testosterone."

"I think I'm going to hide in the kitchen," Josie whispered back.

Josie ended up doing the dishes and wiping down the counters and making a fresh pot of coffee, then she went back into the dining room to check the progress of the tournament. Izzy had advanced to the second round, but was clearly about to lose her next match. Susie had already trounced Doc and was taking on Bob.

"You can cut the tension in here with a knife," Frank told her, accepting the cup of coffee she handed him.

"It's riveting," Josie responded.

"Okay!" Stu said as Susie cornered Bob's final piece, causing him to surrender. "Me and Frank are up next. Lena, baby, I need you to be my cheerleader."

"Go suck an egg, Stu," Lena said in her delightful accent.

Stu sat down across from Frank and put his elbows on the table. "Ready for some ass kicking?"

Josie wasn't exactly sure what transpired in the next twenty minutes. All she knew was that when she left the dining room to give Izzy a quick bath and help her change, Frank and Stu were facing off across a checkerboard.

When she returned, they were rolling around on the floor, fighting.

"Frank! What are you doing?" she shouted. "Stop it!"

Doc and Bob were already moving to separate the two. Doc grabbed Frank and Bob pulled Stu away.

"Am I going to have to throw ice water on you boys again?" Susie asked. Josie looked at her, stunned. Susie's voice was casual, as if it were no big deal to have her two grown sons fighting on the floor.

Susie misinterpreted Josie's look. "That's how I used to separate them when they were teenagers."

Frank and Stu were standing now, both breathing hard. Frank's shirt had been partially pulled out of his jeans, and Stu's hair was sticking up.

Lena was shaking her head. "Really, Stu? This is how you illustrate to our children how to settle a dispute?"

"He touched his checker!" Stu protested. "You have to move the checker once you touch it. You can't move a different checker!"

*Are you kidding me?* Josie thought. That's what the fight was about?

"Outside," Lena told Stu. "We need to go for a walk. Everyone, I apologize for my husband's boorish behavior."

Bob moved to clean up the checkers, which

were scattered on the floor, while Susie rounded up the kids, telling them she needed them to help her with something in the kitchen.

Josie just looked at Frank. She'd always thought of him as the peacemaker, the guy who defused tension.

"What happened?" she asked.

Frank was watching Stu shrug into his parka and head out the front door, trailing Lena.

A slow smile spread across Frank's face as the door closed.

He stood there for a moment, and when he finally answered Josie, instead of looking at her, he continued staring ahead, as if Stu were still there.

"I won."

"But you're not a supercompetitive person," Josie said to Frank on the drive home. The gentle buzzing sound of the tires spinning across the pavement had lulled the girls to sleep. It was around nine o'clock, and the sky was very dark. Few cars were on the road. It felt very intimate to Josie, as if she and Frank were cocooned together.

Frank shrugged. "My brothers bring it out in me."

This wasn't about a game of checkers. Josie began to recast everything she'd assumed about Frank's family dynamics. The teasing, the comparisons about height (Frank was the shortest of the three, but Bob was only half an inch taller) and weight and hairlines. The old jokes, like the one about the time Frank had been competing in a quarter-mile race as a high school junior and had spectacularly fallen, wiping out two other runners in the process. Stu and Bob called him "Usain Dolt" sometimes.

Josie had assumed it was all in good fun. The verbal equivalent of roughhousing. And Frank certainly gave as good as he got.

"Did you fight a lot growing up?" she asked.

Frank shrugged. "They were older and bigger than me, so no. I mean, sometimes we did but it ended quickly."

*They won,* Josie almost said.

She'd always considered Frank the prize in the family. He was the funniest, the best father, the most easygoing—at least in her eyes.

But some men didn't value those traits the same way they would, say, a football trophy or a Mercedes (which Stu drove; Bob had a Lexus).

Josie wondered whether Frank felt as if he didn't measure up in other ways. At Thanksgiving Bob's eleven-year-old son had caught at least one touchdown pass—maybe even two; Josie couldn't remember. But she did recall Bob picking him up and swinging him around and shouting, "That's my mini-me!"

Josie twisted around to make sure the girls

were still asleep before she spoke again. They were, but she still whispered her words: "Did you want a son?"

"No, God, Jos, I can't imagine not having Zoe and Iz," Frank said instantly.

"I know, sweetie, I just meant . . . if you could still have them, too, would you want a son?"

Frank looked at her sideways. "We always said we'd only have two. Are you saying you want another one?"

Josie shook her head. "I'm happy with the girls. I just want to make sure you don't feel like anything is missing."

Frank reached over and covered her hand. "I have everything I want."

He was so good at saying the right thing, at making Josie feel as if they were connected. At ending a sensitive conversation on a positive note.

But when everything erupted, she also began to reevaluate what she'd once considered a strength in Frank. When he cut short conversations with a line that he must have known would satisfy her, was he doing it because he was sharing his actual feelings, or was he dodging true intimacy?

It made Josie wonder whether she'd ever truly known Frank's deepest vulnerabilities, his most secret thoughts. If she had married a man who had always been, in some ways, a stranger to her.

# Chapter Thirteen

*Present Day*

There were two reasons that she had to call Dana's husband.

First, she needed to verify that it was actually Ron who had left that voice mail message. Josie had lost her ability to gauge whether it was far-fetched to suspect that Frank had lied about that, too. She no longer had faith in her own judgment, given how she'd blindly trusted her husband for so long.

Second, it wasn't logical that Ron was being so protective of Dana. Perhaps this was because Dana had told him she'd merely kissed Frank once, and now Frank's psycho wife was hounding her. Since Ron was in the middle of this, it seemed only right that he should know the facts.

The truth was what Frank and Dana had stolen, what Josie needed to reclaim. Josie wanted to hand Ron at least a piece of it back.

Plus, Dana had gotten away with too much already.

*Hi, Frank Moore,* Dana had said in her weird voice. Josie pictured her wearing a teasing little smile as she'd looked up at Frank that first night.

Her salutation would have thrown Frank off, because he was as good at remembering people's names as he was bad with numbers. He would've made a joke, probably, because they always sprang easily to Frank's lips. He would have been intrigued.

It was a pretty masterful opening line, Josie had to admit. It was designed to spark more than a superficial initial contact. She wondered whether Dana had planned it, whether she'd had her eye on Frank for a while. Or maybe Dana had just craved some excitement and had wanted an affair in general, and Frank happened to wander into her line of vision at the right time.

Her throat tightened as she imagined Frank and Dana on the phone together, discussing a strategy to keep as much of their relationship concealed as possible in the aftermath of Josie's discovery.

How had they ended that particular conversation?

Not with "I love you," surely. Not after less than two months. But maybe they'd said something like "Talk to you later."

Josie began to pace tight circles around the living room. Her thoughts felt choppy and sharp, jerking her between memories and images.

Frank pulling away from her embrace on the night she'd gone to see *La La Land* . . . Maggie, their neighbor, standing on her front walk, saying, *I loved having the girls visit yesterday* . . . Frank on their wedding day with red-rimmed eyes, repeating their vows: *Until death do us part . . .* Frank after her discovery, with red-rimmed eyes: *I am so sorry. I will say that to you until the day I die . . .*

Then a possibility she hadn't considered muscled through the chatter in her mind like a battering ram. Maybe Frank and Dana hadn't talked on the phone when they'd both returned to work after the discovery. They could have met in person instead, at a corner booth in a quiet coffee shop. Dana might have become distraught, and Frank could have put his arm around her to comfort her.

The thought of Frank tenderly soothing Dana while she, Josie, was feeling flayed by her discovery was so abhorrent that Josie ran to the sink and retched.

She ran water into her cupped palm and rinsed out her mouth, noticing her hand was shaking. She wondered whether she'd ever fully trust anyone again. Whether she'd ever know peace.

Dana deserved to be punished for that, too.

Josie opened a cabinet and reached for a box of peppermint tea, leaning against the counter and staring into space while she waited for the kettle to boil. When it finally emitted a little shriek, she was so lost in thought that she flinched.

She sat at the kitchen table, cupping her hands around her mug. Huck ambled over and flopped down next to her, releasing a sigh. She lifted her bare foot and rubbed it over Huck's back while she tried to organize her thoughts.

She was taking a break from work. She'd already set up an automatic email response for clients who might be trying to place an order. The automated message explained that she would respond to any sales requests as soon as she returned. Josie's little side business brought in about eight thousand dollars a year, so losing the commission on a few boxes of toys or missing an application deadline to lease a booth at a festival wouldn't torpedo their family financially.

She was only going to do the bare minimum to keep their household running right now. She'd order groceries online and arrange for Peapod to deliver them. She'd let the girls watch television and choose their own outfits, no matter how outlandish the combinations. Huck would clean the crumbs off the floor, and the laundry could wait. The things that had once mattered so very much to her—like giving the girls vitamins every morning, and making sure they used cavity-fighting mouthwash every night—were of so little import now.

She didn't have the luxury of choosing her battles; she needed to eliminate every potential conflict in her life so that she could focus on the seismic one currently gripping her.

In two hours, she was scheduled to pick up the

girls at school. She'd call Ron before then, Josie decided. But she needed to do more investigating before she dialed the number on the Post-it note she'd tucked into a slot in her wallet. Dana had known something of Frank before they'd met in Atlantic City. It seemed only fair that Josie had the chance to learn a bit about Dana's husband.

She sipped her tea, then opened her laptop computer, which had been resting on the kitchen table next to a crooked blue bowl Zoe had made in art class last year.

She began with Ron's Facebook page. It displayed only a few things publicly, but among those things were a handful of "notes," or journal-like musings. Josie got up and found a pen and small spiral notebook in a kitchen drawer, then began going through Ron's notes. Unfortunately, they weren't very illuminating. Ron wrote about his enjoyment of gardening—*The sunflowers are growing at an astonishing rate*—and he compared two different Chinese restaurants in his neighborhood, rating them on the quality and value of their entrées. He wrote almost nothing about Dana, other than a brief mention of a marathon his wife was competing in.

Josie continued to search the Internet but could find little else about Ron.

She reached into her wallet and extracted the pink Post-it, smoothing it out on the kitchen table. She would use her cell phone to dial Ron's number, she decided. If he truly wanted to, he'd be able to ascertain their address and home phone number. But for now, she intended to keep up this firewall between the affair and her children.

She dialed and listened to it ring twice before going to voice mail.

"Hello," she said. "This is Josie Moore. I think you called my husband Frank's cell phone yesterday . . . I'm sorry to bother you, but I needed to make sure it was really you calling, or if it was another lie . . ."

Her voice broke and she quickly recited her phone number and ended the call. She wondered whether Ron was at work today, or whether he and Dana were talking at this very moment. Perhaps they were in emergency counseling.

Josie was trying to think of what to do next when her phone rang, less than a minute later. She knew even before she looked at the screen that it was Ron.

She stood up abruptly as a fresh surge of energy flooded her body. Her heart throbbed so powerfully it was almost painful.

"Hello, this is Josie."

"Hi, it's Ron calling you back." His voice sounded far less forceful than it had on the message on Frank's machine. "Um . . . so . . ."

"So, how are you? No, dumb question." Josie tried to give a little laugh but the sound stuck in her throat.

She was talking to Frank's girlfriend's husband, on an ordinary Wednesday afternoon, in front of the refrigerator where Zoe's latest art project was secured with a Smurf magnet. It was ludicrous. It was a scene from a reality show, or a French arthouse movie.

"I got your message and I wanted to ask you . . . you said there were a lot of lies?" Ron said.

"Yeah, I just have been trying to sort everything out . . . and, well, it's hard. Do you know anything?" Josie asked.

"Only that they saw each other twice, and then they felt so horrible about it, they met a few more times to discuss what to do."

Josie frowned. Could Ron truly believe this?

"Do you know how long it has been going on?" she asked.

"Just those few times, I think," Ron said. "They met in Atlantic City."

"Yeah, that's what Frank told me, too." Josie hesitated. She lowered her voice, as if she were making a confession. "I found their messages on his cell phone. That's how I learned about it."

"Wow. You know, I'm not even mad yet." Ron sounded as if he was marveling at this fact. "Isn't that weird?"

"I wasn't right away either," Josie said. "The shock."

The thought briefly popped into her mind that in the next scene in this reality show, she and

Ron would meet in person to commiserate. Then they'd fall into each other's arms for revenge sex.

"I just want to get past this." Ron sighed. "We need to move on so we can heal."

Josie's head jerked back. He believed Dana's version of events? He must, if he thought their relationship was salvageable.

"I guess I feel as if I need to know the truth," Josie said carefully. "I need to know if there are more lies out there."

She hesitated, then said, "So in the emails, Dana seemed like . . . she was the one who initiated it." This was technically true, even though Josie hadn't learned that information from an email. But Dana had originated most of the email conversations with Frank, like the one about the killer margaritas.

"Oh," Ron said.

He should have been asking for more details about what Dana had written to Frank. He should have sounded more upset.

"Was there anything else she revealed to you that I should know about?" Josie asked.

"Not really," Ron said. "She just kept saying that she was sorry."

He wanted to get off the phone. He wanted to tidy up this mess and go back to his sunflowers and his Chinese food. Dana would get away unscathed; she'd shed a few crocodile tears and move along with her life, while Josie remained mired in misery.

The marathon.

"Okay, it's just that Frank has been acting differently for a while," Josie blurted. "He took up running a few months ago, out of the blue. Is Dana a runner? I wonder if they jogged together, if they shared that."

She held her breath. Silence. She pressed the phone tighter to her ear. She wished she could read Ron's mind.

He said: "I'm sorry, I have to go now. Thank you for calling."

She heard the click of the call ending, and she slowly lowered her right arm, wishing she could snatch back her words.

*I didn't mean to hurt you, Ron,* she thought. *I only told that lie because I wanted to hurt* her.

Physical intimacy was the only thing that set a marriage apart from all of the other relationships in your life. Josie knew she was far from the first person to make this observation, but she'd never thought deeply about it until now. You could love your friends, and fight with them, and share inside jokes with them. You could commingle funds with a business partner, and stake your financial futures on each other. You could enjoy meals with coworkers and trade deep confidences with strangers on a train. You could even share a bed with a close friend, as Josie had on several girls' trips in her early twenties, when money was too tight to pay for extra hotel rooms.

But the specific line separating a romantic partnership from other relationships existed for a reason. Sexual contact was the only thing you shared with your spouse that you shared with no one else.

Imagining Frank and Dana together—entwined in his car, in her office, in the hotel room—made Josie feel such an intense swell of emotions that she felt as if she were about to explode. She fantasized about throwing open the door to Frank's car and seeing the sudden light shine down on the two of them before she grabbed Frank by the hair and yanked him away from Dana. She imagined kicking open the door to the hotel room and stalking over to them as they lay in bed kissing, saying something so cutting they would both wither. In some of her daydreams, she threw a vase at Frank while Dana cried and Frank insisted that Dana meant nothing to him, that she was a terrible mistake and that it was Josie he loved.

Josie had an actual dream in which she'd clawed Frank's face with her fingernails. In her dream, he just stood there and silently endured her assault. When she'd awoken, she'd had trouble breathing for a few moments.

She needed to talk to someone.

Karin was still calling and texting every day,

but Josie knew she needed a professional's help. She phoned her doctor for a referral.

Josie's physician was a small, trim, white-haired woman who was brisk yet kind. "So now you're trying to decide if you should stay for the sake of the kids, or leave the bastard," she said once Josie had summed up the situation. The doctor's tone was softer than her words.

"Yeah . . . I guess that's it."

"I've got a great therapist for you. She has helped a lot of my patients."

"With this sort of thing?" Josie asked. "Do a lot of your patients have this happen?"

The doctor's answer was stunning: "I see it almost every week."

It really was an epidemic, Josie thought.

"Is there anything else you need?" the doctor asked.

Josie recalled those moments in the dark when her chest had felt so tight and heavy that breathing was difficult. "I was wondering if I could get a prescription for Xanax, too."

"Absolutely. Just don't mix them with alcohol, and be careful about driving if you take more than a quarter milligram. I'll phone in the script now."

"Thank you," Josie said.

"And Josie? Call the therapist today. She books up quickly."

*This is what it would be like if we were divorced.*

Josie rolled the thought around in her mind as she lay in bed, staring into the dark. Beside her, Zoe slept on—she'd crawled in sometime around two in the morning—but the queen-sized mattress still felt too large without Frank's big body sprawled across it. He was a restless sleeper; once, early on in their relationship, Josie had awoken shivering. She'd tried to tug a corner of the comforter over herself, but it was twisted around Frank, as if he were in the process of wrestling it. She'd given up and plastered herself up against Frank, soaking in his body heat. From then on, she'd always kept an extra comforter folded at the foot of the bed.

But she'd rarely needed it, because Frank was better than a hot water bottle. No matter how icy her feet were, he never shied away when she pressed them against his legs.

The bedroom felt cold again, even with warm little Zoe next to her. The thermostat was programmed to turn up the heat at six thirty, but that was still a half hour away. Josie reached down to tug the second comforter over both of them.

She lay there until light began to slowly seep in through the slatted blinds she hadn't fully closed. Then she eased out of bed and turned off her alarm.

Frank's sheets and blanket were folded neatly at the end of the couch when she walked through the living room on her way to the kitchen. She knew he'd brought his toiletries down to the basement shower, which was only partially finished, and that he had stored some clothes down there, too.

Frank was at the kitchen table, in the same chair she'd used when she'd called Ron. This gave her a tinge of satisfaction. She, too, had secrets now.

"Hi," Frank said. He gestured to the platter in front of him. "I made some pancakes for everyone."

She couldn't meet his eyes, so she just nodded in his general direction. Then she grabbed a mug, filled it with coffee, and went back upstairs to rouse the girls.

They couldn't go on like this for much longer. She needed to tell Frank he had to move out. She'd do it tonight.

But Frank caught Josie by surprise when he came home early from work. She was on her knees, cleaning out the refrigerator, scrubbing hard at an old ketchup stain with a sponge soaked in hot water.

"Oh, honey, you don't have to do that—I mean, I would have," Frank said.

Josie blew away the hair that had escaped from her ponytail and was dangling in front of her eyes. So much for her plan to do the bare minimum around the house. She'd begun that way this morning after she'd fed the kids Frank's pancakes and had taken them to school. She'd spent hours in bed staring at game shows, until a pretty young contestant was chosen on *The Price Is Right.* "What's your name, darling?" Drew Carey had asked the young woman as she'd jumped up and down. "Dana," she'd squealed.

In an instant, Josie had leapfrogged from inertia directly into a tornado of energy. She'd thrown aside the covers, feeling a compulsion to sort through the kitchen cabinets and throw away any cans that had passed their expiration dates. She'd also washed, dried, and folded three loads of laundry before turning her attention to the refrigerator.

"Don't," she said.

"Don't what?"

"Call me honey."

"Sorry." Frank set down his briefcase on the floor next to the kitchen table. "Do you— Can I talk to you for a minute?"

"Hang on," she said. She walked into the living room, where the girls were watching *Wild Kratts,* turned up the volume, and returned to the kitchen.

Frank cocked his head to the right. "Could we go upstairs?"

*What now?* Josie thought. But she just pushed

past him and went up to their bedroom without looking back to see whether he was following.

She crossed the threshold into the room they'd once shared and stood there, her arms folded. It felt too intimate to have Frank in here. To be alone with him in the space where they'd undressed and cuddled and made love.

He seemed to grasp this, and he paused about a foot away from the entryway.

"So?" Josie prodded.

"I've been reading a lot about affairs," Frank said. He rubbed the toe of his right shoe into the carpet. "I, uh, haven't really been able to work. So I'm Googling articles and reading stuff on HuffPost—there's so much stuff there, you wouldn't believe it—and I bought a few books, and—"

"Frank."

He nodded. "Right, the point. So I need to be completely honest with you. It's only fair to you. I need to answer your questions truthfully."

It was all she'd wanted. Yet she felt a quiver of fear at his words.

"What do you need to tell me?"

He looked down at his toe. It had made a track in the carpet by now. Josie would have to run the vacuum over it several times to erase it.

"Just tell me, Frank!"

She was so tired of wondering what else was out there, of waiting for the next avalanche to hit her.

"It was those five nights, that part is true," Frank said quietly. He met her eyes. "We didn't have sex but, ah, we did other things. It was purely physical. I didn't care about her at all."

"How long did you kiss?" Josie demanded.

Another pause. "Maybe an hour the first two times, when we were at the hotel," Frank said. "Less on the other nights."

"An *hour?*" Josie repeated.

He nodded miserably. "I know."

"Where did you go on the other nights?" Josie asked.

Frank squeezed his eyes shut before speaking. "We were in my car one time. We went to the house of one of her friends who was out of town the other two times."

"There is something wrong with you," Josie hissed because she couldn't scream.

Tears filled Frank's eyes. "I know."

"Did you buy her a Christmas present?" Josie asked.

"What? No. I swear. It wasn't like that. She didn't mean anything to me."

"So it was just about the fooling around. That doesn't make it any better, Frank." Josie's fists clenched at her sides. The rage swelled inside her, spiraling upward, filling her lungs and thickening her throat. "I want to hurt you."

"I wish you would," Frank responded. "I deserve it."

"You just did these things with her, then you came home to me and never gave any indication that anything was wrong! What kind of a person does that?"

"I'm going to get help," Frank said. "I called a marriage therapist today. Would you consider going with me?"

"No!" Josie said. "There isn't any marriage to fix. You would've slept with her if I hadn't found out."

Frank's features crumpled. "You are probably right."

"What did you spend the four hundred dollars on in Atlantic City?"

Frank physically recoiled. "What— How did you know about that?"

Josie just stared at him.

"I gambled," he said. "Blackjack. It was stupid. I started out winning, then I lost it all on a few big hands, and I thought . . ."

His voice trailed off. Then: "And I told you another lie."

Something icy wrapped around Josie. She nodded for Frank to continue.

"When I dropped the kids off with Maggie that first day and I told you I was out looking for you . . . I, ah . . . I wasn't. I went into my office because I thought I had Dana's number there. I wanted to reach her to tell her you had my cell phone. But I couldn't find it so I just came home."

Of all the things he might have said, this felt relatively innocuous. But it didn't make sense, Josie thought, frowning. "You had her email address there, though."

"Yeah, I sent her an email but I knew she probably wouldn't check it until she got back into the office on Tuesday," Frank said.

Josie regarded him. There was no reason for him to reveal that information. Perhaps Frank *was* finally being truthful with her. And Dana would not have confessed to the five encounters had she and Frank communicated.

"You didn't have sex." Josie couldn't complete the sentence. She didn't want to say Dana's name.

"Absolutely not," Frank said.

Her anger ebbed. Frank looked awful. He'd definitely lost weight, and his face seemed to be suddenly etched with lines. He was truly sorry; no one could fake such pain.

"Jos . . ." His voice was a plea. Perhaps he could read the softening in her stance. He took a step toward her.

An hour of making out, like teenagers who were madly in love and couldn't keep their hands off each other. It had been ages since Frank had kissed her like that. She would never be able to look at him again without that vision intruding.

"No!" she cried. She jerked back. "You need to move out. Go find an apartment or something."

She expected Frank to protest, to fall to his knees again and beg. But he didn't. His posture sagged as he kept looking at her.

"I learned from the books that I need to respect whatever you want," he said. "So I will. But Josie, I'm going to spend every single day showing you how much I love you and the girls and how much I want you back. You three are the only people who matter to me. I know I didn't act that way. But I'm going to prove it to you."

"It's too late."

She turned and walked into the bedroom, shutting the door. She walked directly to her dresser and opened her jewelry box. Then she took off her slim gold wedding band, wincing as it scraped across her knuckle, and placed it on the blue velvet.

# Chapter Fourteen

The therapist's eyes were large and soft. They seemed to regard Josie without agenda or judgment.

Her office was in the basement of her home, which made going to the appointment less intimidating than it would have felt if Josie had to visit an impersonal building. To get to the private entrance, Josie followed a stone path that wound through a side yard filled with herb gardens and a bird fountain.

When Josie walked through the door, she saw two chairs and a small table containing magazines in the waiting area. Even the magazines were nonthreatening and homey: *Reader's Digest*, *Cooking Light*, and *Highlights for Children*.

When the therapist opened the door to her inner office, Josie glimpsed a cozy-looking beige couch, a coffee table, and a fabric-covered chair in the main seating area. A far corner held a wooden desk and a second chair. Bookshelves lined the walls, filled with heavy volumes addressing various psychological issues: coping with anxiety, raising explosive children, thriving in the aftermath of divorce.

Josie sat down on the couch and put a crimson

chenille throw pillow on her lap, running her fingers over the soothing fabric. The therapist— "Call me Sonya," she'd said during the initial phone call—settled into the chair and crossed her legs at the ankles. She gave Josie a smile. Her voice and manner were unhurried. "What brings you here?"

Josie looked into Sonya's understanding eyes and began to tell her story, the words streaming out of her like water from a faucet.

"I asked him to leave," Josie concluded. "But I don't know if I want a divorce right now. How would I tell the girls?"

Sonya nodded. "You need some space from Frank, so you've asked him to leave. That's a good step."

Sonya spoke slowly and soothingly. Her hands remained still in her lap. Her gentle eyes were steady on Josie. The tight knot Josie didn't realize she'd been carrying around in her chest eased a bit.

"It's hard to feel all this uncertainty." Josie reached for a tissue from the box on the coffee table and dabbed at her eyes. "I keep bracing myself for Frank to unload another bombshell. And when I think about divorce and what it will do to the girls, I just feel frozen. But I can't even bear to look at Frank. How could I ever be married to him again?"

Sonya nodded again and Josie had the feeling

that no matter what she said, Sonya would validate her. Not even Josie's revelation about calling Ron had provoked a reaction. But then, Sonya saw women like her every single week.

"You don't have to decide that this minute," Sonya said. "All you know right now is that you need more time to decide. That's okay. That's good. You're going to take the time and make a careful decision."

They talked for a while longer, then Sonya told Josie their time was up. "For your homework this week, I want you to do three things that used to make you happy. Can you do that?"

"I can't imagine anything making me happy right now."

"Three things," Sonya repeated. "Tell me what you did during our next meeting."

Getting dressed for a night out when your relationship had just shattered felt very different from when you were married.

Gone were the moments when Josie would look across the bedroom and realize Frank was putting on jeans and a black shirt, just as she was, and they'd have to negotiate who was going to change. She had no one to help her zip up, or tell her to go with the polka-dot dress instead of the navy one.

Josie held a scoop-neck, cream-colored shirt up against herself and looked in the mirror, wondering whether it would make her look even paler. She always grew pasty during the depths of the Chicago winter. She decided she could pull it off with some extra blush on her cheeks, then she pulled on her favorite jeans.

They were loose. She pulled out the waistband with her thumbs, noticing she had at least two inches of extra space. She walked into the bathroom and stepped on the scale. She'd lost nine pounds without any effort at all.

She assumed it was mostly water weight, but when she tried on her pair of skinny jeans from the bottom of the stack in her dresser, they fit perfectly, even though they were a size smaller than Josie was used to wearing.

She looked in the mirror. Her collarbones seemed more defined, as did her cheekbones. She'd been eating less than usual, but not so much as to make such a pronounced difference. It must be the adrenaline surge she'd been experiencing; it had probably boosted her metabolism.

Josie thought of the woman she'd encountered outside the preschool, the one whose husband had had an affair. *I get it now,* Josie thought. She wished she hadn't recoiled from the woman's explosion of information. She should have stepped closer and put her hand on the woman's arm, as Karin had done. That's how she would have treated a victim of a car wreck who was in shock.

But maybe Josie had recoiled because she recognized, on an instinctual level, that she had come too close to a dangerous truth.

She wouldn't think about that now. She was going for drinks with Karin and Amanda—a night out with the girls was one of her happy things—and she needed to act even-keeled, because she wasn't sure yet if she was going to tell Amanda about the affair.

Amanda was a genuinely kind woman, utterly without malice or guile. She never spoke a bad word about anyone. She also had a genius-level IQ, a fact Josie had pried out of her when she'd learned Amanda had gone to college at sixteen. But Amanda occasionally lacked a filter, and she was incapable of keeping a secret. She never meant to violate anyone's trust, but she had a habit of repeating information without consideration of how such news would be received.

"She's completely clueless, but we love her anyway" was Karin's take on Amanda.

Josie paired the cream top with her skinny jeans and camel-colored boots, then applied more makeup than she usually wore, swiping on two coats of mascara and stroking highlighter over her cheekbones. Her mother's voice intruded in her mind with an admonition Josie had heard her say at least a dozen times: *If you look good, then you can't help but feel good.* Josie answered: *I haven't looked this good in years, Mom, and I feel like complete crap.* That seemed to end the conversation in her head, so Josie went downstairs.

Frank was cleaning up the dinner dishes. He turned at the sound of her boots tapping against the floor as she approached.

"I'm heading out," she said. Zoe was practicing writing her spelling words at the kitchen table, and Izzy was playing with her Bratz dolls in the next seat over.

"I love you girls," Josie said, dropping a kiss on each of their foreheads.

"You're going out *again?*" Zoe asked.

It was only her second night this week—and her third night of the past month—but the girls always took note when she was gone. By now they were used to the fact that Daddy traveled for work and didn't get home from the office until dinnertime. They were far more sanguine about his changing schedule than they were about Josie's.

"Mommy deserves a night out with her friends," Frank said.

Josie ignored him and answered the girls for herself. "Just for a bit. I'll kiss you good night when I come in, even if you're asleep."

She scooped up her purse from where it was hanging on the back of Zoe's chair.

"You look nice," Frank said.

She hesitated. "Thank you." She couldn't avoid replying to him in front of the girls, but it chafed that she had to be gracious, that she couldn't say what she really wanted to: *If I look so nice, why'd you have an affair with another woman?*

She saw bright headlights as Karin's minivan pulled into the driveway. "I'm off, girls, see you soon." She deliberately excluded Frank from her good-bye.

Josie was dying to tell Amanda what was going on.

Amanda would be warm and sympathetic, but more important, she'd give Josie a fresh perspective. So few people knew about what had happened. Maybe Amanda would say something that would help Josie figure out what to do next.

"No, no, a thousand times no," Karin said when Josie floated the idea on their way to pick up Amanda. "You know what she's like. She'll stand up at the next PTA meeting and say, 'Should we set up a meal delivery schedule to help Josie during this awful time?' "

"She's not that bad. But, yeah, she probably would let something slip." Josie sighed. "You're right. I won't tell her."

When they arrived at the bar, they found it surprisingly crowded. Louie's had two big connecting rooms, each filled with high round tables and wooden booths. An event was taking place in the back room. Josie could see men and women wearing name tags and mingling.

"Is it a high school reunion?" Amanda wondered. The hostess had seated them at a table that afforded them a direct view into the gathering.

"I bet it's an office thing," Karin said, squinting. "Everyone looks uncomfortable. Check out their body language."

The waitress approached and all three women ordered glasses of chardonnay. "The universal frazzled-mom beverage," Karin said. "Now, how about food? Hummus and pita? Maybe a cheese plate, too?"

"Yum, yes," Amanda said. "You look so skinny, Josie. What's your secret?"

"Oh, I'm just cutting down on carbs." She knew if she met Karin's eyes she'd give something away, so Josie reached for her glass of water and took a big sip.

"Wait, this is interesting," Karin said. She tilted her head in the direction of the back room. "Everyone just sat down. But they're all at tables for two. They went from a group into couples just like that."

Josie studied the pair nearest to them. The guy was staring down at his drink; the woman's teeth were clenched in a smile. If she had to guess, she would've said they were out on a first date, and that it wasn't going particularly well.

"I don't know," Amanda said. "Check out the man in the purple sweater. He's, like, a hundred years older than the woman he's with. They can't be together."

"And what about those two?" Josie flicked her eyes toward a corner of the room. "She's in a little black dress, and he looks like he just came from the gym."

When the waitress arrived with their wine, Karin asked: "What's happening in there?"

"Speed dating," the waitress replied.

"Seriously?" Josie looked more carefully into the room. She would have said most of the speed daters were in their late thirties or early forties. If she divorced Frank, these would be her people.

"Jeez, I'm glad I'm not out there anymore," Amanda said. "Remember what it was like? All those awful dates, all those lonely Saturday nights."

Josie took a sip of her wine, noticing Karin's eyes flick toward her.

"Hey, Miss Lonelyhearts, what universe did you exist in?" Karin said. "I loved being single. Never having to compromise on what movie you'd see or whether you had to have your husband's obnoxious law school roommate stay with you when he came to town . . ."

"It almost sounds like that isn't a hypothetical,

Karin," Josie said. She knew Marcus's former roommate drove Karin nuts, and that he visited every couple of years.

"All I'm saying is that being single now, in our forties, when we know ourselves so much better and can make wise choices, wouldn't be the worst thing in the world," Karin declared.

*No, that isn't all you're saying,* Josie thought.

Amanda began talking about the dog her children were begging her to adopt, and although Josie tried to listen, her gaze kept being pulled back to the speed-dating room.

One of the men was actually quite attractive. She could only see his profile. He had very close-cropped hair, probably to camouflage his receding hairline, but on him it looked good. His shoulders were muscular and his nose was strong and straight.

Everyone in that room had a story of heartbreak, a tale of loneliness. She wondered what the man's narrative was. Perhaps his wife had left him. Perhaps she'd died.

He was the sort of man Josie would be interested in getting to know if she were single.

Wait, *was* she single? Josie wondered. Not technically. But in spirit, yes.

It was far too soon to go on a date, though. Aside from the fact that she'd only seen the guy's profile and knew nothing about his character, this wasn't like when Josie was nineteen and tried to speed through heartbreak by meeting a new guy as soon as possible. You couldn't use a hookup to smother the emotions that stemmed from the implosion of a twelve-year marriage.

"You're so quiet tonight," Amanda said. Amanda was one of those people who really seemed to see you when she looked at you. She regarded Josie as she waited for a response.

"Sorry, long week . . . I guess I'm just tired," Josie said.

"Everything okay?" Amanda asked.

"Yeah, it's just . . . Frank and I are having a thing. A fight."

"Hoo boy," Karin said, her foot nudging Josie's under the table in warning.

The waitress passed by their table. "Another round?"

"Not for me, I'm driving," Karin said.

Josie didn't realize she'd drained her glass. "Sure, I'll have one."

"Me too," Amanda said, even though she still had half of her drink left. "So, what are you fighting about?"

"I just . . ." A lump formed in Josie's throat and she shook her head. It was the kindness in Amanda's voice that did it.

Amanda's right hand reached across the table and covered Josie's left one.

"He had an affair. You can't tell anyone, okay? Please."

When Amanda spoke, her voice contained no surprise.

"I thought it was something like that," she said.

Josie's head jerked up. "What? How'd you know?"

If lovable, clueless Amanda had already caught on, then Josie had no hope. Everyone else would figure it out, too.

"Because of this." Amanda squeezed Josie's hand. "You aren't wearing your wedding ring."

Two glasses of wine later, she'd told Amanda everything. "What do you think?" Josie asked. "There's no way I can stay in this marriage, right?"

Amanda didn't answer immediately. She just kept looking at Josie, a thoughtful expression on her face. "You don't have to decide right now," she finally said.

"That's what my new therapist seems to think, too."

"It's hard when your life is following a certain direction, then it veers onto another path," Amanda said. "Uncertainty can be terrifying."

Josie nodded and dabbed at her eyes with the napkin Karin passed to her. "Yes. That's it exactly."

"I think you need to talk to Frank," Amanda said. "Once you really understand why it happened, it'll be easier for you to decide what to do."

"Why it happened?" Karin echoed. "It happened because he's a scumbag—sorry, Josie, but it's the truth—and he doesn't deserve her understanding."

Josie dragged a triangle of pita through hummus and popped it into her mouth. She immediately regretted it; the bread was tough and chewy and the hummus was as bland as paste. She took a big swallow of water to wash it down.

"Frank wants us to go to a marriage counselor," she said.

Amanda shrugged. "Just because you go doesn't mean you're promising to save the marriage. But it might at least calm things down. At the moment you hate him, right?"

Josie nodded. "Passionately."

Amanda looked directly into her eyes again, and Josie had the feeling Amanda had never seen her more clearly. "It's one thing to hate your husband," she said slowly. "But it's another to hate the father of your children, isn't it?"

# Chapter Fifteen

*One year earlier*

It was moms' night out at Louie's, and the waitress had just delivered a round of chardonnay to their table of three. Josie and Karin were treating Natalie, another parent from the elementary school, who was moving to Cleveland because her husband had secured a tenure-track teaching job at a university there.

Josie hadn't known Natalie long, but they'd sat together in the back row of a bumpy school bus on the way to a field trip at a petting zoo at the very beginning of the year, and the experience had bonded them. "Like war veterans," Natalie had joked.

The night had started with cocktails and conversation about their kids—Izzy's tantrums, Natalie's comic tales of her potty-training attempts for her two-and-a-half-year-old, Karin's worry that the twins had begun to stockpile snacks beneath their beds, which could lead to hoarding (though Josie was pretty sure Karin was exaggerating in an effort to entertain them).

Then Karin held up her palm: "You know what?

We talk about the kids all the time. Let's put the kibosh on that tonight."

"Are husbands off-limits, too?" Natalie asked.

"No, they're good," Karin decided. "As long as it's something relating to *you*. Like, let's not talk about their jobs or how busy they are or that kind of bullshit."

"What about the fact that Charles and I haven't had sex in three months?" Natalie asked.

"Hang on," Karin said. She signaled the waitress and ordered a fresh round. "You were saying?" she prompted.

"It's not his fault, poor guy. I just look at him and think"—Natalie gave a little shrug—"Eh. The sex was never spectacular, to be honest," she continued. "Maybe if we hadn't known each other forever it could have been different. But I remember Charles in the second grade, crying because someone's shoe flew off and hit him in the head during kickball. I used to think the fact that we knew each other so well was a good thing. But now I wonder . . . would life be more exciting with someone else?"

Karin shook her head. "No," she said decisively. "The problem is, when you live with someone for years, there isn't any mystery. How can you be expected to want to rip off someone's clothes when you've picked up their gross tissues because they missed the trash basket, and when they walk past you and you realize ten seconds later that they farted?"

"Husbands are disgusting," Josie said, laughing.

"So what about you?" Natalie asked. "Do you guys have, like, regular sex?"

"Marcus would want it three times a day if I let him," Karin said. "He's the horniest guy I know. But we only do it about twice a week. Maybe three times."

"Three times a week is good!" Josie exclaimed. "Wow, don't tell Frank or he'll be jealous."

"What about you?" Natalie asked.

Josie shrugged. "Maybe twice on a good week," she said. The number still sounded low. "It was more before Izzy was born," she added.

"Yeah, the second kid is the sex killer," Natalie said. "I don't even know if I'd want to have sex with anyone else at this point. I mean, a hot bath, a good movie, a night alone in my bed without a little kid crawling in and kicking me . . . that's probably my biggest fantasy right now."

"Even if Brad Pitt showed up and begged me to sleep with him, I'd probably be too worried about how I looked naked to enjoy it," Josie joked.

"Do you think our husbands care?" Natalie asked. "I mean, that we don't look the same as we did when we first met them."

"Marcus says he loves my stretch marks

because they are from carrying our babies," Karin said.

Josie felt a surge of envy. Sweet, adoring Marcus, who always put his wife first. No wonder Karin was so confident. Josie drained her glass of wine.

"I read this article in a magazine once," Natalie said. "It talked about how most women need to feel an emotional connection with their husbands in order to enjoy sex. But the thing is, it's the opposite for most guys. They need to have sex to feel emotionally connected to their wives. So when one side gets out of whack, the whole relationship falls apart. It's like a catch-twenty-two."

"Well, you know what they say," Karin said. She looked at Natalie, then at Josie, and raised her eyebrows. "If you don't have sex with your husband, someone else will."

The first time Josie suspected something, she let herself be convinced it wasn't real.

It was the night of one of Frank's big business events. A cocktail hour would lead into dinner at a fancy hotel in the heart of town. Tons of people from his industry would be there; Frank's company had purchased three round tables.

Zoe was six years old then, and Izzy was three.

"Are you sure you should drive?" Josie asked that morning as Frank looped his tie into a knot around his neck.

"Yeah, I won't drink that much," he said.

"Just take a cab home if you do," she said. "I can drive you into work tomorrow."

The dinner was an annual event. Frank always looked forward to it because he got to catch up with old colleagues. Spouses were never included. Josie wasn't sure whether she felt relieved or disappointed about that; it would have been nice to dress up and be served a fancy dinner, to chat with other adults and sip martinis. But Frank was always so busy networking at these events, and although she was friendly with some of his coworkers, she didn't know them well enough to sustain a long conversation, so she often felt bored.

Even worse, she felt boring. "What are you up to?" people would ask. She could talk for a few minutes about her little toy-sale business, but those conversations ran out of steam quickly. "And the kids? They're good?" Frank's colleagues would say, their expressions indicating they were only interested in a superficial answer. Josie didn't know about the intricacies of their jobs, or the personalities of the players in the industry; Frank and his colleagues spoke a language she couldn't infiltrate. "Oh, they're a handful!" Josie would laugh, and Frank's colleagues would laugh, too, then move on.

Maybe she'd suggest to Frank that they get a sitter next weekend. The two of them could go out to a nice dinner on their own. It had been a while since they'd done that.

As for tonight, she'd order pizza and pop the cork on a bottle of cheap rosé and put on a movie for the kids, she decided. It wouldn't be as good as a custom-made martini, but it would still be a treat.

Her evening passed uneventfully. They watched *Beauty and the Beast*—the great version with Emma Watson; Josie fast-forwarded through the scary parts—and at around eight o'clock, right after the credits rolled, Josie told Izzy it was time for bed.

"My tummy hurts," Izzy complained.

"Too much pizza," Josie said, hustling Izzy into the bathroom and squirting toothpaste onto her toothbrush. "You'll feel better when you lie down."

Izzy fell asleep easily, leading Josie to deduce that the claim of a stomachache was a ploy to delay bedtime, and a half hour later, Zoe was tucked into bed, too.

Josie took a hot shower—she'd been so rushed she'd skipped one that morning and had felt grimy all day—then she'd tidied the kitchen before letting Huck out the back for his final pee of the evening.

She'd intended to read in bed, but the shower and rosé and low-key evening had left her feeling so relaxed that she'd dozed off at around nine thirty.

She'd awoken to the sound of retching.

"Izzy?" she'd called as she'd run toward the bathroom. But Izzy hadn't made it that far. She'd vomited on her bedroom carpet.

"Oh, sweetie," she said.

Izzy started to cry. "I'm sick," she said.

"I'm so sorry, baby," Josie said. "Does your tummy still hurt?"

"Yes," Izzy wailed miserably.

She carried Izzy into the bathroom and helped her rinse out her mouth with tap water and left her sitting on the bath mat, promising that she'd be right back. She dampened a towel and cleaned up the mess on the carpet as best she could, but the room still smelled awful. She grabbed a fresh towel, threw it over the stain, and pulled the door shut. She'd have to deep-clean the rug tomorrow, but this was the best she could do for now.

Then she looked at her phone.

It was 12:17 a.m. Where was Frank?

She sat on the closed lid of the toilet and rubbed Izzy's back while she called his cell. It rang a couple of times, then she heard his voice mail message, ending with "Hit me at the beep." Maybe his group had decamped to a bar. If it was loud, he wouldn't hear his phone. She didn't bother leaving a message, knowing he'd see the missed call once he checked his phone.

She helped Izzy gargle with a bubble gum–flavored kids' mouthwash, then she carried her daughter to her bed, settling her into Frank's side. She put a plastic trash can on the floor, along with yet another towel, and she left the bathroom light on. Izzy felt slightly feverish, but Josie knew medicine might upset her stomach even more.

"I need Teddy," Izzy said, and Josie sighed and got up and braved Izzy's room again, searching for her little brown bear.

Josie kept her phone by her side, and forty-five minutes later, still wide awake, she phoned Frank again. She listened to the ring, then heard his voice mail message again. "Where are you?" Annoyance turned her whisper into a hiss. "Izzy is sick. Come home!"

It was after one in the morning. Bars in the city were still open, but it was a weeknight. This was ridiculous.

Why wasn't Frank answering his phone? He was probably in the center of a group, holding court, entertaining everyone with one of his endless stories. Josie wasn't truly angry, because Frank couldn't have known Izzy would become ill. But she was peeved that he hadn't checked his cell phone. She never would have stayed out so long without doing so. The rules were different when you were a parent.

She fell asleep curled around Izzy. Her phone woke her a little past two.

"Frank?" she said. She sat up and rubbed her eyes. "Where are you?" In the background, she could hear the echo of his footsteps. It sounded as if his hard-soled dress shoes were slapping against concrete.

"Sorry," he panted. "I'm just getting my car from the garage now. I'll be there in a minute."

"Izzy threw up!" Josie said. "It's all over her room."

"Should I stop and get her Pedialyte or anything?"

"Frank, it's the middle of the night," she said. "Just come home."

She ended the call and remained motionless. She suddenly felt wide awake. Her skin prickled. She lay in bed, her hand absently stroking circles on Izzy's back, until she heard Frank's key in the lock twenty minutes later.

He came into the bedroom, still in his suit jacket and tie, a contrite expression on his face.

"We were at the hotel bar," he explained. "I didn't hear my phone."

"What if the house had burned down?" she asked. "What if I'd had to take Izzy to the hospital?"

"I'm sorry." He approached the bed. "How is she?" He reached down and smoothed Izzy's hair back from her face. The look on his face was so loving, so kind, that Josie felt her heart soften. It wasn't intentional that he hadn't heard his phone. He probably had a little too much to drink and hadn't been paying attention to the time.

"Her bedroom is a disaster," Josie said.

"I'll clean it," Frank said, standing up. "Let me just change. Do you need anything else?"

"Can you get her more water?" Josie asked, gesturing to the glass on the nightstand.

"Sure," he said. He went into Izzy's bedroom. She heard him rustling around, then heading downstairs. When he came back five minutes later, he poked his head into the doorway.

"That was gross," he said, smiling. "I threw her comforter and sheets into the washing machine."

"Ew, it got on those, too?" Josie asked. "Can you wash your hands before you come to bed?"

"Yes, I'll wash my hands," Frank said. His voice sounded a little exasperated, but he was still smiling at her.

The exasperated tone was what did it. It proved that this was just an ordinary night, that nothing strange had happened, and that Frank had been doing exactly what he'd said. If he'd had something to feel guilty about, he wouldn't be acting so normally.

Josie felt the tightness in her abdomen relax as she inhaled deeply. Frank eased into bed, gently moving Izzy into the middle.

"I love you," he whispered, right before Josie fell asleep.

The next morning, she'd woken around seven. Izzy was asleep, splayed out like a starfish. Josie touched her daughter's forehead. Izzy's fever had broken.

That could have been the end of it.

Across the room, Josie saw Frank's iPhone on the bureau, plugged into a charger.

She could hear the shower running, and the muffled sound of Frank's singing. He was fond of belting out Sinatra in the morning.

One detail from last night kept nagging at her. The sound of Frank's footsteps rapidly slapping against concrete, echoing as if in a stairwell.

Wouldn't a hotel have an elevator to deliver you to the parking garage?

Perhaps Frank had left his car at the office and had taken a cab or Uber to the dinner. That was plausible. He could have been let off at the front entrance of his office building. He could have used his key to gain access to the building, then taken the stairs down one level to the parking garage because he was in a rush.

The thing was, Josie had driven Frank to work before, on weekend mornings when the office building was closed, to retrieve his car. Instead of entering the lobby, he'd used a device on his key chain to unlock the giant metal garage door. She'd watched it grind upward, folding into the ceiling, and then Frank had given her a wave and disappeared inside, emerging a moment later with his car.

He hadn't taken the stairs, because it was faster to enter through the garage directly.

And he'd been in a rush last night.

Josie looked at his iPhone again.

*"Fly me to the moon,"* Frank sang. He always took long showers, often draining their small tank of hot water.

Izzy was still sound asleep. Zoe must've been, too, since she hadn't come into the room.

Josie lifted up the covers and slid out a leg. The mattress shifted and creaked as she stood up, but Izzy slept on.

She walked to the bureau and stared down at his phone. She swept her index finger across the screen and typed in the code.

If someone—say, Karin—had asked Josie to articulate what was going on in her head at that moment, she would not have been able to explain her actions. She was operating on instinct alone. But she was aware that she didn't expect to find anything on Frank's phone. She was looking at it for reassurance, not because she truly doubted her husband.

There was one new text.

It was from a woman whose name Josie recognized instantly. Melissa was a sales associate Frank had worked with for the past year. Frank had mentioned her several times.

Josie knew Frank admired her professionally; she was smart and hardworking. Josie had met her once or twice and had found her to be pleasant if somewhat bland. Melissa wasn't particularly attractive, either—or at least, Josie had never considered that she might be to Frank. She was tall and gangly, with knobby elbows and knees. Her complexion was pasty and her hair a mousy brown.

Josie had never considered her a threat.

Melissa had texted Frank at 6:58 a.m., just a couple of minutes ago. Perhaps the buzzing sound of an incoming text was what had woken Josie.

She stared down at the message, feeling her skin prickle again.

Fun night. Let's do it again soon.

Had Melissa written more? Only the opening two lines were displayed on the screen. If Josie touched the text, the entire note would appear— but then Frank would also know she had opened it.

She touched the text.

The green dot next to the message, which indicated it was unread, disappeared. Now there would be no hiding from Frank what she'd done.

But Josie hadn't needed to view it, after all. The full message was only those two lines.

Josie carefully set the phone back down on the dresser and walked over to the bed, perching on the edge of the mattress's foot.

*Fun night.*

The rushing water ceased, and Josie could hear Frank, humming now, pull back the curtain. There was a rustling noise that she knew meant he was rubbing a towel over his hair. Next he'd put on his thick robe, the one she'd gotten for him at L.L.Bean for his birthday, and he'd spread shaving cream on his cheeks.

*Let's do it again soon.*

That phrasing. It seemed deliberate. Cautious. Purposefully vague. Perhaps in case someone other than Frank saw the message.

What, exactly, had been fun? The industry dinner, or something else?

Melissa lived in a small apartment building downtown. Josie knew this because Melissa had hosted a cocktail party months ago that Frank and Josie had attended, along with many of their colleagues.

Josie and Frank had parked on the street that night. Josie closed her eyes and tried to visualize the apartment building. But she couldn't recall whether it had a basement garage.

Frank had been running when he'd phoned her back. He'd been out of breath. Frank, who had never been big on exercise. If he'd been innocently hanging out in a group after the dinner, would he have run to his car? It seemed more like the action someone might take if he was guilty of something.

She heard the buzz of Frank's electric toothbrush. He would open the bathroom door and walk into the bedroom at any moment.

She waited. The bathroom door swung open.

"Sweetie?" Frank sounded surprised. "You okay?"

She looked up at him. "Melissa texted you. I read it."

"Okay," Frank said. He remained standing in the bathroom doorway. He seemed utterly calm. "What did she say?"

"That she had a fun time last night and wanted to do it again soon."

Frank took a step closer to Josie. "Yeah, I talked to her a lot last night. She's had a rough year. Her dad got really sick—he needed a bone marrow transplant—and she had to help her mom through it all. I think she was happy to get out."

Josie's brain felt thick and sludgy. It was difficult to think.

"We were all hanging out at the hotel bar," Frank said. He moved a step closer. "Other people were there, too. You remember Dean, right? He was with us. And Cindy."

"So if I called Dean and Cindy, they'd tell me they were at the bar with you until two a.m.?" Josie asked.

Frank nodded. "Of course. Sure. Call them if you want."

He couldn't be lying. His expression radiated sincerity.

"Okay, I may just call Cindy," Josie said. That didn't provoke a reaction. "And the next time you see Melissa outside of work, I want to come."

"Sweetie!" Frank looked wounded. "Of course! You would have been there last night if they'd let us bring spouses."

Zoe woke up a moment later, and Josie went downstairs to pour Kix cereal into bowls and slice up oranges.

"You okay?" Frank said before he left for work. He was holding one of his to-go mugs with flowers and butterflies drawn on it. *We love Daddy,* Zoe had written. Frank's forehead creased as he looked across the kitchen at her. "Come here, Josie."

He folded her into his arms and whispered, "I love you."

She inhaled his woodsy cologne and closed her eyes, her ear pressed so closely to his chest that she could feel his strong, steady heartbeat. This was real; this was the truth. He simply could not have been with another woman seven hours ago. It was impossible.

"I love you, too," she said, clinging to Frank.

"I'll be home early tonight," he promised, and she finally let him go.

But as soon as the door closed behind Frank, the words in the text floated back into her mind. It was as if Melissa were leaning close, whispering them.

Would a hotel bar really remain open until two on a weeknight? The kitchen tile felt cold under Josie's bare feet and she shivered. Frank hadn't been upset that she'd read his texts. Did that indicate guilt, or was he merely being kind because he knew she'd had a rough night and was feeling fragile?

It would be easy enough to check. She'd feel better once she confirmed that small fact. Then she could let this go completely.

She settled Zoe in front of a video, then she ran upstairs and put on socks before she found the reservations number for the hotel chain and dialed it.

She was transferred around until she finally reached the concierge at the Chicago location where Frank's dinner had been held. The concierge was initially confused, thinking she wanted a reservation at the bar, but she managed to convey her question.

"No, miss, our bar has last call at twelve o'clock," he said.

Josie froze. She felt as if she were going into shock. "So no one could be there at, say, one o'clock?" she asked. Her voice sounded strangled.

*He lied,* Josie thought. *He was with Melissa, in her apartment.*

"Well, sure, they could be," the concierge said.

"Wait—is the bar closed or open after

midnight?" Josie asked. She rubbed her forehead.

"You see, the bar has last call at twelve, but the seating area for it is in an open area of the hotel, with lots of couches and chairs. So if your group wants to relax there, that would be fine. You just couldn't be served drinks that late."

Maybe Frank hadn't lied.

"So last night, people *could* have been in the bar area until one thirty or two?" Josie asked. The concierge still seemed to think she wanted to make a reservation; it was critical that he understand what she was asking.

"The bar *area* is open all night," the concierge said. "It's more like a lounge for our guests. We have complimentary water and newspapers there as well. There is plenty of seating for large groups."

He'd probably still missed the point of her call, but he'd given her some information. Josie thanked him and hung up. She felt more uncertain than ever. Was it plausible that Frank and his friends had hung out for nearly two hours without any alcohol being served? Perhaps they'd all ordered drinks for last call at midnight. They could've nursed their cocktails, then switched to water.

She tried to picture it. Soft, comfortable chairs and couches. Everyone settling in after the long dinner. And Frank did always hate to leave a good party. They could have lingered, a small group of good friends who didn't get to see one another enough. Frank was a night owl. He wouldn't have felt the lateness of the hour the way she would have.

Maybe she should go to the bar area. Perhaps if she saw it for herself, she'd have a better understanding of what might or might not have happened.

She'd do it. She'd take Izzy into the city for lunch, then make up an excuse to wander through the hotel.

With that settled, Josie turned her attention to the laundry and breakfast dishes.

She'd intended to go into the city around noon. But first she had to run to the store to pick up rug cleaner. When she pulled back into her driveway at around eleven thirty, she discovered Izzy had fallen asleep in her car seat. Josie let her doze while she ran into the house and saturated the rug with the spray cleaner. When she went back outside, Izzy was still sleeping. Josie picked her up to carry her into the house, thinking Izzy might need to nap a bit longer after her rough night. Josie settled her on the couch and covered her with a blanket, putting cushions on the floor in case Izzy rolled off.

Josie finished scrubbing and vacuuming the rug, then she sank into the recliner next to the couch, intending to just close her eyes briefly. But she slept for nearly an hour and a half. By the time she woke up, it was too late to go into the city and still make it back in time to pick up Zoe.

She'd go another time, Josie told herself. But already, the errand seemed less urgent. She was warm and drowsy and the intense emotions that had battered her last night and this morning were fading. Frank had texted while she'd been sleeping—How are my beautiful girls doing?—and Huck was whining to go out the back and Josie needed to make one more pass over the rug because it still smelled a bit.

The pull toward everyday life had already begun to reassert itself.

At the time, Frank's explanation seemed plausible, when Josie held it up against the scanty facts she'd secured. Only much later would she begin to question whether she truly believed Frank, or only *wanted* to believe him. But, at least on that afternoon, as she looked at her sleeping daughter in the cozy living room of the home she loved so, the distinction didn't occur to her.

# Chapter Sixteen

*Present day*

"Tell me your three happy things," Sonya the therapist said.

Josie wrapped her arms around the chenille pillow that she'd pulled onto her lap again. It was soft and squishy, and she wondered whether Sonya had chosen it for those reasons.

"I had drinks with my friends. Then I took my daughters out and we all got manicures; that was kind of a big deal because it's expensive and I usually do my own nails. And I bought some trashy magazines to read."

"How did it feel when you did those things?" Sonya asked.

"Everything reminded me of the affair." Josie sighed. "I talked about it during drinks. The manicurist pointed out I've been biting my cuticles. And in the magazines—my God, is everyone having an affair? It seemed like it was all about celebrities being caught with strippers."

"So the reminders are everywhere."

"I can't escape them," Josie said. "It's like if I manage to stop thinking about it for thirty seconds, then, bam! I drive by a Starbucks, or a song comes on the radio and the lyrics are all about cheating. Or, the song is by Gwen Stefani and it makes me think about how she caught her husband with the nanny or whatever. I overhear someone talking about the new Kristen Stewart movie, and I instantly remember how she cheated on Robert Pattinson with that director years ago. It's like the six degrees of separation game, but everything in my world is one degree away from cheating."

Sonya let Josie's words sit for a moment. "You are experiencing post-traumatic stress disorder."

Josie looked up in surprise. "I am?"

Sonya nodded. "In many ways, a discovery like yours can feel like a death. It's a tremendous loss. With time, you will find that those constant reminders ebb. You'll be able to find joy in everyday activities at some point, I promise."

Josie sighed. "I'll take your word for it," she said.

Sonya glanced down at the yellow legal pad that was resting in her lap.

"Has Frank found a place to move into yet?"

"Yeah, an apartment," Josie said. "He's sub-letting it from a woman who is moving to Asia for six months. It's already furnished, so he doesn't have to deal with that."

Sonya jotted something on her notepad. Josie wondered what her notes said: *Married twelve years, two kids, affair*. Those were the bullet points of her life.

"That will make things simpler, if he doesn't have to furnish it. Especially since you haven't made a decision yet. And when does he move out?"

"In a few weeks." Josie dropped her head into her hands. "How am I going to tell the girls?"

When her sobs eased, Sonya spoke again. "Keep it simple, but tell them the truth. That you and Daddy need a break."

"They think Frank hurt his back and that's why he's sleeping on the couch," Josie said. "That's what I told them, anyway. But the other night Zoe crawled into my bed and wanted him, and she started to get upset, so Frank came upstairs and lay down in her bed with her until she fell back asleep. I heard her asking why he could lie in her bed but not in the big bed. I don't know how he answered her . . . The girls have to know something is going on."

"They probably do," Sonya acknowledged.

"Should I use the word 'divorce' when I tell them?" Josie asked.

Sonya's eyes seemed gentler than ever; looking into them felt soothing. It was as if Sonya was trying to transfer some of her own tranquillity to Josie.

"I would not use that word until you are certain you want a divorce."

Josie nodded. "I'm not one hundred percent certain yet. But I think I'm moving in that direction."

Josie sat at the kitchen table in the darkened house. The only illumination in the room came from her computer screen. It was eleven o'clock at night, but numbers were keeping her awake.

Therapy was expensive. Frank's new apartment was expensive, even though it was a small studio. They'd been saving a little every month for retirement, but they'd have to cancel those automatic withdrawals now.

Josie could go back to work full-time—assuming she could even find a job after so many years out of the workforce—but it would be a big change for the girls, on top of everything else. Plus by the time she paid for a nanny and transportation and new work clothes, she'd probably end up netting so little that it wouldn't be worthwhile.

Josie looked at the budget she'd been creating in a spreadsheet. No matter how many times she tried to find a chunk of fat to trim off, she came up short.

She turned her head at the sound of a floorboard creaking. Frank was approaching the doorway, wearing athletic shorts and an old T-shirt. It had a hole in the collar.

"Um, can I get you anything?" Frank asked. By

now he knew not to ask how she was doing; her icy responses had trained that instinct out of him.

"No," she said. She could feel the rage coming off her in waves. It seemed like a tangible thing; an angry red force in the room. She wondered whether Frank could feel it, too.

"I thought I could leave early tomorrow and pick up the girls from school," he said. "Give you a little time to yourself."

"Fine." She bit off the word.

He reached up to scratch his head with his left hand and she caught a glimpse of gold against his dark hair.

"Take off your wedding ring," Josie ordered.

"What?"

"You touched her while you were wearing that ring. Get it off. Now I don't ever want to see it again."

"Can I get another one?" Frank asked.

She turned back to her spreadsheet, willing him to leave.

Then she heard a muted sound, almost like a hiccup.

"I don't know what's wrong with me," Frank whispered. He wiped his face on his bare forearm and she struggled against the urge to get up and tear off a paper towel and hand it to him. "Please, will you help me? I know I shouldn't ask that and I don't deserve it, I don't deserve you or the girls. But I am so lost without you."

He'd definitely lost weight. His shirt hung on him. And maybe it was a trick of the dim blue light, but deep shadows seemed etched under his eyes.

"I didn't feel anything for her," he said, his voice breaking. "You are the woman I love, the only woman I have ever truly loved. If I could go back . . . God, I never would have done it. I can't believe how much I hurt you. I feel sick. I despise myself."

"Why?" Josie asked. It was the only question that seemed to matter now.

"I don't know," Frank whispered. "You're so much prettier and kinder and better than she is in every way. I never really wanted to be with her. That's what scares me . . . I have absolutely no idea why I did it."

He didn't make any move to come closer. Josie had the sense that he wasn't trying to sway her. It seemed more like he was in a confessional, revealing his deepest truths. His raw honesty smoothed the rough peaks of her anger.

They hadn't talked like this in years. Even when they'd gone out for date nights, their conversations had revolved mostly around the logistics of running their family. Josie didn't know when or how it had happened, but they'd stopped sharing intimate pieces of themselves long ago.

"I don't know if I can ever get past this," Josie

232

said, trying to match his honesty with her own. "Sometimes I think I want to, but other times I feel like I would remember it every single time I look at you."

"I understand," Frank said. "I think of it all the time, too. When I'm at work I imagine you in the house and I wonder what you're doing and if you're crying or hating me or both and I start beating myself up again."

She hadn't thought about how Frank might be suffering, not even once, Josie realized. She'd been too focused on her own pain.

"I found a counselor," he said. "I thought I should make an appointment for myself and try to figure things out . . . One thing I've realized is that we were growing apart before this happened."

At her sharp intake of breath he quickly added, "That's not an excuse and I'm not blaming you for anything. It's all on me. I just meant I don't think I noticed it until . . . I mean, I think I felt disconnected and that's part of the reason why I was able to do all the horrible things I did. I need to fix myself, Josie. I know it might be too late for us, but I need to do it for the girls."

Josie slowly nodded. She didn't want Frank to leave and end the conversation, not exactly, but she also didn't want to prolong it.

"The counselor . . ." Frank hesitated. "Would you consider coming with me?"

Josie sighed. "Let's just see how things go."

After Frank left the doorway, she sat there for a moment. Then a deep exhaustion abruptly crashed over her. She closed her computer and crept upstairs, feeling her way through the darkness. She reached her bed and crawled into it, and she fell asleep almost instantly.

The creak of the front door opening woke Josie a little before five in the morning. She rolled over in bed to nudge Frank awake, remembering at the exact same moment that her arm landed in the empty space beside her that he wouldn't be there.

She climbed out of bed and hurried to her window, which overlooked the front yard.

Frank was heading down the walk, toward his car. He wore jeans and a down coat, and his hands were buried in his pockets.

Josie watched him get in his Honda Civic and drive away slowly, then she walked downstairs. His bedding was folded at the end of the couch. He'd left a note on top of it: *I got an early start today. I'll be home at 6. Love to everyone.*

He couldn't be going to a work meeting, not this early and certainly not in those clothes. Frank had begun to exercise more regularly in recent weeks, but he wasn't carrying a gym bag.

Something else was off; a clue nagged at Josie. She realized what it was when she went into the kitchen. Frank's hands had been buried deeply in his pockets. He wasn't holding his coffee mug.

Perhaps he'd avoided brewing a pot because he thought the noise and aroma might wake her. He'd been awfully quiet this morning; if it hadn't been for that unavoidable creak of the door, Josie might have slept straight through until her alarm at seven. By the time she'd have showered and gotten the girls up and dressed and headed downstairs, it would have been closer to seven thirty. Frank hadn't put a time on his note. Had he wanted her to assume he'd left later than he actually had?

Possibilities whirled through her mind. Josie didn't believe Frank was sneaking off to meet Dana; he was too determined to fix their marriage, and he would have known this would seal its demise. But he could be meeting Ron, Dana's husband. Josie had read an article on Huffington Post about a woman whose husband had discovered her affair and had tried to burn down the house of the other man. Ron had seemed so mild-mannered on the phone. But sometimes those guys were the ones who ended up exploding; maybe Ron was now threatening Frank somehow.

She began to search through the house, looking for the familiar red case of the iPad Frank was so attached to. She found it wedged between two cushions deep in the sofa. Perhaps he'd been using it last night before he'd gone to sleep, and it had fallen into the crack. Or perhaps he'd deliberately hidden it.

She opened the cover and tapped in the pass code, which she knew since the girls occasionally used the iPad. Then she called up all the open pages on the device.

Frank had been on Amazon, and he'd checked the score of last night's Bulls game. He'd also looked at his emails.

Josie stared down at his in-box, feeling an unsettling sense of déjà vu. There was an unfamiliar woman's name, right there on the front page.

Josie jabbed at the line with her index finger to open the email.

*Sunrise service begins at 6 a.m.,* a woman named Kerry had written. *Please don't forget you've signed up to bring donuts.* Her automatic signature contained her title and the name of her organization.

Frank had begun to attend church.

# Chapter Seventeen

*Eighteen months earlier*

Zoe needed new shoes. It was a simple errand, a quick round-trip to the mall. They'd be home within an hour—two, tops, if the girls badgered Josie into stopping at Build-A-Bear or the candy store that was cannily located just across from the children's shoe store.

"Izzy, where are your socks?" Josie asked. She was in the kitchen, packing up the diaper bag. Izzy was newly potty trained, which meant she had an accident every few days.

She didn't expect Izzy to respond. Izzy was two, and she had the focus of a gnat sometimes.

"Let's hurry, girls!" Josie called, knowing her admonition was falling into a void.

"Iz? Zoe?" Josie walked through the house, finally locating Zoe in her room. She'd changed out of her shorts and T-shirt. Now she was clad in a Little Mermaid bathing suit.

Josie felt a hitch in her blood pressure. She had a dentist's appointment at two; a filling had fallen out of her back tooth weeks ago and she was just now getting around to having it replaced. And her tank was almost empty, so she also had to stop at the gas station on the way or she might not even make it to the mall.

"Sweetie, come *on*."

"I'm ready!"

"No, you're not. You can't wear a bathing suit to the mall."

"Yes I can! Everyone does it!"

"No! The police won't like it," Josie said, wondering where the bizarre warning had come from even as she said it.

Zoe walked over to her toy chest and pulled out a puzzle, accidentally scattering its pieces over the rug.

"Zoe! We don't have time for puzzles! We need to go get you some shoes!"

Josie threw open a dresser drawer and found a soft blue skirt.

"Here." She shook it in front of Zoe. "Wear this over your bathing suit, okay? Zoe, put down the puzzle and move it!"

Josie grabbed a T-shirt out of the drawer, intending to wrestle Zoe into it before they went to the mall. Then she discovered Izzy in the kitchen, playing with Huck's kibble while Huck watched with sorrowful eyes.

"Oh, Izzy, yuck, here, baby, let's wash your hands." She lifted Izzy up and held her to the sink, using her raised knee as a stool and reaching with one hand to twist on the tap. She felt a painful twinge in her lower back.

"Here's the soap," she said.

"Do it self!" Izzy howled. It had been her favorite phrase for the past few weeks.

Josie knew independence was an important developmental phase, but the process would take forever. "No, I'm doing it!" she said, grabbing the bottle of soap out of Izzy's hands and squirting a dab into them. She ignored Izzy's outraged protest as she rinsed the suds and then she carried Izzy to the door, scooping up her sneakers along the way. Izzy could survive without socks.

"Zoe? We are leaving. Right. This. Minute."

Five minutes later—naturally Zoe needed to go to the bathroom—they were finally settled in the car, and Josie was sweating. It was mid-July, and the sun had turned the vehicle into an oven.

"I'm hot," Zoe whined.

"It's going to take a second for the air-conditioning to kick in," Josie said. Her shorts had hiked up and the cloth seats felt itchy against her thighs. It was only ten o'clock, but she was exhausted.

She wondered what Frank was doing right now. He'd left for the office around eight, wearing a shirt that was crisp and fresh from the dry cleaner, whistling as he'd walked out the door. She knew Frank's job wasn't easy—he was constantly schlepping around, meeting with doctors and other health care professionals—but at least there was a little dignity to his stress. He didn't have to passionately argue with a toddler about whether he could help her wipe her bottom on a daily basis.

It wasn't supposed to be like this.

Josie had planned to return to work when Zoe was four months old. She'd been working as director of accounts for a public relations agency, which sounded more glamorous than it actually was. She was still putting together mailings, just as she'd done when she'd started at the company, but instead of stuffing envelopes, now she was in charge of helping to coordinate branding and taglines on the glossy materials that went into the envelopes.

She'd found a good day care for Zoe, run by a trio of women who seemed capable and kind. But as the final day of her maternity leave approached, Josie found herself more and more reluctant to return to the office. She knew Frank wanted her to stay at home for at least the first few years of Zoe's life. Frank had said he'd accept whatever decision she made, but it was clear where his preference lay. His mother had left her job as a librarian when her oldest son was born, and Frank wanted to replicate that experience for their children.

Since Frank made about twice what she did, the subject of his becoming a stay-at-home dad never came up. The ideal solution would have been for each of them to work part-time, but they didn't even bother proposing it to their bosses; it was an impossibility.

As it turned out, Zoe never spent a single morning in the day care. Josie gave up her spot to a woman on the waiting list. She handed in her notice at work and told Frank she'd think about going back after a year. But that year turned the corner and approached two, and she and Frank began trying for another child. They had a miscarriage before Izzy came along—an event so bleak and painful that Josie always had difficulty talking about it—which made them all the more grateful for their second daughter.

But the whole point of her quitting to be a stay-at-home mom had gotten blurry somewhere along the way. Josie had imagined building forts out of the dining room table and a sheet. She'd thought she'd spend lazy afternoons reading to her children before they took long, rambling walks around the neighborhood, discovering the magic in flowers and wiggling worms.

Never in her fantasies did she see herself like this: ten pounds overweight and having snacked on a few semisweet chocolate chips immediately after breakfast, brushing sweaty hair out of her face while she drove two cranky kids to the mall.

In two months, though, everything would change again. Izzy would start going to preschool three days a week and Josie would have regular blocks of time to herself for the first time in nearly seven years. She'd been fantasizing about those breaks, imagining that she'd go to the gym, build up the little business selling educational toys that she'd begun just a few months earlier, and finally organize her home. But right now, September seemed like a mirage.

She pulled into the mall parking lot at the exact moment that she realized she'd forgotten to stop for gas.

"Pronated?" she asked the shoe salesman, who was frowning as he stared at Zoe's feet.

"See how they turn in?" he said. "Sweetheart, walk down to the door and then come back."

Zoe obeyed. Josie had never noticed it before, but now she saw. "How do we fix it?"

"Orthotics," the shoe salesman said. "They're like custom inserts for her shoes that will help train her foot to stay in the right position. Does your insurance cover it?"

"I have no idea." Josie sighed and tried to think of what to do next. "I'll call them. Should I hold off on getting the shoes?"

"Yeah, you'll want to go up at least a half size or so because the orthotics will take up room. And you'll need to have those made first. There's a guy I can recommend who works at a place in the city. He works with a lot of our customers."

"Okay," Josie said, accepting the card the salesman pressed into her hand. The store was busy, and he hurried off to help someone else as she called, "Thank you."

A simple errand had sprouted into three: she had to phone the insurance company (the last time she'd called she'd been placed on hold for more than fifteen minutes); take Zoe into the city to have the orthotics made; and then buy new shoes.

"Want Build-A-Bear," Izzy said.

"No!" The word came out more sharply than Josie had intended. She softened her tone. "You can each get a tiny bag of candy—five pieces only—but no eating any until after lunch."

"I'm hungry now," Zoe said.

"It's barely eleven," Josie started to respond. But the girls had been awake for hours, and Josie felt hungry, too. "Fine. Let's go to the food court."

They stopped by the candy place first, and after only one minor catastrophe—Izzy spilled Starbursts all over the floor when she tried to scoop them by herself—they made it to the food court.

Josie bought them all slices of pizza and cups of lemonade, then they settled in at a table.

"Cut it self," Izzy said when Josie began to slice her pizza into bite-sized pieces.

"No, Iz, I don't—"

"Self!" Izzy bellowed.

The knife was plastic and flimsy; Izzy couldn't

hurt herself with it. "Fine." Josie sighed, trying to remember how long this stage had lasted with Zoe.

She raised her own slice to her lips, opening her mouth to take a big, greedy bite, and two things happened simultaneously: Zoe knocked over her cup of lemonade, which splashed the liquid across the table, and it began dripping onto Josie's lap. And Josie caught sight of a pretty woman in a flowered sundress sitting at the next table over, enjoying a healthy lunch of apple and avocado slices and string cheese with her perfectly behaved daughter.

The woman was staring at Josie, too.

"All I'm saying is it isn't fair for me to come home after a long day at work and have to clean up the house!" Frank snapped that night.

"I work, too!" Josie yelled. "I have never worked harder. I actually made a big sale today, Frank. I'm supplying all the toys for a new summer camp. And I did it while the girls were napping."

"I'm not saying you don't work hard! But this is the third night in a row I've had to clean up the kitchen and it doesn't seem fair when I'm working so late."

"I clean it up eighteen times a day! All I do is clean and clean and clean and things get messy five seconds later."

"Zoe is big enough to help you," Frank said.

"Really?" Josie put her hands on her hips. "You're welcome to start teaching her, Frank. Why don't you do it this weekend?"

Frank loved to do this, to say that it was time for Izzy to give up her pacifier or for Zoe to keep track of her own library books. Then he'd back away and expect Josie to undertake the hard work of implementing the change.

But maybe that's what stay-at-home mothers were supposed to do; the avocado woman's daughter probably cleaned up after herself with a miniature dustpan and broom.

Frank exhaled slowly. "Is there anything for dinner?"

"Hamburgers," Josie said. "Yours is in the fridge."

Pizza for lunch and hamburgers for dinner; she'd never even thought of packing a nutritious snack to bring along on their errands.

"I'm going to bed," she said.

"Jos, it's only nine thirty. Come on."

She shook her head. "I'm exhausted." When she'd come home from the disastrous trip to the mall and had discovered the email message from the director of the summer camp, she'd felt her body unclench. It wasn't just the money, although her commission would be several hundred dollars. The email had been a victory she'd needed desperately.

But Frank didn't even care about that; he only saw a sink full of dishes and an inadequate meal. She'd felt alone all day, but never so much as in this moment. It felt as if Frank were jabbing at the most tender, vulnerable parts of her.

She ducked her head so Frank didn't see her blinking back tears. He didn't have to criticize her; she knew all too well that she wasn't doing a good enough job.

She climbed the stairs, her footsteps heavy. As she neared the top, she could hear the sound of the television coming to life. Frank would remain on the couch, eating his reheated dinner and watching a baseball game. She'd read in bed for a while. By the time he came to bed, she'd be sound asleep.

She knew this, because it was becoming their pattern.

# Chapter Eighteen

*Present day*

She'd completely forgotten about the Valentine's Day party for Zoe's class. Frank had been the one to remind her. All of the parents were invited to attend. There would be games, a valentine-making station, and a snack table.

"Is it still okay if I go?" Frank asked that morning.

"Zoe would be disappointed if you didn't," Josie responded.

She'd felt some sympathy for him after his confession the other night in the darkened kitchen, but now she was back to hating his guts again. If he'd just come to her and said he felt disconnected and that he missed her, she would have acted. She would have called a therapist. She would have talked to him. She would have worked with him to fix things.

Instead of turning in toward her, though, he'd looked outside of their marriage for a solution.

"It's at two o'clock, right?" Frank asked.

He knew the appointed time. He was just trying to reestablish communication with her. She picked up her mug of coffee and said "Mmm-hmmm" as she strode out of the room. She didn't look at him. But somehow she knew his shoulders were slumping.

Frank was in charge of running the bingo station. He'd printed out special cards from a website, with Valentine's images like Cupids and hearts forming the columns. He sat on a small metal chair, a circle of kids around him, pulling various images out of a paper bag.

"Ladies and gentlemen, I have the next picture in my hand. Who's ready to see it?"

Predictably, the kids erupted in shouts and squeals.

"All right, I think one or two of you is ready . . . Who . . . has . . . this . . . word?" Frank asked, holding up a square of paper.

"It's backward!" "We can't see it!" "Turn it around, Zoe's dad!"

"Oops," Frank said, playing to his audience. "Is this better?"

"Now it's upside down!"

Kids were literally falling out of their chairs with laughter by the time Frank showed them the clue, a picture of the word "love" written in puffy red letters.

Josie circled the table, pointing out the square to a child who hadn't noticed it on his bingo sheet and handing out a napkin to another kid who had cupcake icing on his face.

"Bingo!" a girl shouted.

"Let's see your sheet," Frank said, peering at it. "Oh, sweetie, you are so close! See, you put a marker on the fish kissing but I haven't pulled out that image yet. You just need one more and you've got it. Keep an eye out for the smooching fish."

"Smooching!" "Eew, that's gross!" "Why do fish kiss?"

A mother Josie didn't know well leaned over and whispered: "He is so amazing with kids. I wish my husband were more like that!"

Josie dredged up a smile. "Yeah."

She could tell her lackluster response surprised the woman, but Josie was in no mood to do damage control. She circled the table again to escape more conversation.

When the game ended, she accompanied Zoe to the valentine-making table. There were lacy doilies and construction-paper hearts and stickers and glitter and glue.

"Who do you want to make one for?" Josie asked as Zoe sat down and reached for a pink doily.

"It's a secret," Zoe said. "Don't watch."

"Okay," Josie said. She went to tidy up the snack table, to the sounds of Frank's next raucous bingo game.

The party wrapped up fairly quickly, its end coinciding with the conclusion of the school day—first-grade teachers were savvy enough to put time constraints on anything involving kids and sugar—and Josie and Frank helped Zoe gather up her backpack and lunch sack and coat before they walked down the wide hallway toward the school exit.

Clustered in a group right by the front door were several parents Josie recognized, including Amanda. Her stomach clenched. Surely Amanda wouldn't say anything, not here in front of Zoe and everyone else.

"Why did you stop?" Zoe asked Josie.

"Sorry," Josie said. "I just— I wanted a drink of water." She walked over to the silver fountain attached to the hallway wall. When she pressed the button for the water flow, the lukewarm spray hit her in the chin. She wiped it off with the palm of her hand and straightened up without taking a sip.

Amanda and the other parents were still there. Amanda looked up and caught Josie's gaze. She waved and smiled. Then her eyes widened and the grin left her face as she took in Frank walking beside Josie.

*Don't say anything.* Josie willed Amanda the message. She didn't truly believe Amanda would do anything overt. But she could very well touch Josie's arm and speak in the sort of hushed, sympathetic tone one used at a funeral. It would draw the attention of the other parents and spark their curiosity, even if all Amanda said was a simple "How are you?"

She was only a few feet away now. Josie reached for Zoe's soft little hand and held it. If need be, she'd yank her through the front door quickly.

She drew close to Amanda, then passed her. Amanda kept staring at her, but she didn't say a word.

Josie pushed through the heavy double doors, and then she was outside.

Frank came through the door after her, completely unaware of the near miss.

"Do you want to drive home with me or Mommy?" he asked Zoe.

Zoe looked confused. "You didn't drive here together?"

"No, Daddy came from work," Josie said quickly. She hoped Zoe's sense of direction wasn't well enough developed for her to realize that their home was between the city and the school.

"Let's keep walking while we figure it out," Josie suggested. Amanda could still come through the door at any moment.

"I'll go with Daddy," Zoe decided.

"Okay," Josie said. A few weeks ago, she would have been glad for the chance to run a quick errand on the way home unencumbered. But now it felt like rejection. Frank was the fun, spontaneous parent; she was the steady one who preferred schedules. When Frank moved out, would the girls beg to go with him?

"What's this?" Frank was saying.

"It's for both of you," Zoe told him. "Read it together!"

Josie looked at the pink folded heart in Frank's hand. She moved closer to him to view it.

*I love Mommy and Daddy,* Zoe had written. She'd put kitten stickers around the edges of the heart.

"Oh, sweetie." Josie's voice sounded strangled. It was the kitten stickers that did it, that caused a lump to form in her throat. Zoe was still so very little, and so innocent. She believed in Santa Claus, and the tooth fairy, and in the security of her family.

"Josie?" Frank whispered. She shook her head. She could feel herself begin to shake.

She was going to lose it, right here in the parking lot. She was going to begin sobbing and she wouldn't be able to stop, and Zoe was going to see everything, then Amanda and the other parents would come through the door . . .

She felt the pressure of Frank's hand briefly squeezing her arm, and then he shouted, "I love it, Zoey-Boey! And I love you!"

He scooped up Zoe in his arms, blowing platypus kisses on her cheeks and tossing her around while he walked to his car. She was laughing and squealing and she didn't even look in Josie's direction. Frank opened the rear door to his car while still holding Zoe, then flipped her right side up and eased her into her seat. "Buckle up, and let's race Mommy home!"

He closed the door and met Josie's eyes over the roof of his car. He raised his eyebrows and she understood the question conveyed by his expression: *Are you okay now?* She took in a deep, shuddering breath and then she nodded. Frank nodded back. He held her gaze for another few seconds, then he got into his car and slowly drove out of the parking lot.

Josie climbed into her Sienna and sat there for a little while before she turned the key in the ignition and headed home.

The counselor wasn't what Josie expected. He was perhaps fifty, and very fit. He wore an earring, and there was a mini basketball hoop hanging on the back of his office door. "I'm Michael Ambrosi. Call me Mike," he said, and Josie wondered whether this was a thing now, that every therapist wanted to be called by their first name.

There was a large leather sofa in the seating area, across from a single chair that Josie assumed was for Mike. What Josie liked about the sofa was that it was big enough for her to stake out a spot far away from Frank. The therapy sofa didn't try to force them together.

"Tell me what brings you here," Mike said, leaning forward like an athletic coach.

Josie looked sideways at Frank.

"I screwed up," Frank began. He laced his hands together over his knee. "I, ah, I had an affair with another woman."

Mike nodded. "And you are here because you wish to try to save the marriage?"

"I'm on the fence about that," Josie interjected.

Mike smiled. "Noted."

"I want Josie to know how much I love her, and how sorry I am," Frank said.

Mike looked at Josie. "If you're comfortable doing so, I'd like to try a technique to ensure the two of you really hear each other."

Josie shrugged. "Sure. Okay."

"Either you or Frank can start, whichever you'd rather. And you can say whatever you'd like to each other. The person listening should repeat back exactly what they've heard."

"Frank can start," Josie said.

"Okay." Frank twisted so that he was directly facing Josie from the other end of the sofa. "I want you to know how deeply sorry I am. How much I regret what I did. I feel awful."

The thing about doing this in front of a therapist was that it encouraged better behavior, Josie thought. No one wanted to seem like a shrew in front of a witness.

"Josie? Can you echo what Frank just said?"

She felt silly, but she complied. "You're sorry and you regret what you did."

"Could you try to repeat him as close to word for word as possible?" Mike asked.

"You are deeply sorry and you regret what you did."

"And I feel awful."

"And you feel awful." She felt her posture relax.

Saying those words made Frank's feelings incrementally more real to Josie. That was unexpected.

"Josie, is there anything you would like to say to Frank?"

Frank kept his eyes trained on her, but she refused to allow herself to feel pressured. She knew she could say no, or get up and leave the therapy room. She'd told Frank on the ride over that she wasn't promising to stay for the whole fifty minutes.

When she spoke, the emotion in her words surprised her: "What you did completely devastated me, Frank. Nothing has ever hurt me so much."

Fresh pain filled his eyes.

"Our family was everything to me. And I felt like you made me a laughingstock, that you just threw away everything we built together."

Mike waited a beat, then prompted, "Frank? Could you repeat this back to Josie?"

"I hurt you more than anyone ever has before," Frank said slowly, looking into her eyes. "Our family was everything to you. And you felt like I made you a laughingstock. You felt like I threw away everything we built together."

Josie had considered this exercise silly. She didn't see any point to it. But when she heard Frank carefully echo her without making an excuse or apology, something happened. She didn't know what it was, exactly. Maybe it was simply the relief that came with the fact that she and Frank were truly listening to each other, and being heard, for the first time in a long while.

"Would you like to schedule another appointment?" Mike asked them at the conclusion of the session. "I can see you next week."

"I would like to," Frank said. "Josie?"

She nodded slowly. "Okay."

It had been seven weeks since Josie had learned about the affair. Frank's affair had also happened over the course of seven weeks. The dual passages of time had each lasted an eternity.

Josie sat on her back steps, bundled up in her coat, a wool blanket over her shoulders and head. It was a clear, icy night, and the sky held a scattering of silvery stars.

The girls were asleep, and Frank was attending a business dinner. "I'll leave my phone on the whole time with the ringer turned up high," he'd said. "Call anytime. I'll be home by nine at the latest. I can come earlier if you need anything." But Josie was grateful for the time alone.

Frank would move out next week. His lease was temporary, though. They would need to make another decision when it expired.

Josie had no idea what her life would look like seven weeks from now. But something had compelled her to come outside and sit in the absolute stillness on this strange, sad, sort-of anniversary.

She wanted to ensure that whatever decision she made carried intention. That she went forward with clear eyes. She could not slide back into her marriage because she didn't know how to be without Frank, or out of guilt because of the children.

*Whatever happens, I will be happy again,* she promised herself. *I will make the right choice carefully.*

She peered into the sky, hoping to see a shooting star or some other physical manifestation to mark this moment, to sear it into her memory. But the sky remained stagnant, so she closed her eyes and cemented the vow within herself.

# Chapter Nineteen

"I want to come over every night and help put the girls to bed," Frank said. "I can bring dinner, too, or make it here. Whatever you want."

Josie nodded. They were in the car after their second therapy session with Mike.

"I thought I could pop by in the mornings, too, and see them before school," Frank said.

"But that's going to make you late for work."

"I don't care. It doesn't matter."

"You're going to be with them all the time." Josie's voice broke. "We're still going to do stuff as a family."

"Izzy is so little." Frank blew his nose on a crumpled napkin he pulled out of his pocket. "She's not going to understand. What if she thinks I don't love her and that's why I'm leaving?"

"She's not going to think that, Frank. She knows you adore her. You're a good father." When Frank shook his head, she added, "You are!"

"A good father wouldn't cheat on his children's mother," Frank said. "Whatever you think of me, however much you hate me, it's nothing compared to what I feel about myself. *I* did this to them."

Josie could see his knuckles whiten as he gripped the steering wheel. The car wasn't moving, though. They were sitting in front of their house.

Inside, a babysitter was watching the children, a teenaged girl from a few blocks over whom they both adored. The girls were probably playing Candy Land or Zingo! with the sitter right now. They'd have eaten the snacks Josie had set out—grapes and bagel chips and chocolate milk—and they would be happy.

Josie pulled down the visor and checked herself in the mirror. She rubbed concealer under her eyes and on the tip of her reddened nose. Frank's skin was darker than hers; it didn't reveal that he had been crying.

It was time.

Josie opened her car door. "Are you ready to go tell them?"

"Are you getting a divorce?" Zoe asked.

"No, no!" Josie said, wondering how Zoe even knew the word. "All we are doing is taking a break."

"Why can't Daddy just keep sleeping on the sofa? Isn't that enough of a break?" Zoe's eyes were pleading.

Frank bent over, his arms crossing his stomach, but he managed to smile reassuringly.

"I'll see you every single day, Z-girl," he said.

"Every day, every night, every weekend. You too, Busy-Izzy. You'll get sick of me. And my new apartment has a pool! You can come swim there."

"I hate swimming," Zoe said.

"Zoe! You love it," Josie protested.

"Not anymore."

"There's also an elevator," Frank said.

"For me?" Izzy asked.

"Sure, it's for you!" Frank said. "You can push all the buttons. We'll ride it up and down."

They'd planned to take the girls to Benihana for dinner tonight, the place where chefs cooked your dinner on a sizzling grill right in front of you while flipping shrimp tails into their tall white hats and slicing onions with the speed and dexterity of magicians.

But Josie realized that felt all wrong. This wasn't a celebration. They needed to stay here, hunkered down in the security of their home.

"Why do you and Mommy need a break?" Zoe asked. "When Izzy and I fight you make us stop!"

"I know, baby," Frank said.

"It's different with adults," Josie said.

"It's stupid and I hate it," Zoe said. Her lip was trembling.

"We are a family," Josie said. "We will always be a family."

Zoe exhaled. Josie waited anxiously for whatever she might say next.

"Can I watch *Backyardigans*?"

260

Josie looked at Frank, confused. Did Zoe need a retreat from the intense emotions? Or was it healthier to make her continue talking?

"I think a little *Backyardigans* would be okay," Frank said.

Josie reached out and stroked Zoe's hair. "Okay," she said. "*Backyardigans* it is."

Neither of them left the girls' sides for the rest of the evening. They ended up heating frozen chicken nuggets for dinner, then they all watched a Disney movie.

Zoe fell asleep before it ended, much earlier than her usual bedtime, almost certainly because of the stress the day had carried. Would she always be looking for signs that the separation was harming the girls? Josie wondered.

"I'll carry her up," Frank said. He gathered Zoe into his arms and headed for the stairs.

"How are you feeling, sweetie?" Josie asked Izzy.

"Good," Izzy said, her focus on the screen. When the movie's credits began to roll, Izzy went upstairs without protest. She brushed her teeth and washed her face, then changed into her footsie pajamas, all without complaint or delaying tactics. That was unusual, but perhaps she was worn out, too.

But when Josie tried to tuck her in, Izzy began to wail: "I want Daddy."

"Okay, okay," Josie said quickly. "No problem."

She ran downstairs. Frank was unfolding his bedding and spreading it out on the couch. "Frank? She wants you."

Josie went into the kitchen to make a cup of herbal tea. She was stirring a spoonful of honey into her mug and contemplating taking a Xanax when Frank reappeared: "Josie? She wants you now."

Josie hurried upstairs. "Iz? Mommy is here."

Izzy lay in her small twin bed, rubbing her eyes. "Can I lay next to you?" Josie asked. She crawled into bed and began rubbing Izzy's little back. "I love you, sweetie. Everything is okay."

But Izzy abruptly pulled away and sat up. "Daddy!" she yelled.

Frank thundered up the stairs and appeared in the doorway in an instant. "What is it?" he asked.

"May Daddy come too, please?" Izzy was using her best manners, her most polite words, in an effort to bring her parents closer together. She was trying to fix her family in the only way her three-year-old mind knew how.

Frank approached the bed. "Jos—is it okay? I mean, I won't . . ."

"There's room on the other side of her," Josie said. Her voice sounded choked and she hoped Izzy didn't know why. She shifted over, pulling Izzy with her.

Frank climbed in slowly, turning sideways so

he would fit on the narrow mattress. He reached out and took Izzy's hand.

They lay like that, curled on either side of their daughter, for a long time.

# Chapter Twenty

"What would you need to feel safe with Frank again?" Sonya asked.

Josie shook her head. "I have no idea."

"Let me put it another way. What steps would Frank need to take to make you feel certain he wasn't cheating on you again? You could say, for example, that Frank would need to let you check his iPhone every night when he came home from work."

Josie wrinkled her nose. "I would hate that. I would feel like a prison guard."

"So maybe not every night. But maybe whenever you felt like seeing it. You could simply ask Frank to hand it over, and he would need to immediately."

"But aren't relationships supposed to be based on trust? Okay, I just realized the irony in that comment . . . I guess what I meant to say is how could I have a relationship with Frank if I felt like I constantly had to check his iPhone?"

"No one expects you to suddenly start trusting Frank again, just like that." Sonya snapped her fingers. "But if you wanted to, you could think about steps that might help you rebuild trust."

Okay, Josie thought. She could play this game.

"I would need to be able to check his iPhone whenever I wanted," Josie said slowly. "I think just knowing I could do it would help me feel safer. And I guess it would keep Frank from doing anything sneaky."

"Anything else?"

The affair had happened during a trip. "When he traveled, I would want him to call me when he was in his room for the night. And I guess I'd be upset if he stayed out really late when he's out of town."

"Define really late."

"After ten p.m.?" Josie posed it as a question.

"He'd need to be in his hotel room, and on the phone with you, by ten p.m. That would be your second condition." Sonya was writing on her yellow legal pad.

"Actually, let's change that to nine thirty p.m.," Josie said.

"Done." When Sonya looked up, she said, "It's important to be specific. So rather than say, 'I don't want you to stay out late when you travel,' you should say, 'The latest I'm comfortable with you staying out when you travel is nine thirty p.m.' "

Josie nodded. She'd thought of something else. "And all the work events he goes to—I'd want to attend more of those with him."

*Fun night. Let's do it again soon.*

"That woman I told you about, Melissa—

I'd want to be around whenever there's a work function that they both attend. I don't know if I'll ever know what happened, but that message still bugs me. Is that fair?"

"Absolutely," Sonya said.

"Okay," Josie said. "Well, as long as we're at it, there is one more thing."

It was a physical reminder that made her feel ill every single day. It must be a reminder for Frank, too.

"He'd have to get rid of his car and get another one," Josie said. "He was with *her* in it. I can't ever get in that car again. I can't sit where she sat when they were out on their little date."

Sonya didn't react, predictably. Josie wondered what it would take to spark one in her.

"Number five, get rid of his car." Sonya finished writing and looked up. "Is that all?"

Josie thought about it. "More stuff might come up. But yeah, that would be for starters."

Sonya put her pad in her lap and leaned forward. "Let me ask you one more question. I want you to think carefully before you answer it."

For some reason, Josie's stomach tightened, even though Sonya's expression was as kind as ever.

"If Frank promised to do all of those things, would you feel able to give him a second chance?"

266

Josie leaned back. She tried to consider the question as deeply and honestly as she could.

"I don't know," she whispered. "I'm scared."

"Scared of . . . ?"

"Scared I might start to love him again. And then, if he cheated again, what would happen to me?"

Sonya regarded Josie thoughtfully. "You think that you'd be completely destroyed if Frank cheated again."

"Yes!" Josie felt almost angry. Wasn't it obvious?

"But why?" Sonya asked. "He didn't destroy you this time, did he?"

On the Saturday that Frank was to move out, Josie arranged to have the girls stay with Karin.

Frank wasn't going to take much, other than his clothes and toiletries and a few odds and ends. Still, his belongings would require a few trips to the apartment.

Josie had thought about staying at Karin's while he packed, but something compelled her to return home after she dropped off the girls. Perhaps it was because if this were truly the beginning of the end of her marriage, she needed to witness it.

She found Frank on his side of the closet, folding clothes and putting them in a Hefty trash bag.

"Frank, you can take a suitcase," she said.

267

He looked up. He was sweaty, despite the chill in the day, and his hair was tousled.

"I have a duffel bag," he said. "But I could only fit all my T-shirts in it. Trash bags are fine. You guys might need the suitcases."

She watched him for a few moments as he turned back to work. Then she reached for an armful of suits and carried them down to the back of his Honda. She laid them on his hood while she folded down the rear seats, then she went back upstairs for another armful.

His car: a reminder.

"You don't have to do that," Frank said. He'd moved on to his shoes by now.

"I don't mind," Josie said.

She looked down at the suits in her arms: another reminder. Which ones had he worn when he'd gone out with Dana?

Frank's trunk was nearly full, so she loaded her second armful into her car.

They finished the clothing within twenty minutes. Then Frank walked over to the bureau.

"Is it okay if I take this?" It was a framed photo of him with the girls on Christmas morning a couple of years ago. Frank was wearing a Santa hat, and both girls were on his lap.

"Of course," Josie said.

Christmas: he'd been seeing Dana this past one.

She watched as Frank found a towel from the linen closet. He carefully wrapped the picture in it before tucking the bundle inside his Hefty bag.

The emotions battering Josie felt so huge and overwhelming that she yearned to freeze right here, in this moment, until she amassed the strength to keep moving again. But she couldn't. The girls needed to be picked up in a couple of hours.

"You should take another towel," Josie said. "Here." She reached for a second one and added it to the bag.

"I think that's it . . . Oh, my mugs," he said, almost to himself. They went downstairs, Josie holding the railing for support as she descended.

"Do you want any pots and pans?" Josie asked as Frank retrieved his mugs from the cabinet. "Or, um, silverware?"

"Nah," Frank said. "I think all of that comes with the apartment."

"Okay." His belongings looked so meager. One duffel bag, two trash bags, and the suits.

Josie looked around, trying to think of what else he might need. Frank would be back tonight to have dinner with the girls, she reminded herself. But that didn't make this moment feel any less like an ending.

Frank went to the closet and pulled out his down coat, which he stuffed into one of the bags. He slipped on his dressier work coat.

"I've got some of your clothes in my car, so I'll follow you there," Josie said.

"Thanks," Frank said. "I'll, ah, meet you outside. Give me a second?"

"Sure." Josie put on her coat and slowly walked back out to her minivan, turning on the engine to warm it up. She glanced back at the house, as if seeing it anew. It should look different today, she thought, which reminded her of how on that first day, as she'd waited for Frank to come out of Starbucks, she'd wondered whether he would look any different.

But it was just the same two-story, redbrick house they'd brought Izzy home to from the hospital, the same house that had witnessed birthdays and snow days. Zoe's scooter leaned against the side of the front steps, and an old plastic tube of bubbles was under the bare forsythia bush on the side of the yard. Josie kept meaning to pick it up and bring it inside, but by now it had been there for so long that she'd almost stopped noticing it.

Her eyes drifted up to the second level. There was a silhouette in one of the windows. Frank was in Zoe's room.

Josie squinted and leaned her head closer, trying to see what he was doing.

He was just standing there.

The apartment was nicer than Josie had imagined. It was on the second floor of a tall, narrow building located about a half mile away from their home. Bright African artwork decorated the walls, and a colorful screen separated the bed from the small living and kitchen area.

Josie hung up Frank's suits in the closet, wincing at the loud clink of the hangers against the metal rod. The apartment was so clean and still, so unlike their bustling home.

"We should have brought you some coffee for the morning," she said. "You can get that when you come over tonight."

"Or I can just run to the store," Frank said. He lifted a shoulder. "No big deal."

She watched as Frank reached into his Hefty bag and unwrapped the photograph from the towel. He glanced around the room, then set it on the kitchen counter, where it could be seen from nearly any angle.

"Do you need some help with . . ." Josie gestured to the bags. She couldn't just stand still, as she'd wanted to do earlier. Now she needed to keep moving, to stay ahead of her emotions.

"No, no, I've got it," Frank said.

"Okay." She wondered whether the apartment reminded Frank of the place he'd lived in when they'd first met. That apartment was bigger, a one-bedroom with a decent-sized kitchen. The first time Josie visited, Frank had offered her a choice of beer or tap water. When he'd gone to get ice for her water, she'd seen only a single Hungry-Man dinner entrée in the center of his freezer, as if it were on display. For some reason, it had struck her as hilarious.

He hadn't learned to cook for himself. He'd done it for their children.

She looked at Frank with his rumpled T-shirt and Hefty trash bags. Her insides twisted. She was still furious with him, but she ached for him.

"Josie . . . I want you to know I'm going to do everything I can to become the man who deserves to be with you," Frank said. "I'm not ever going to give up on us."

"Can you . . ." Her throat closed up and she couldn't continue.

"What?" Frank asked quickly. "I'll do anything you want."

She wiped her eyes. "I want to give you a hug. But that's all I want it to be."

Frank nodded. "Okay." He took a deep breath.

She moved toward him slowly as he opened his arms. She stepped into them and he squeezed her tightly. After a few seconds, he released her.

"Was that okay?" he asked.

It was the first time they'd touched in two months. Josie had stayed in the present; she hadn't thought about the way he might have embraced Dana. But she doubted she'd ever be able to make love with Frank ever again without the intrusion of Dana. His affair hadn't just ruptured their marriage; it would be a wrenching interference in their future intimacy.

She didn't see how she could ever reconcile with Frank.

But she could do this: "Do you want to come with me to pick up the girls?" she blurted.

"Yeah, let's go," Frank said.

# Chapter Twenty-One

When she was six years old, Josie had nearly drowned. She had only patchy recollections of that early summer afternoon, perhaps because the incident had terrified her so deeply that she'd suppressed some of the details. Her parents had told her the story enough times that she could almost claim it as her own faded remembrance, though.

They'd been visiting Josie's father's parents in Florida. Grandpa Sam and Grandma Jocelyn—whom Josie had been named for—had enough money to retire to Palm Beach and live in a three-bedroom condo right on the beach, with a terrace overlooking the Atlantic.

They rarely stepped onto the sand, however. Instead, they sat in lounge chairs under big striped umbrellas at the pool. Her grandma Jocelyn's favorite thing was to play cards with her friends—games that sounded exotic to Josie, like canasta and rummy—and her grandfather listened to baseball games on a radio and kept score on a special notepad he filled with slashes and dashes and numbers.

On the first day of the vacation, they all went to the pool. They'd flown in the previous night and had spent the morning hours in the apartment, which was filled with china platters and glass figurines that Josie and her sister, Elizabeth, were told they mustn't touch.

Perhaps it was the lure of the crashing ocean waves that birthed the impulse within her. Or perhaps she'd been cooped up for too long, first in a plane and then in a corner of the apartment, and she'd simply seized the chance at freedom.

Their family took the elevator to the lobby, then exited through the glass doors in the back that led to the pool area. They strolled along the cement deck, heading toward the far side of the patio and the seats Josie's grandparents preferred. Then Grandpa Sam spotted a golfing buddy.

Grandpa Sam stepped forward first to greet his friend, then Josie's father was introduced. Josie imagined there had been a comment along the lines of "He's a chip off the old block," because the two looked so alike. Next her mother stepped up to meet the golfing buddy, and then Elizabeth was gently nudged forward and told to say hello politely. Everyone realized a few seconds later that Josie was missing.

"It was like you simply vanished," Josie's mother would say. "We all scanned the deck and you simply weren't there. There was only one place you could be."

Josie used to try to imagine those lost moments. She saw herself running to the edge of the pool, her feet never slowing as she reached the concrete lip. Then she was sinking, the cool blue swallowing her whole as ambient sounds were snuffed out. Had she seen the legs of any swimmers scissoring through the water, or had she felt utterly alone? She only remembered the silence.

Before her parents could act, there was a giant splash, and then an old man, who was so tanned his skin was like leather (Josie's mother always included that observation with a tinge of disdain), surfaced, holding a sputtering, coughing Josie up by the back of her sundress. She'd been under for maybe twenty seconds.

Josie's grandmother wanted to call for an ambulance, just to be safe, but Josie was screaming so loudly that her parents felt certain her lungs were undamaged (her mother included that detail every time, too).

What she remembered most clearly was her mother fussing over the sodden dress, which had been purchased especially for the trip. She recalled her father asking, in a voice loud enough to carry to the onlookers, how Josie had suddenly forgotten to swim when she'd been able to do a perfectly adequate dog paddle the previous summer.

She had felt her lips begin to quiver, but she

knew if she cried, it would make everything worse.

She remembered wanting to disappear again.

Later that night, she awoke to the sounds of her parents' loud voices. They sounded as if they were in the next room, but when Josie slipped out of bed and peered into the hallway, their voices grew softer. She returned to her room, and the voices increased in volume again. It was like playing a game of hot and cold.

She finally realized their argument was taking place on the beach, directly under the open window of the bedroom she was sharing with Elizabeth. Elizabeth slept through it all, but Josie clung to the window frame, watching.

Her parents didn't yell, ever. Usually they were almost too polite with each other. They never cuddled on the sofa or called each other by nicknames.

They stood on the beach, facing each other but with several feet of distance between them, hurling grievances back and forth like a volleyball. One of them would shush the other, and their voices would briefly lower, but a second later, they'd crescendo again.

What Josie learned was this: her mother and Grandma Jocelyn, who always greeted each other with smiles and kisses on the cheek, didn't actually like each other. Her father was trying to convince her mother otherwise, but her mother's rebuttal floated up toward Josie:

*She called me the name of your old girlfriend for the first* year *we were married!*

Her father, who organized their annual trip to Florida to see his parents, actually hated coming here.

*You think I* want *to spend a week of my vacation time sitting around a pool all day long?*

The argument ended a minute or two later when Josie's father abruptly turned and stalked away. Her mother stared at the ocean for a few moments, then she slowly began to walk back toward the condo building.

Josie ran to her bed and slipped under the covers, pulling the sheet up over her head. She grew warm and sweaty, but she didn't poke out her face. Her parents might have seen her in the window. They might be standing in her doorway, waiting for her to ease the sheet down to take a breath of fresh air. She knew that the moment her mother and father glimpsed her expression, they'd realize she'd heard everything.

She finally fell asleep, and when she woke up, her mother was shaking her shoulder, saying it was time for breakfast. Josie sat up in bed, rubbing her eyes until her mother left the room, in an effort to hide her face. She waited until her father called her, this time with an edge in his voice, then she slowly walked into the dining room.

They were all seated around the shiny, dark-wood table, staring at her: her mother, her father, Grandpa Sam, Grandma Jocelyn, and Elizabeth.

Josie's breath caught in her throat. The room was too quiet.

"Well, look who's finally awake!" Grandma Jocelyn said.

"She's a sleepyhead," Josie's mother chimed in. "Jocelyn, would you mind passing me the syrup?"

"Of course, honey," Grandma Jocelyn said.

Josie eased into her chair. A pancake was on the plate before her.

"Here," Josie's mother said, pouring a thin trail of syrup around its edge. She was always skimpy with the syrup. "Eat up."

"It's a gorgeous day out," Josie's father said. "What time are we going to the pool?"

They were all smiling and talking. It was as if the previous night, with its sharp-edged words, had never happened at all.

Everyone was faking it, Josie thought as she looked around the oval table. The adults who admonished her to always speak the truth, who scolded her when she told a lie, were the biggest fibbers of all.

"You're not feeling ill, are you, Josie?"

Her mother's question cut through her thoughts.

For a terrible moment, Josie thought she wouldn't be able to stop herself from crying out *I heard you last night!* She imagined her mother's face falling, her father turning red with embarrassment. They might have to pack up and leave right away if Josie spoke the words she was yearning to release. She would ruin the vacation.

She shook her head and picked up her fork and took a bite of pancake.

The adults continued their conversation. The moment passed.

She'd joined in their game of pretend. She had become a faker, too.

Josie had signed her daughters up for swim lessons at the YMCA at an early age, possibly in a reaction to her own early childhood trauma. She'd managed to find group classes for both of them held simultaneously at the same pool on Tuesday afternoons, which had felt like a gift from the scheduling gods. Most of the parents sat on the bleachers that folded down from the wall on one side of the pool, passing the time on their phones or reading newspapers, occasionally looking up to shout "Good job!" at their kids.

There was a woman named Gabriella who had a son who'd been in the same class as Zoe for four years straight. She and Josie had fallen into a casual friendship during the confines of these thirty-minute sessions each week.

When Josie arrived at the pool on the Tuesday after Frank had moved out, it was the first lesson of the new winter session. The fall session had ended in December, before the holidays. Before Josie had learned about the affair.

Gabriella waved to her from the bleachers. Josie waved back, then walked Izzy over to her instructor, who held the class for the threes in the shallow end, before joining Gabriella.

"Have a good weekend?" Gabriella asked as Josie sat down beside her.

Josie's mind flashed to Frank standing motionless in Zoe's room. She recalled how still and empty the house had felt after he'd put the girls to bed and had returned to his apartment, how she'd lain awake for hours.

"Yeah," Josie replied. "Just the usual. How about you?"

"We tried this new restaurant, Elbas, have you been?" Gabriella asked.

"No, what kind of food is it?"

"Mediterranean. It's a little pricey, but so delish. You and your husband should go sometime."

Josie nodded and tucked her ringless left hand, the one that was closest to Gabriella, behind her purse.

How did one drop into the conversation with an acquaintance that you were a completely different person than you were the last time she'd seen you?

"Yeah, that sounds good," Josie said. Josie didn't think she could handle sympathy right now. She didn't want to have to reassure Gabriella that she was fine, and that the girls were, too. Nor could she fake it, not completely.

"Things with Frank are— Well, we're in a bit of a rut." Those words felt like a compromise. "We haven't had a date night in a long time."

Gabriella looked at her sharply. "Is everything okay?"

"Oh, sure, we're just not in the best place," Josie said. She quickly added: "But it'll be fine. We just need to go to marriage therapy and get a tune-up."

She must have sounded convincing, because the worry in Gabriella's face eased. Gabriella touched Josie's arm. "Well, you're lucky one of you didn't have an affair," she said.

*Do not react.* The command burst into Josie's brain.

Josie forced herself to smile. "I know, right?"

She pulled her eyes away from Gabriella and turned to glance at Izzy in the pool, making sure her movements were fluid and unhurried.

"I mean, so many people are these days!" Gabriella lowered her voice; she seemed to be settling in for a juicy chat.

*Do not cry.*

"It's true," Josie said. Her mind whirled. She could pretend to be sick and say she needed to

282

wait in her car. No, that would be too obvious.

"My college roommate told me she went on vacation with three other couples a couple of years ago. You are not going to believe this story. Anyway, they were all away for a week—just the adults, it was a kid-free trip—and they'd rented this big house in the Caribbean. And one night one of the women woke up, and oh my gosh, this is so awful—can you imagine?—but she woke up and her husband wasn't in bed next to her. So she walks into the living room and sees him having sex with one of the other wives in the group!"

"Oh my gosh." Josie was fascinated, despite herself. "What did she do?"

"She screamed so loudly she woke everyone in the house up. And then she packed her stuff and went to the airport even though it was the middle of the night, and she waited three hours for a flight home. And now they're divorced."

"Wow."

If she revealed her story to too many people, this is what would happen: she would become a cautionary, gossipy tale. How would it begin, if Gabriella were telling it? *Once I knew this woman who seemed so happy . . .*

"Soooo scary," Gabriella said. "I mean, it could happen to anyone." Her attention was drawn to the pool. She jumped to her feet and clapped. "Oh my gosh! Did you see that? Noah just did the butterfly!"

"That's amazing!" Josie cried. "Wow, I don't think Zoe will be ready for that for another year." She reached into her purse and pulled out her ChapStick, making sure to keep her left hand hidden.

The air was overly warm and moist. The chemical smell of chlorine filled her nose. She had to escape.

*Wait one more minute.*

"How is your son liking school this year, by the way?" Josie asked.

After Gabriella finished answering, Josie stood up.

"I need to run to the bathroom," she said. "I think I'm going to hit the vending machine, too. Want anything?"

"No, I'm good." Gabriella was already looking at her phone.

Josie eased out of the bleachers and walked slowly around the pool, trying to eat up as many seconds as she could. She went into the bathroom and ran cold water over her wrists, practicing taking slow breaths. Then she walked to the vending machines.

She surveyed the offerings, then pressed the button for a ginger ale. It thudded into the bottom of the machine and she popped the top, sipping the fizz that spilled over the lip of the can. She took a long drink, closing her eyes.

Then she slowly walked back into the pool area.

For the rest of the session, she peppered Gabriella with questions about how her holidays had been, and whether she'd read any good books lately, steering them into the safety of superficial topics. It was the type of conversation she'd had countless times before with other parents at school or sports functions, but never before had it taken so much effort.

At the end of the class, she was as spent as if she'd swum for the entire half hour.

She helped Izzy change and she gathered the wet suits and towels, tucking them into her mesh beach bag. She'd intended to swing by the grocery store on the way home, but she felt too depleted. She'd throw a frozen pizza into the oven, again, she decided. It was all she could handle.

She was strapping Izzy into her car seat when she received a text from Frank: Is it okay if I bring over stuff for tacos and cook for everyone tonight?

Their next session with Mike—Josie privately thought of it as separation therapy, rather than marital therapy—was scheduled for Friday evening at seven.

Frank picked up the girls to take them out for an early dinner. While he helped them into their coats, he asked Josie whether she wanted to ride together to the appointment.

She hesitated. "Okay. But let's take my van."

"Are you sure?" Frank asked. "I'm happy to drive so you can relax."

Josie lowered her voice and twisted farther away from the girls. "You can drive the minivan. I'd rather not be in your car."

She saw the understanding come into his eyes a moment later and he hung his head.

As soon as the door shut behind them, she walked upstairs, shucking off the hoodie and jeans she'd worn all day. She ran warm water in the bathtub and added a capful of the organic bubble bath she'd bought for the girls.

As she soaked in the tub, she tested herself, as she did from time to time. She allowed herself to imagine Frank and Dana together in the hotel room.

The scene, while still painful, was losing some of its overwhelming power over her. More recent images, like the intensity in Frank's eyes as he'd told her he felt nothing for Dana, were commingling with her imaginings of what had happened between them that night.

Frank had never loved Dana. His memories of Dana would forever be tainted, too. It helped a little.

Josie pulled the plug and stepped out of the bathtub, into her terry-cloth robe. She ran a brush through her hair, then smoothed lotion over her skin.

She walked to her closet. Frank had left some of his summer things behind, and she'd spread out her clothes to fill in the gaps he'd left. But it still looked empty.

She reached for dark slacks and a sweater, then put on high-heeled boots. The high school senior from down the street, the one the girls adored, was coming at six thirty to babysit.

It occurred to Josie that to someone viewing her, it would appear as if she were getting ready for a date.

She pushed aside the thought and checked the clock. It was only a few minutes after six.

She went downstairs to sit in the quiet of her living room and have a glass of wine.

"I've got it," Frank said, hurrying ahead of Josie to open the door to Mike's office. He'd opened her car door for her, too.

*This isn't a date,* Josie wanted to say.

The long leather therapy sofa was waiting for them. Josie claimed her usual end, and Frank sat on his. They'd positioned themselves on the same sides they'd always slept on when they'd shared a bed, Josie realized.

Mike greeted them with his usual smile, a coffee cup in his hand.

"Who would like to start?" he asked.

"If it's okay with Josie, I would." Frank looked at her and Josie nodded.

Mike liked to begin with what he called house-keeping—smaller logistical issues—before Josie and Frank delved into their deeper feelings.

"My parents are coming to town next month," Frank said. "My dad has a conference in Chicago, and my mom wants to hang out with us during the day. They asked if they could spend the weekend with us."

"Do your parents know about the separation?" Mike asked.

Frank shook his head. "Ah, no. I hadn't gotten a chance— No. They don't."

"Have you told anyone?" Josie twisted to face Frank. "Your brothers?"

"God, no, they'd be the last ones—" Frank cut himself off. "I've only told Tony."

One of his oldest buddies, a guy Frank had known since high school. Tony lived in South Carolina and had been divorced for about a year. They barely saw him these days. Perhaps that was why Frank had chosen him, Josie thought.

"So if your parents come and stay with you, they would realize you and Josie are separated, and that you are no longer living in the house," Mike said.

"Yeah, or— I guess I was thinking that they could stay in the guest room and they wouldn't need to know I wasn't living there."

Josie frowned. "How would that work, exactly?"

"Well, we could all have dinner and I could hang out in the living room until after they go to bed. And then I could come back the next morning and bring bagels. If they woke up and noticed I was gone, the bagels would explain it."

"You've given this a lot of thought." Mike summed up what Josie was thinking. "Would you really rather create this scenario than tell your parents the truth about what is going on?"

Frank looked down at his hands. Josie had always found it endearing, somehow, that his strong-looking hands had chewed-on nails.

"I didn't think it would be that big of a deal," he said. "It's just for two nights."

Frank and Mike both looked at Josie.

"Why don't you just tell them, Frank? Say we're having some issues. You don't need to explain what it is. They can stay at the house with me and the girls or they can stay at a hotel."

"Okay. If that's what you want," Frank said.

"Have you told your parents, Josie?" Mike asked.

"Sort of." Josie sighed, remembering the conversation of a few days earlier. "I called my mom and I downplayed it. I just said Frank and I were having some issues and we were taking a little break to figure things out."

Mike took a sip of coffee. "What was their reaction?"

"My mother didn't ask any questions. She

289

was the one I told. She'll relay everything to my father; pretty much everything gets funneled through her. She just said she was sure everything would work out. It was a ten-minute call if that."

"Oh." Frank sounded surprised. "I didn't know you told her."

"Yeah . . . well." Josie couldn't think of anything else to say so she shrugged.

"I'm sorry she wasn't more supportive. You deserved better, Jos."

Josie looked at Frank and felt her throat tighten. She'd forgotten this, how he'd always tried to make up for what her parents lacked. She wanted to say thank you, but she felt as though sobs might escape along with those words.

Mike set down his coffee cup and leaned forward. "Do you feel as if your parents wouldn't be supportive if you revealed the truth to them, Frank?"

Frank shook his head. "No, they would be."

"What would they do?" Mike asked. "Can you describe how each of them might act, and how each of them might feel upon hearing the news?"

Josie watched, fascinated. Mike was taking Frank down a path that was unfamiliar to Josie; she'd never asked him to dissect his relationship with his parents this way.

"My mom would want to talk about it endlessly, and she'd flutter around and make casseroles or something. My dad would clap me on the back and say something like 'We're here for you, son.' But he wouldn't bring it up after that unless I did. He might suggest we go play golf or something. That would be his equivalent of the casseroles."

If she left Frank, she'd lose his family, too, Josie realized with a start. Maybe the girls would go home with Frank on some holidays. Instead of poker and silly movies, she would be left alone to endure a Christmas dinner served atop her mother's heirloom lace tablecloth, while her father made a production of carving the turkey. Frank wouldn't be there to create elaborate games to choose who got to pull the wishbone apart; he wouldn't catch her eye and wink to take the sting out of the moment when Zoe's and Izzy's voices rose in excitement and Josie's mother's lips pursed.

"So that's how your parents would act." Mike steepled his hands and leaned in closer to Frank. "How would they feel?"

Frank shook his head. "Ah, you know." He tried to smile but it looked more like a grimace. He shifted and started to rise to his feet, but then he seemed to catch himself and he sat back down.

Josie didn't know if she'd ever seen him look so acutely uncomfortable.

Mike allowed the silence to stretch on.

"They'd, um, you mean, how would they really feel?" Frank finally asked.

Mike's voice was as calm and soothing as

ever. "Yes. Can you tell me how your parents would feel if you told them you and Josie were separated?"

Frank lowered his eyes. "They'd think I was a fuckup. They'd all think it. My brothers, too."

What struck Josie almost as much as Frank's surprising words was the note of defeat in his voice.

"You don't think they'd feel sympathetic that you're going through a hard time?" Mike asked.

"Maybe. But deep down, that's what they'd be thinking: 'Frank fucked up again.'"

Josie couldn't stop looking at Frank. Did he really think his entire family saw him in such a poor light? Or maybe it was he who saw himself in that role when he was around his family. Frank had never talked to her about this; he'd hidden this piece of himself. But to be fair, Josie had never thought to ask the questions that Mike was making seem so basic.

"I'll tell them," Frank said. "I'll say they should stay at a hotel when they come to visit. Is that okay, Josie? I'll do whatever you want."

She exhaled. "I don't know. I don't like the idea of creating a pretense for them." What she didn't add: there has been too much lying already.

"Frank . . . say we're going through a rough patch, okay? If they ask questions, you should tell them the truth, but if they don't . . . you can just let it go. You can do the bagel thing. And we can all go out to dinner together, with the girls."

"Does that sound like a good plan?" Mike asked.

"Yeah," Frank said. "I'll tell them tonight."

Mike smiled. "I'd like to commend you two. You were faced with a problem and you came up with a solution that satisfies you both. You're presenting a united front and you're working together."

Frank looked pleased at Mike's words. But Josie could only think about how they hadn't worked together when it counted most, when it would have made a real difference.

When they left therapy a while later, Frank asked whether Josie had eaten dinner.

"Not yet," she said. She'd nibbled on some cheese and crackers with her glass of wine before the session, but she was still hungry.

"We have the sitter, so . . . I was thinking, would you want to stop and get a bite?" Frank asked. He must've seen the wary look that she knew came into her eyes, because he quickly added: "That's all it would be. Something to eat. Anywhere you want, and I'll bring you home the second you say you want to go."

She knew how eagerly Frank was awaiting her answer. She also knew that if she said no, he would bring her directly home and would leave if the girls were already asleep.

Josie tried to think of what she truly wanted. Not what Frank wished, and not what Karin or her mother or anyone else would urge her to do; she sought to excavate her own honest feelings, which was harder to do than she would have thought.

"I wouldn't mind a cheeseburger and fries," she finally said.

# Chapter Twenty-Two

"How could he do it?" Josie looked across the table at Karin and Amanda. "That's the thing I can't get past. I know he's sorry, I know he regrets it, I know he wants to take it back. And I don't hate him as much as I used to. The other night we went out for burgers and I was able to talk to him without wanting to throw the ketchup bottle at him . . . but I keep wondering what was going through his mind when he left Dana and came home to us. How could he live with himself?"

They were settled at a corner table at a small French café, and the waitress had just brought a china pitcher of real cream for their coffee, which was served in bowls rather than mugs.

"This place is insane," Karin had said when she'd suggested the three of them meet there. It had opened only a few weeks earlier, and although other coffee shops were closer to them, Karin insisted the trek was worth it. "You'll eat like twelve brioches and not even feel full because they're so light. And you look like you need a few brioches, Kate Moss."

Josie had intended to decline—she'd been throwing herself back into work, since money was becoming a real concern—but she realized she'd made no progress unspooling her thoughts about Frank since he'd moved out. Perhaps her two most blunt, honest friends could help with that.

Karin fussed with the pots of blackberry and strawberry jam when their food arrived, making sure they were close to Josie and asking for extra butter. It was lovely, feeling so taken care of, Josie thought.

"If we're going to try to sort things out, let's start at the beginning," Karin said, blowing on her coffee before taking a sip. "You and Frank met at a party, right? Let me guess, Frank walked up to you and said something funny. He made the first move."

"No." Josie shook her head. "I did."

She tore off the top knot from her brioche, thinking about how she'd noticed Frank soon after she arrived at the party given by a mutual friend. He wasn't the most handsome guy in the room. But there was an ease about him, a lightness, that drew her gaze. His smiles punctuated the ends of his sentences. He touched the arm of the person he was talking to, and threw back his head when he laughed.

Josie was working at her job in public relations—at that point, she was only a step or two above entry level. She'd envisioned herself diving into interesting campaigns, sitting around conference room tables with other creative types as they batted around ideas. Instead, she mostly put together mailings and proofread press releases. Still, the job had its perks: fancy parties for big clients, and overtime pay when they were up against crushing deadlines and needed to work through the night. Plus, she was still in her midtwenties. She'd thought she had plenty of time to advance in her career. She hadn't been in a rush to settle down or get married.

"I was in the kitchen getting more beer from the keg when I heard this crash." Josie smiled, remembering. "When I went back into the living room, I saw Frank sprawled on the floor, next to an overturned table. Apparently he'd accepted a challenge to try to walk on his hands."

"And in what universe did he think this would end well?" Karin asked.

"Then I walked over to him and said, 'I bet I can do it.' "

At Karin's raised eyebrow, Josie added, "I took gymnastics for years when I was a kid."

She took a sip of her milky, sweet coffee, feeling it warm her insides. "So Frank starts shouting, 'We have a new challenger!' And I asked him what I'd win if I did it."

"Ooh, you saucy minx!" Karin said.

It was totally unlike her, Josie reflected. She'd never been forward with guys. She couldn't credit it to the two beers she'd had before coming to the party, or even to the two after she'd arrived. Something about Frank simply put her at ease.

"I bet Frank said you'd win a date with him, right?" Amanda asked.

"Sort of. He said I'd win a milkshake."

"Okay, random, but kind of cute," Karin said. "Did you do it?"

"I was wearing a skirt, which complicated things," Josie said. "But I managed to tuck it between my knees and I walked upside down for a good twenty seconds. Then I started getting really nauseous."

"It's making me nauseous just hearing about it." Karin shook her head and reached for another brioche.

"My friends wanted to leave the party a little while after that, so Frank wrote down my number. He walked me outside when the cab came, and I ended up making out with him on the street for so long that my friends left me."

Josie smiled again, despite everything. She could recall how right it felt to be in Frank's arms, and how his lips had warmed her cold ones on that cool fall night.

"We walked about two miles to an all-night diner—it was only a mile away but we kept getting lost—and he bought me my milkshake and we talked. And he called me the next day and we went to go see a movie. There was no game playing or acting hard to get on either side. We just sort of fell into a relationship right away.

"I'd never had a boyfriend like Frank before," Josie reflected. "I didn't feel anxious about whether he'd call. I was never jealous or insecure. He made it clear early on that he cared about me. I never doubted his feelings."

She was staring down at her bowl of coffee, but she sensed her friends watching her intently.

"I felt . . . safe with him," Josie said slowly.

"And he took that away from you," Amanda said gently.

"Yeah." Josie leaned back in her seat and sighed. She felt tired again, even though she'd taken a Xanax last night and had slept for nearly eight hours. "And I don't think you can ever get it back after something like this, can you?"

"I think men and women are built differently," Amanda said. She leaned across the table, closer to Josie, and her wide blue eyes seemed more earnest than ever. "Guys compartmentalize things. I'm not saying they don't have all the same feelings that we do, but they're not socialized to dissect and analyze and put a label on them, so a lot of times they push them away. Do you think Frank has told anyone about the affair?"

"Just one of his friends," Josie said. "He's going to tell his parents that we're having issues since they're coming to visit, but we agreed he'd downplay it."

"So he's going to work as usual and act

normally with almost all of his friends," Amanda said. "Compartmentalizing. He probably couldn't imagine sitting around a coffee shop talking through this stuff for hours with his buddies. Just like you couldn't imagine acting like it never happened."

"Yeah, but . . ." Josie frowned. Amanda had a point, but she was missing something. "So why didn't he come to me rather than stuffing down his feelings? If he had just talked to me, this might never have happened."

"Exactly." Karin set down her coffee mug with a little too much force and it clanged against the table. "If he had told you right away, you might have been able to fix things."

Josie tore off another piece of brioche, but her throat felt too tight to eat it, so she left it on the edge of her plate. "I mean, I know things between us weren't perfect, but I thought we had a pretty good marriage. We were busy, and it was always chaos with the girls, but we loved each other. At least I thought we did."

There was a beat of silence, then Amanda spoke. "How often did you two talk, though?"

If anyone else had asked the question, Josie might have found it accusatory. But Amanda was completely guileless. She was asking for information, not making a judgment.

"All the time, every five seconds," Josie said. She shrugged. "And also never."

"Like everyone," Karin chimed in. "And why is it Josie's job to pull the feelings out of Frank? He's a grown man. He can use his words."

"But we all know most guys have a harder time doing that than women," Amanda said.

It was like an old comic Josie had once seen in the newspaper, in which an angel and a devil sat on a person's shoulders, whispering opposing things. *Try to see if you had a role in any of this,* Amanda seemed to be saying. *Blame everything on Frank,* Karin was urging.

"I guess what I'm wondering is this," Amanda said. "Did Frank want you to find out?"

"Oh, come *on!*" Karin said.

Josie blinked. "About the affair? Are you serious?"

"It was risky, keeping those emails. He had to have known that, right?"

Josie nodded slowly. She could see Karin roll her eyes, but Josie ignored her.

"And when you were in that parking lot and asked for his phone, he could have just told you he was expecting a call or that he'd phone in the prescription," Amanda continued. "He didn't have to give it to you."

Josie gaped at Amanda. She felt as if she'd received an electric shock. Amanda's theory was outlandish. Yet Josie recognized a kernel of what felt like truth in it.

"He did this thing right before he handed it to

me—he started tapping on it," Josie blurted. "I wonder if that's why, when I finished the call, his email account popped up. Because he'd just been tinkering with it."

Josie sat up ramrod-straight, her pulse quickening.

"You're right. Frank thinks quickly on his feet. He could have waited while I made the call, or offered to do it himself," she said. "Do you seriously think he *wanted* me to see those emails?"

"Not consciously." Amanda reached over and touched Josie's hand. "But I do believe he wanted to stop having the affair, and that he wanted to tell you about it, and he didn't know how."

They said good-bye on the sidewalk outside the coffee shop a few minutes later. Amanda had driven separately, so they walked in different directions to pick up their cars.

Josie was so busy thinking about what Amanda had said that she didn't notice how quiet Karin was being. It wasn't until Karin was pulling out of the parking garage that she spoke.

"I'm sorry."

The surprise of hearing those words made Josie jerk back. "For what?"

"For being so hard on Frank." Karin twisted the wheel to the right, turning toward the highway.

"I don't think you're being too hard on him,"

Josie said. "But you do seem pretty angry at him."

Karin drove another mile or so before she answered. "I don't think it's him I'm really mad at, Josie. I think I'm still mad at myself for what I did."

# Chapter Twenty-Three

Some days, Josie felt as if she might actually be able to give Frank a second chance. She wasn't able to imagine having sex with him—though Sonya predicted it would be possible, if Josie chose reconciliation—but Josie envisioned inviting him to live in the house again. Frank could stay in the basement. They could present themselves as a couple until they learned whether it would be possible in actuality.

Other times, she knew it would never work. Her emotions were still skittering all over the place, like a handful of marbles thrown on a wood floor. And she hadn't even checked out the other loose threads she'd collected. There might be unseen pieces to the story.

She'd put off resuming her investigation because she hadn't felt able to absorb more pain. But the not knowing was becoming worse than the knowing. She needed more answers.

Josie started by obtaining duplicate copies of their credit card statements for the duration of Frank's affair. This was surprisingly easy. She simply phoned the credit card company, answered a few security questions, and less than an hour later, an email containing the documents pinged into her in-box.

At the noise, her stomach clenched. Her body grew rigid.

She stared at the attachment, her hand resting on the computer's mouse. If Frank had charged hotel stays to their credit card—if she caught him in another lie—the fragile relationship they'd rebuilt would be demolished. Josie would close her computer and call the lawyer Karin had recommended, the woman who was supposed to be a shark.

She felt as if she'd been plunged back into the icy void that had nearly swallowed her immediately after she'd learned of Frank's affair. She was so angry at him for putting her through this again and again.

She muttered a curse, then quickly clicked the attachment and began scanning the charges. She finished, then read through them again.

There were no line items for a hotel stay, other than Josie's escape to the Marriott.

She expelled the breath she hadn't been aware she was holding, relieving the tightness in her lungs, and slumped in her chair.

Then she went through the charges more carefully.

There were fees for groceries, gas, a vet's visit for Huck, and a few restaurants they'd gone to as a family, including the place where they'd celebrated her birthday. Josie had bought some things for the kids at the Gap outlet, and Frank had lots of lunches at the salad bar across from his office, where he never actually ate salad but instead got an overstuffed sub and chips.

There were no charges for dinners Josie didn't recognize. That was a relief, too. Frank must have paid cash for those killer margaritas, because the only charge listed as originating on that date was a small one from the dry cleaner's.

Near the top of the statement, on the date that everything had changed, was the charge for Starbucks. Josie closed her eyes, trying to remember how her last normal day had felt. She'd chatted with Frank in the kitchen that morning as she'd tidied the kitchen and he'd poured Cinnamon Toast Crunch into a bowl and ate it noisily. She knew he'd put the bowl in the sink without rinsing it, which would mean a few hard shards of cereal would stick to the bowl even after it had gone through the dishwasher.

"The present for the birthday party," Josie had said. "Don't let me forget it."

"Yup," Frank had responded, slurping up more cereal. She was certain he hadn't eaten this sloppily when they'd first been together.

She saw herself setting her phone down on the kitchen counter as she reached into a lower cabinet for a bag of fruit gummies, then walking out of the room, leaving her phone behind.

What would have gone through her mind if someone had told her that an hour later, because of that simple, absentminded moment, their marriage as she knew it would no longer exist?

She wouldn't have believed it. She would've looked at Frank singing *"Mary had a little rhinoceros,"* and Izzy giggling, and Zoe saying "That's dumb" but trying to hide a smile behind her DS, and Josie would have shaken her head. She would have said, "Nope, not us. You've got the wrong family."

Josie rubbed a hand across her forehead as she looked at the credit card statement again, making sure nothing had slipped through her scrutiny. Then she reached for her phone to begin the next part of her investigation.

She scrolled through her photos until she found the ones she had taken in the Marriott when she'd been in possession of Frank's iPhone. The photos revealed the names and numbers of unfamiliar women in Frank's contact list. There were a dozen or so. They were likely work contacts, people Frank interacted with during the course of his professional day.

She could reach out to each of them, maybe using a borrowed phone from Karin so caller ID wouldn't reveal her name. She could see whether the number connected her to a business line, and pretend it was a wrong number if anyone answered. But what would that really reveal?

It was also possible Frank had the cell phone numbers of clients.

When she'd checked Frank's call history in the hotel, she hadn't seen any recent contact with any unfamiliar women, Josie remembered. And his emails, other than the exchanges with Dana, were clean, too.

This she could let go, Josie decided. Her gut told her that these contacts weren't threatening.

Still, she would save the photos.

There was one more piece left.

Josie could still hear the echo of Frank's footsteps slapping against concrete as he ran for his car in the middle of the night.

*Fun night. Let's do it again soon.*

She needed to finally have an answer about what had transpired on that night.

"How could you find out?" Sonya asked.

Josie shrugged. "I have no idea. I asked Frank about it at the time, and he said he was getting his car from the hotel garage. Then when we were in couples therapy again last week, he swore nothing ever happened with Melissa when I brought it up."

"But that isn't enough for you."

"I just wonder if he knows that admitting to another affair would mean the end of us," Josie said. She hugged the familiar chenille pillow to her chest.

"Would it?"

Josie nodded. "I think so. One is bad enough. But if he had two . . . and especially with someone I've met. Well, I'd have to leave him."

"So you think he may be hiding the truth because he's terrified you'd divorce him."

"Yeah." Josie put down her pillow and pulled a tissue from the box on the end table next to the couch. She began to tear off little pieces and roll them into balls.

Sonya nodded and jotted something on her legal pad. Then she changed the subject.

"You've talked about how at night sometimes, Frank wanted you to remain downstairs with him and watch TV, and how you often went to bed to read," she said. "How regularly did that happen?"

"Pretty regularly, I guess," Josie said. "We had a couple of shows we watched together—*Modern Family* is our favorite—but Frank really likes sports, and I don't. And he's into violent shows like *Game of Thrones*, and they kind of freak me out, all those beheadings, especially right before I go to sleep."

"So you'd go upstairs how many nights a week?" Sonya asked.

"Most of them," Josie said. "By the time I'd gotten dinner cleaned up and given the girls baths and put them to bed, I'd be so tired, even though it was only around nine. I liked to unwind with a bath and then herbal tea and a book in bed."

She hesitated. "I was thinking about something the other day. This isn't really relevant, because nothing happened, but I did have some affairs in my mind. I did think about other men, like that guy who invited me and the girls over to swim."

"You fantasized about them?"

"Sure," Josie said. "I had crushes, I guess."

"How many were there?"

"Two or three. Like, there was this old boyfriend I found on Facebook. We dated freshman year in college, then he transferred to a school in California so I haven't seen him in ages. Anyway, we reconnected a year or so ago and we chat now and then."

"How did you find him on Facebook?" Sonya asked.

Josie rolled another tissue ball with the pads of the thumb and index finger of her right hand. "I did a search for him."

Sonya nodded. "And now you have a crush on him?"

"Sure," Josie said. "But that's all it is. A harmless crush."

Sonya looked at Josie with her clear blue eyes. "I'm just curious about why you brought it up."

"I guess because I can see why Frank wanted something new, something fresh," Josie said. "Maybe I wanted that sometimes, too. But I never would have acted on it."

Sonya seemed to be waiting for her to elaborate, but Josie didn't have anything more to add.

"Can we explore the state of your marriage before he had his affair?" Sonya finally asked.

"I guess I thought it was pretty good." Josie's words came slowly; she felt as if they were being pulled from somewhere deep inside of her. "I think we coparented well. And the kids took up so much of our time and energy . . ."

"But you didn't want to be with him at night, and you had crushes," Sonya said. Her voice was so soft that it was almost as if she were sympathizing with Josie—except Josie suspected Sonya was really trying to get her to see Frank's point of view.

"He had crushes, too, apparently." Josie lifted a shoulder. "And he could have come upstairs to be with me. He could have read in bed next to me."

"Yes, he could have," Sonya acknowledged, and Josie felt her flare of temper subside. "Did you ever ask him to do that?"

"Sure, I . . ." Josie reconsidered what she'd been about to say. She was paying an awful lot of money for therapy, and the whole point of it was to be honest with herself.

"Does it sound awful to say that I didn't want him to?" Josie asked. "That maybe I only asked him when he wanted me to watch TV with him, kind of throwing it out there as a rebuttal, because I knew he'd say no? Frank isn't a big reader. And

I liked being upstairs alone. I have so little time to myself. And he'd be wanting sex—"

She abruptly stopped. Then she felt her cheeks heat up.

"Just because I didn't want to have sex with Frank all the time doesn't mean he should have gone out and found someone else to fool around with!"

"Of course it doesn't." Sonya was as unflappable as ever.

"He should have talked to me! He should have told me how he felt!" Josie blinked back tears. "Okay, so our marriage wasn't that great. Maybe it was at one point. But Frank was downstairs emailing his girlfriend and I was upstairs trying to get some space away from him. So clearly it was a disaster."

"Or you'd just grown apart, as so many couples do," Sonya said mildly.

"Do you think that's all it was?"

"Couldn't it be? Perhaps the affair was a symptom of the distance between you. That does not in any way excuse or diminish the devastation it caused both of you. It does not absolve Frank. But is it possible that it was at least partially in response to the fact that your marriage was stagnating?"

Josie exhaled slowly. "Maybe. Yeah, I guess."

Sonya leaned forward. "You may not be able to get past this. Only you can decide. It's going to be difficult and painful if you try. But I don't want you to lose sight of the fact that if you do leave Frank for good, that's going to be difficult and painful, too."

"I can't win," Josie said. She blinked back tears. "I know I need to stop putting off a decision. It's probably not good for any of us to be in limbo like this. But whatever I choose, it's going to be awful. Stay with a guy I don't trust, or tell my kids their mom and dad are getting divorced."

"What would be the best case?" Sonya asked. She must have predicted what Josie was going to say, because she added, "Obviously the best case would be for Frank to never have had the affair— but since that's not an option, what would be the ideal way for you to move forward?"

Josie tried to think carefully before she answered.

"If I could guarantee that Frank would never, ever have an affair again—and if I knew that this was the first time it had happened—I think I could try to reconcile with him," Josie said. "I don't know if I'd do it if we didn't have the girls. But he's an amazing father. I don't think I could ever fully forgive him, though."

"So you would need to make sure that this was the only time," Sonya echoed. "And then you would need to rebuild the trust that has been demolished."

At Josie's look, Sonya added, "It can be done, you know. The rebuilding."

"Not if he had an affair with Melissa, too. I guess I'll have to accept that I'll never know for sure." Josie slumped, feeling defeated.

She thought of the words in Melissa's text, which felt branded into Josie's soul. The absence of tone muddled their meaning.

They could have been delivered in a rushed, friendly way—*Fun night! Let's do it again soon!*—which was exactly the kind of thing Josie might have said to Karin after a night out.

Or they could have been intended to be flirty and seductive.

Her fifty minutes were up. She felt more tangled inside than ever.

"Josie?" Sonya usually stood up quickly to walk her to the door, but she remained seated.

"I think you should tell Frank how important this is to you," Sonya said. "Let him know exactly how you feel."

"Do you think he'll tell me the truth?" Josie asked.

Sonya didn't answer for a long time.

"I wish I had an answer for that," she finally said.

# Chapter Twenty-Four

*Nine months earlier*

"Zoe, in your room now!" Josie yelled.

"She ruined it!" Zoe yelled back. Izzy was wailing, too, and clutching at her hair, which Zoe had just pulled. "She scribbled all over it."

"She's a little kid!" Josie said. It took all of her willpower to speak calmly. "She thought she was helping you with your painting."

"I hate her!" Zoe said, but her lower lip was trembling.

"We don't talk that way," Josie said. "Those words are hurtful." She set the stove timer for twenty minutes, then reached for Zoe's hand and led her upstairs.

"Babe?" Frank appeared on the landing, his hair wet from the shower, a towel tied around his waist. "What's going on?"

"She pulled Izzy's—" Josie began, but Zoe interrupted.

"She messed up my painting! She did it on purpose!"

"She pulled Izzy's hair, and she is going into time-out," Josie said firmly.

"Daddy, it isn't fair!" Zoe looked at her father with imploring eyes.

"Come on, Z, you know you can't hurt your little sister," Frank said. Then he walked back into the bathroom, removing himself from the conflict.

"Twenty minutes," Josie said as she began to pull closed Zoe's door.

Zoe burst into tears.

"Zoe, calm down. I'll be back soon to get you. But you knew this would happen if you pulled Izzy's hair." Plus, it was hardly a severe punishment. Zoe had a soft bed and books and toys in her room; she wasn't being exiled to Siberia.

Josie went downstairs to attend to Izzy, who was already over the trauma and scribbling on the construction paper that Josie had set out before the sibling crisis had erupted.

"Beautiful," Josie said over the sound of Zoe's wails, which carried through the house. She gave Izzy a kiss on her head, aiming for the injured spot.

Zoe abruptly stopped crying. *Good,* Josie thought. Zoe wasn't often rough with Izzy, but her little sister was barely three. Zoe was twice her size. She needed to learn to control her temper.

Josie checked the timer. Sixteen minutes left.

She cooked a pot of mac and cheese and

sliced up some Granny Smith apples, which she distributed between two plastic plates from Ikea. She hesitated, knowing she should take an apple slice to munch on. Instead, she scooped up the last few spoonfuls of macaroni and cheese from the pot and ate them over the sink.

Then she walked back upstairs.

She could hear Zoe laugh. She pushed open her door and saw Frank sitting on the edge of Zoe's bed, while their daughter lay sprawled on the floor.

"Hi, Mommy," Zoe said.

Josie looked at Frank. "What are you doing?"

"She was crying," Frank said.

"Frank, she hurt Izzy!"

"I know, but she feels badly about it."

"Frank, for God's sake!" Josie snapped.

"Don't be mean to Daddy!" Zoe leapt to her feet and put her arms around Frank.

"I'm not— Zoe!" How did this situation morph from Josie instructing Zoe on how to be kind to Zoe admonishing Josie?

It was Frank's fault. He could never stand to be the bad guy, so she always had to take on that role. And now he was deliberately undermining her.

She knew that if she stayed in the room, she'd start to model the very sort of behavior she was trying to teach her daughters to avoid, so Josie whirled around and stepped into the hallway, shutting the door behind her. She went into her bedroom, and a moment later, Frank followed her.

"Hey," he said.

"I can't believe you did that," Josie snapped.

"I know, I know . . . I just thought I'd calm her down, and then . . ."

"Frank, how is she ever going to learn how to behave if her parents contradict each other? If we can't even be consistent?"

"You're right," Frank said.

"You need to tell her she has to start her time-out all over again because the last one didn't count."

"She hasn't even eaten lunch."

"So we'll put her lunch in her room. She can eat it at her desk."

Frank threw up his hands. "Okay." She heard him go back into Zoe's room. She waited for Zoe to erupt, but Zoe didn't.

Frank left the room and went downstairs, and came back a moment later with Zoe's plate and a glass of juice. "Here you go, sweetheart," he said. "I'll be back soon to get you."

She heard Zoe's voice but couldn't make out her words. Zoe's tone seemed pleasant enough, though.

"She's in time-out again," Frank said, coming back into the bedroom. He looked at Josie's face. "What?"

"I just . . . You can't . . ." Something still felt wrong and unfair, but she didn't know how to explain it.

"I did what you said!" Frank's tone straddled the line between wounded and huffy.

"You know what, just forget it," Josie said.

It wasn't worth arguing about. It would take too much effort, and there was so much else to do: the laundry was piled up, and Huck needed to be walked, and she had to call a plumber because the pipe under the kitchen sink had been slowly dripping for three days and Josie had had to stick a big Tupperware container beneath it to catch the water.

"I'm going to take Iz to Home Depot with me in a little while," Frank said. "She loves it there."

"Okay, then I'll take Zoe to gymnastics at three," Josie said.

Frank turned toward the stairwell and Josie pivoted into the bathroom; they headed in opposite directions.

# Chapter Twenty-Five

*Present day*

Josie almost missed the incoming call.

She'd spent most of the morning immersed in work, signing up to secure booths at two new spring festivals and creating a marketing email to send out to her existing clients. She'd taken a quick break for lunch, then she'd begun to vacuum up the Cheerios that Izzy had spilled that morning.

One of the Bratz doll's plastic purses got sucked up along with the Cheerios, causing the machine to emit a high-pitched squeal. She was thinking about how she regretted ever buying a value pack containing a hundred miniature accessories when the phone rang.

So few people dialed their home number these days. Josie checked caller ID, but the number was unfamiliar. Even though she assumed it was a telemarketer, something compelled her to answer. Perhaps because she couldn't bear to have even an extra ounce of uncertainty in her life these days.

She didn't recognize the tentative voice of the woman who asked, "Is this Josie?"

Josie leaned against the handle of her vacuum. Her heartbeat quickened. "It is."

"Hi, it's Gemma."

It took Josie a moment to place the name in context. Gemma was married to Evan, one of Frank's poker buddies. Josie didn't know her well, but she'd found Gemma engaging and friendly the few times they'd met.

"I hope I'm not intruding," Gemma began.

"Not at all," Josie said. "I just accidentally vacuumed up one of Zoe's toys, so it's a typical morning in paradise."

As soon as she said it, it hit her: She'd made a joke. She'd responded normally to an acquaintance. A few months ago, this would have been impossible.

Gemma gave a little laugh. "Um, yeah, I do that all the time, too. Anyway, I was calling because Evan mentioned that Frank had been ill, and I just wondered if I could bring by dinner for your family."

"Ill?" Josie couldn't quash the high note of surprise.

"Oh, did he get that wrong? I'm so sorry. Evan said that Frank had dropped out of the weekly poker game, and none of the guys had seen him for a while . . . I didn't mean to— If it's private, don't worry."

Frank had been at the house almost every single night, helping Zoe with her reading homework and giving Iz a bath, or offering to take the girls out for pizza to give Josie a break. He usually stayed until the girls were asleep. Sometimes Josie wondered why they were paying so much for a rental apartment when Frank spent all his spare time away from it.

On Thursdays, though, Frank came by earlier, around five o'clock, but he only stayed for an hour. Josie had assumed he was seeing his friends on those nights.

"It's a little complicated," Josie said. "Frank is okay, though, so please don't worry. But that's really nice of you."

"I understand," Gemma said. Josie was grateful her voice contained no curiosity, and that she refrained from asking a single question. "I'll let you go."

Josie hung up and stared into space. If Frank wasn't seeing his friends on Thursday nights, what was he doing?

When trust was demolished, it needed to be rebuilt.

Josie silently paraphrased Sonya's words as she sat in her minivan, occasionally turning on the ignition to run the heater and keep warm.

Frank thought she was out with her girlfriends on this Thursday night. When he'd asked whether he could come by from five to six to see the girls, as usual, she'd texted that it was fine—but that a sitter would be there, too. I won't be home until 8 or 9, she'd typed.

She could have asked Frank for his whereabouts. But he hadn't volunteered the information, and she was curious about the reason behind this.

She didn't believe Frank was seeing Dana, or anyone else. Well, that wasn't completely true. A tiny, panicky part of her wondered whether she'd gotten it all wrong, again. But it seemed more likely that Frank was exercising, or doing something with the church he'd joined.

Josie hadn't mentioned to Frank that she'd checked his email, and he hadn't brought up the sunrise service. It seemed more meaningful that he was keeping it private. His effort would have been cheapened if he'd told her about it as evidence of his redemption.

It was a quarter to six.

Josie had already circled the block to see which way Frank's car was pointing so she didn't meet him head-on when he drove away from the house.

Now she shifted into drive and eased around the corner, parking toward the end of their street. She could just barely see Frank's Civic in the distance.

Seven minutes later, she caught sight of Frank's maroon coat as he moved down their front walk; then his taillights came on.

She followed him to the end of their block,

turning left about twenty seconds after he did. She tried to maintain enough distance between them so that he wouldn't spot her if he looked in the rearview mirror. She felt a little silly, but her need to better understand Frank propelled her forward.

She followed him for nearly four miles as he headed into the city. Most of the rush-hour traffic was going the other way, for which Josie was grateful. She would have lost him otherwise.

When Frank finally pulled over and parked on a narrow street lined with buildings, it was dark enough that Josie felt confident he couldn't see her by the top of the road. She found an illegal spot—the sign warned that she'd be ticketed and possibly towed—but she couldn't drive around the block again or she'd miss seeing which structure Frank entered.

Josie shut off the minivan and stepped out. She could see Frank in the distance, striding briskly, and she quickened her step. A homeless man walking in front of her momentarily blocked her view, and she almost missed catching Frank turn into an entrance.

When Josie reached it, she stared at the two-story, nondescript building. Another homeless man passed her and walked through the door.

Josie walked closer to the entrance. There was a metal engraved sign attached to the brick facade. SALVATION ARMY, it read.

"Excuse me."

Josie turned and saw a man and woman standing behind her. She was blocking the doorway.

"I'm sorry," she said, stepping aside. "Is there anything else in this building, or . . . ?"

"You lost?" the man asked.

"No, no," she said. The man shrugged and he and the woman went inside.

Josie followed them. At the end of the hallway was a second door, a heavy-looking swinging one. Josie approached it and peered through the pane at the top. By then she'd heard the murmur of voices and clatter of silverware against plates. She'd smelled the aromas of meat and hot bread.

Dozens of people—mostly men, but a few women, too—sat at cafeteria-style tables lining the room. Toward the back of the room, serving the buffet-style meal from enormous containers, was a line of four volunteers. Frank was second from the left.

Josie was still awake around eleven when she heard footsteps, too soft and light to belong to anyone but one of the girls.

"Izzy?" she called.

But it was Zoe who appeared in her bedroom doorway. At first Josie thought she was sleep-walking.

Then Zoe said, "I want Daddy."

"Oh, sweetheart." Josie lifted up the side of the covers. "Come here."

Zoe climbed into bed and Josie wrapped her arms around her daughter. "Daddy loves you so much."

"Why isn't he here?" Zoe asked. Her voice sounded so small.

Heartbreak felt like no other kind of sadness. It was walking through a barren, winter-gray landscape. Her daughters were too young to experience such bleakness, Josie thought, wishing she could absorb it on their behalf.

"He'll be here tomorrow," Josie whispered. "We can call him as soon as we get up in the morning and check what time he'll be here."

"I shouldn't have told him to stop giving me platypus kisses."

"Zoe, this isn't your fault!" Josie hugged her daughter tighter. "Daddy and I were fighting and we needed a break. It has nothing to do with you or Izzy. You two are the best"—Josie's voice broke, but she fought her way back—"You are the best things in the world. You have to believe that. Daddy and I love you so much."

"I just miss him," Zoe whispered.

Josie thought about Frank scooping food out of a huge silver tin at the Salvation Army and smiling at the man standing before him as he carefully put it on the plate.

*I miss him, too,* Josie thought.

# Chapter Twenty-Six

Ever since Frank had moved out, he'd taken to ringing the doorbell when he came to the house. Josie appreciated that he was respecting their new boundaries, even though it still felt strange.

Usually the girls raced to meet him, but today they were down the street at their favorite teen-aged babysitter's house because her cat had had kittens. So Josie greeted Frank.

"Hey," she said. "I just walked the girls over to Alice's. Can you pick them up there and bring them back?"

"Would you mind if I went upstairs first?" Frank asked. "I need to get a few more things from the bedroom. Maybe it would be good if I did it when they weren't here."

"Sure," Josie said. She moved aside to let him pass over the threshold, then followed him upstairs.

"Do you need a bag to put stuff in?" she asked when he disappeared into their closet.

"Nah, I'm just getting my old basketball shoes and a pair of cuff links," he said when he emerged.

He looked around the room, his eyes landing on the dresser. "Our wedding picture," he said.

Josie shrugged. "I put it away."

Frank looked as if she'd stabbed him. "Why?"

"Why, Frank?"

A rushing wave of anger and pain nearly knocked her physically off-balance. "Do you think I can ever look at pictures of our wedding again?"

His eyes widened.

"I'm sorry, I'm sorry," he repeated, but it was too late.

She fell back onto the bed and curled up in a ball and began to cry as she hadn't since she was a child. She thought about how Frank had kissed her twice right after the minister pronounced them man and wife, drawing laughter from the onlookers, and how he'd stepped on her foot during their first dance. They'd spent lazy Saturdays leading up to the wedding wandering around Crate and Barrel to create a registry, choosing silverware and plates and a panini maker that they'd never actually used. They'd sampled cakes at two bakeries, swooning over layers of zesty lemon and Bavarian chocolate and coconut cream, while Frank had joked that they should pose as an engaged couple every weekend and go to tastings.

In the kitchen, high on a shelf so that it wouldn't get broken, they had a china platter decorated with Izzy's and Zoe's handprints. They had a yard with a bare patch in the middle of the grass because they'd left a plastic Little Tikes slide in that spot for too long. They had a growth chart along the doorjamb in the kitchen with Sharpies marking all of their heights, even Huck's.

Frank had dismantled it all.

"Josie—please—" Frank approached her with an outstretched hand, then withdrew, as if he were afraid to touch her. He sank onto the floor next to her and held his head between his palms.

"I want to hit you!" she cried.

"I wish you would," he said.

"I don't know how I can ever live with you again," she sobbed. "You hurt me, Frank. You hurt me so much."

"I know I did," he whispered.

He sat there until her sobs grew hoarse and quiet. "I did this to you," he finally said.

She was too drained to speak.

After a while, he stood up and reached for the comforter at the bottom of the bed. He unfolded it and placed it over Josie. "Your poor feet." His voice was uneven. "I have to cover them because they always get cold."

Josie could hear the front door opening, then Alice's high voice calling out, "Hello? Mrs. Moore?" She started to sit up, but Frank was already moving toward the hallway.

"Be right down," he called.

She turned over onto her other side as he left the room.

· · ·

She must have slept for a bit, because when she rolled back over, she caught sight of a plate on her nightstand. There were three Mint Milano cookies—her favorite—and a glass of water. She suddenly felt desperately thirsty. She gulped down the water without pause.

She got to her feet and nibbled on a cookie before she went into the bathroom. She'd thought her eyes would be red and puffy from crying, but they weren't. She splashed water on her face anyway, then changed out of her clothes and put on her softest old pajamas and went downstairs, bringing her plate with her.

Frank was seated at the dining room table with the girls, playing a game called "Pretty Pretty Princess." He was wearing a big blue plastic ring and a tiara, which had slid down the side of his unruly hair.

He and the girls all looked up at the sound of her footsteps. Frank's expression was worried, but her daughters were smiling.

"Mommy!" Izzy said. "Do you want to play?"

She could make an excuse and go back upstairs, to the comfort of her bed. Or she could do something that felt a little frightening. She could test out what it would feel like to sit across from Frank, to join the game.

She looked at the empty chair between her

330

girls, the one she always sat in during family dinners. They'd saved it for her.

She took a deep breath, and on the exhale, she said, "Okay."

# Chapter Twenty-Seven

Josie hadn't intended to walk this far when she'd set out on a stroll with Huck. But Frank and the girls were spending the morning at a children's museum in the city, and the empty Saturday hours seemed to stretch out endlessly in front of her. Frank had invited Josie to join them, but she'd wanted some space from him after the intense emotions of the other night.

She found herself passing by a playground she occasionally drove to with Zoe and Izzy. Though the early spring days were warming up, the air still held a chill. But a few parents were there, pushing children on swings and squatting at the bottoms of slides, clapping in encouragement.

Josie remembered days when she'd been so desperate to get two high-energy girls out of the house that she'd hit playgrounds before nine in the morning. She'd also known the schedule of every indoor recreation room's open house by heart.

But life had shifted. Yesterday Izzy had lifted the plastic jug of apple juice out of the refrigerator and poured herself a glass without spilling a drop. And Zoe already had secrets;

she'd told Josie that one of the cafeteria ladies was mean, but she'd refused to elaborate.

Josie folded her arms across the top pole of the chain-link fence, watching the children play. One little boy had on an alligator hat. He was about a year older than Izzy. Josie found her eyes trailing him as he tore around the playground, the mouth of his hat flapping open and shut as he ran.

He caught sight of Huck and raced over to the fence.

"Is he a German shepherd?" the boy asked.

"No, he's a golden retriever."

"I always confuse those ones." The boy gave himself a theatrical punch on the head. "Can I pet him?"

"Sure," Josie said.

The boy stuck his hand through one of the diamond-shaped openings in the fence and Huck sniffed it, then gave him a lick.

"Dogs love me!" the boy shouted happily, then he ran off.

The baby Josie had lost would be about his age now.

Early on, the miscarriage had consumed her. She couldn't stop hearing the terrible silence of her twelve-weeks doctor's appointment, the one in which she was expecting to listen to the baby's heartbeat.

Josie had blamed herself for the wine she'd drank before knowing she was pregnant, and for failing to take her vitamins every night, even though her doctor had assured her it was almost certainly due to a chromosomal defect. "You're over thirty-five, after all, and sometimes this is what naturally happens," the doctor had said, her hand patting Josie's shoulder. "I promise you, there is nothing you could have done to prevent this."

Josie still had the miniature pair of sneakers she'd purchased for that baby the day after her EPT test had shown a positive sign. They'd been an impulse purchase. She'd taken Zoe to buy a birthday present for one of her little friends and had seen a display of brightly colored shoes. Even though the new baby could wear all of Zoe's neutral-colored hand-me-downs, Josie had reached for a yellow pair. Every child should have something new, she'd thought.

The sneakers were up on a shelf in her closet, still nestled in their small white box. Josie didn't think she'd ever be able to give them up. On some days, though, her eyes were able to skim past the box without it causing a reaction in her.

Perhaps the same would be true of Frank's affair. Maybe, in time, they would be able to tuck it away on a shelf.

She couldn't compare her two private sorrows, though. She'd had Izzy after the miscarriage, her sweet reward following so much pain.

A father followed his daughter over to the swings by Josie and began to push her.

"Higher!" she shouted, tilting her head back, her long hair streaming out behind her.

Josie looked around for the little boy with the alligator hat, but he was gone. He must have left with his parents while she'd been lost in her memories.

"Come on, Huck," she said, giving his leash a gentle tug.

Frank was trying so hard, she thought. If he'd been trying only to win her back, Josie might not have felt herself softening toward him. But he also was trying to become a better man.

She wondered how it was possible that she'd shared a bedroom and a life with Frank and yet had barely known him in some ways. They had become the closest of strangers.

During their last counseling session with Mike, Josie had asked Frank a question.

She'd been angry because of something that had happened when Alexia, a friend of Izzy's, had come over to play after preschool. Alexia's mother had arrived to pick her up and had said, "What a nice house you have."

And Izzy had responded: "My daddy doesn't live here. He has an elevator apartment."

The smile had dropped from Alexia's mother's face. Her eyes had widened. "Oh," she'd said. "Oh, dear—I'm sorry!" Then she'd said too brightly, "Come on, Alexia, let's get on your shoes. Time to go!"

Josie understood that people didn't know how to respond when confronted with unexpected situations; that adults often fumbled for the right words. Perhaps the mother wished she could have a do-over.

But Izzy's little face in that moment . . . the way her eyebrows had tilted up in bewilderment and her soft, sweet mouth had fallen slightly open. She'd probably been expecting Alexia's mother to be excited about the elevator, to say something like, "Ooh, you lucky girl!"

Josie had wanted to absorb every bit of Izzy's confusion and hurt. It killed her that she couldn't.

"Do you really think our marriage could ever be the same?" she'd almost shouted at Frank soon after their session had started.

She'd expected Frank to respond that he'd continue to prove his trustworthiness, that they'd eventually get back to where they were before the affair. She'd thought he'd reiterate that he loved her and the girls and would never hurt them again.

That's why Frank's response had been such a surprise.

"What if we could make it better?" he'd asked.

# Chapter Twenty-Eight

Josie was answering emails when Frank called. Her business was picking back up again, and she'd just sold a hundred wooden toys to an international school downtown that was adding a new music program. She was grateful for her work beyond the extra money it brought in; it also helped to divert her focus.

"I want to invite you to something," Frank began.

Josie felt her brow crease.

"There's a happy hour Friday night," Frank continued. "A big group email went around."

"Frank, I don't—" Josie began.

"It's not like that," he interrupted. "I want you to come because Melissa will be there. I want you to see that there isn't anything between us. That there was never anything between us."

When she'd called Frank after her last session with Sonya, she'd told him she needed to know the truth about Melissa. He'd again begun to deny anything had happened. She'd cut him off.

"I need proof," she'd said. "Please get it for me."

Now she was silent as she considered his proposition. Would he be suggesting this if he and Melissa had been intimate? It seemed unlikely.

"I could come home and pick you up first," Frank said. "That way we could walk in together. We'd stay as long as you wanted."

She could try to read Frank's body language, and Melissa's. Wouldn't one of them exhibit a tell if something had happened?

"Okay," Josie said.

She felt her stomach twist at the thought of coming face-to-face again with the woman she'd wondered about so often.

What she needed, Josie decided, was a killer outfit. There was no way she was going to show up for the happy hour in her usual jeans and a sweater, or even her go-to pink-and-orange patterned dress that could get her through everything from a christening to a wedding.

The next morning, right after she dropped the girls at school, she headed to a boutique she'd passed a hundred times but had never entered. The window displays were geared toward customers with very different lifestyles than Josie's—women who strode about confidently in heels and wore cream-colored slacks without worrying about getting grape jelly smudges on them.

A little bell over the door sounded when Josie entered the hushed, beautifully organized space. Acoustic Billy Joel played over the speakers, and a chunky scented candle—Josie picked up notes of lavender—burned within a glass container.

Josie touched a fringed poncho, admiring how soft the wool felt beneath her fingers, then picked up an embossed leather belt.

A smiling saleswoman approached her unhurriedly. "Good morning. Looking for something special?"

*Oh, just something to intimidate my estranged husband's possible mistress,* Josie thought.

"Yes, but nothing too fancy," she said. "I'm going out downtown for a happy hour."

She found herself checking out the saleswoman's ring finger. She'd been doing that more and more lately—trying to figure out which category people fell into. This saleswoman wore a wedding ring.

"I'm Nina, by the way. Were you interested in seeing our dresses?"

"Sure," Josie said.

"We've got some great ones over here." The saleswoman started to lead the way, but Josie stopped after just a few steps.

In front of her was a mannequin clad in slim-cut black leather pants, paired with an off-the-shoulder black sweater. A trio of hammered silver bangles adorned the mannequin's wrist. The outfit looked like something a chic, confident woman would slip into for a night out on the town.

Josie looked at the price tag on the pants. They were expensive, but not outrageously so.

"We just got that in," Nina said. "Want to give it a whirl?"

"I'd love to," Josie said. She knew before she even entered the dressing room that she'd buy the entire outfit.

Frank was waiting for her outside the restaurant, his shoulders hunched, stamping his feet against the pavement. Josie could see his breath in the cold air as she approached.

"You look gorgeous," Frank said. "Wow."

"Thanks." She'd put more effort into her appearance tonight than she had for her senior prom. She was wearing a long, camel-colored dress coat she'd borrowed from Amanda, and she'd splurged on a blowout. It all felt like a form of armor.

"Does she know I'm coming?" Josie asked.

Frank knew better than to ask who she meant. "Yeah, I replied to everyone on the email chain that I was bringing my wife."

"Did you write those words—'my wife'?"

"I did, is that okay?" Frank's brow furrowed.

Josie nodded. Melissa needed to have that message reinforced. The fact that Josie and Frank were now separated was immaterial. No single woman who sent a text to a married man early in the morning suggesting they get together again soon had completely guileless motives.

Josie remembered her therapist's directive to be clear about her needs. "I do not want you to talk to Melissa unless I'm involved in the conversation. And when I tell you it's time to leave, please don't draw out your good-byes forever."

"Anything you say," Frank said.

"And I don't want you to act like we're separated," Josie said. "I want her to think . . ." She couldn't articulate what she meant, and the wind was messing up her hair. "Forget it. Let's just go in."

Josie saw her immediately. She'd feared that Melissa was more attractive than she'd remembered, but Melissa looked exactly the same. She wore a plain dark suit and a white blouse, and she was sitting at the end of a high, rectangular table in the bar area, along with a few people Josie recognized and a few she didn't.

Josie hadn't instructed Frank on where to sit. She didn't want him to lead her over to Melissa's end of the table. She should have thought of that.

"Hey, everyone," Frank said.

Melissa looked up and caught Josie's eye.

Josie's heart exploded in her chest.

When she'd anticipated this moment, she'd imagined being cool and reserved while she observed the nuances of Melissa's expressions. She thought she'd be able to remain in the role of investigator. But she was the one who pulled her gaze away from Melissa's.

Her breathing grew quick and shallow, as if she were the guilty party. She felt light-headed.

"There's an empty stool here," an older woman to Frank's left said. At least it was a few down from Melissa, Josie thought as she lowered herself onto it. Frank stood on her other side, the one that was closer to Melissa.

"You look great, Josie!" The older woman's name was Lisa; Josie had met her a half dozen times before. She worked with Frank and had been at the cocktail party they'd all attended at Melissa's apartment a few years back, before that early-morning text.

"Did you do something different with your hair?" Lisa was asking.

"Oh, it's a little longer, I guess," Josie said. She tried to sneak a glance at Melissa. Was Melissa looking at Frank?

She could hear someone on Frank's other side ask him a question, bringing Frank into an existing conversation. Josie wanted to turn to Frank, to be included in that group, so they could present a united front. But Lisa kept pulling her the opposite way.

"So, any plans for spring break?" Lisa asked.

"I—ah—we don't have any yet."

A waiter approached and Josie felt a surge of relief. Now there would be a natural break and they could regroup.

"Josie? Chardonnay?" Frank asked.

She nodded. He gave the order to the waiter. "I'll have a Sam Adams. Anyone else?"

"I'll have a Sam Adams, too," Melissa said from the other end of the table, waving.

Josie felt her body grow icy.

"So, we were talking about spring break," Lisa said. "Did I tell you my grandkids are clamoring for a Disney cruise and my son invited me to come with them? I don't know, it's so expensive . . . but on the other hand, it would be nice to see some shows."

Josie could hear snatches of the conversation Frank was involved in—"Worst conference ever"; "Seriously, even the food sucked"—in between Lisa's words.

Coming here had been a terrible idea. There were too many different forces yanking at her; she couldn't concentrate on anything. The waiter hadn't even returned with their drinks, but she already wanted to leave.

If she tugged on Frank's arm and told him so, everyone would be curious about why. She was trapped. Her expensive outfit, her styled hair—none of it mattered. Tears gathered in her eyes. She felt completely vulnerable and exposed.

Then she felt Frank's arm slide across her back.

"You okay?" he whispered in her ear.

She blinked, hard, and looked up at him. Then she reached to hold on to his hand as it draped across her shoulders. His hand felt warm, as it always did.

"So, the guys are talking about this conference they went to last year," Frank said. "It's in Arizona."

Josie cast an apologetic smile at Lisa, then turned back to Frank.

"Arizona would be nice in the winter," she said. Her voice rose and fell like a wave through her words.

Frank's arm rested heavily around her, but not in an unpleasant way. It felt as if it was anchoring her.

"How's your wine, beautiful?" Frank asked. He didn't lower his voice; he intended for everyone to hear.

She should be watching for Melissa's reaction, Josie knew.

But she wanted to keep looking up at Frank instead.

Frank kept his arm around Josie the entire time, even while they said their good-byes. Lisa made a joke about it, telling them they were acting like newlyweds. When they left, Melissa gave them a smile and another wave, then turned to chat with the person next to her. She didn't seem to be behaving strangely.

"Are you okay?" Frank asked as they walked to Josie's van.

She exhaled. "Yeah, that was . . ." She'd been about to say "good," which wasn't what she meant. She let her sentence trail off.

"I took a cab here from my office," Frank said. "I thought that way if you had a few drinks I could drive you home."

He'd taken his arm off her shoulders after they'd left the restaurant, but she could still feel its weight there.

Josie checked the time on her iPhone. It was early. The sitter wouldn't even have put the girls to bed.

She looked up at Frank again.

"Would you drive me home in my car?" Josie asked. "We could make hot chocolate with the girls. Then we can all drive you back tomorrow to get your car . . . I mean, if you want to spend the night on the couch."

Gratitude filled Frank's eyes.

She passed him the keys and he walked around to the driver's side and started the engine.

They were both quiet on the way home, but the silence between them felt different than it had since Josie's discovery. It felt like peace.

"Will he do it again?" Josie asked Sonya the following week.

"Probably not," Sonya said.

"How can you know that?"

"Because you'll recognize the signs. When you

345

and Frank start to feel distant from each other—when you begin to go upstairs to escape him, and when he starts to become addicted to his phone—then you'll remember that your marriage is in a dangerous place. And you can both take steps to correct it, to reconnect."

"It's hard," Josie said. "Why is it so hard to talk to my husband sometimes?"

Sonya leaned back in her chair. "Think of all the habits we replicate in life, sometimes despite our best intentions. You weren't encouraged to express negative emotions as a child. When you were upset, you were given the instructions that you should stay small."

"But I yell," Josie protested. "When I'm really mad at Frank."

"Sure," Sonya said. "But that isn't true communication. It's only releasing steam."

"I like the idea that we can blame this all on my parents." Josie had intended for it to be a joke, but her eyes filled with tears.

"You can do this, Josie," Sonya said gently. "You can talk through difficult things with Frank instead of retreating, even though it feels scary. You can tell him exactly how you feel and you don't have to worry that he'll stop loving you. Just look at how much better the two of you have gotten at it already."

Josie nodded and reached for a tissue.

"Frank asked if I'd go out on a date with him,"

she said. "He said it could just be coffee, even."

"Would you like to?"

Josie thought back to the list of requirements she had created when Sonya had asked her to imagine reconciliation. "I think I can let the Melissa thing go now," she said, instead of answering Sonya's question directly. "I doubt they could have slept together and acted the way they did in front of me. They'd practically have to be sociopaths to do that. I bet she had a crush on him, and he liked the attention, but I doubt it went much further than that."

"That's good," Sonya said.

"How would we do it?" Josie asked. "I mean, would I invite him to come back into the house? Or should we take it more slowly?"

"You can do it any way you want." Sonya smiled. "You get to make the rules now."

# Chapter Twenty-Nine

"Don't forget to have Izzy pee before bed," Frank told his mom.

"I raised three boys," Susie said. "You think I'd ever forget?"

Josie bent down to kiss Zoe, then Izzy. "We'll see you on Sunday. Be good for Grandma and Grandpa."

"Don't worry, the girls will take care of us," Doc said, causing Izzy to erupt in one of her delicious belly laughs.

At Josie's suggestion, Frank had called his parents and asked whether they'd stay at the house during the weekend of Doc's conference. He'd explained that he and Josie had been going through a rough patch and could use some time away alone.

"My mom is going to show up with a casserole," Frank predicted when he got off the phone. She hadn't, but she'd brought a homemade sheet cake covered in tinfoil. Frank had waggled his eyebrows at Josie when Susie had held it out, and Josie had needed to wrestle back a smile.

It seemed incredible that Frank could make her smile again.

Frank picked up Josie's bag in one hand and his in the other. "Ready, Jos?"

She nodded and followed him out to his car. "Can you pop the trunk?" he asked.

Josie looked around for the right lever. It took her a minute to locate it in the unfamiliar vehicle.

Frank had traded in his Honda Civic for a used Acura at CarMax a few weeks earlier.

He climbed in and looked over at Josie before he started the ignition. "Do you want to drive straight there, or should we get dinner first?"

"Let's have dinner at the hotel," Josie said. They were only driving into the city. It wouldn't take long.

Frank nodded and started the car. But he didn't pull away from the curb. Instead he looked at Josie again.

"I'm nervous," he said.

"Me too."

"Like, more nervous than I was on our first date."

"You were nervous?" Josie asked. "You didn't act like it."

"No, I was. I figured if I kept you laughing you'd like me more. But then I picked that awful movie—"

"It wasn't awful," Josie interrupted.

"And I drank so much Coke that I felt hyper. I kept having to use the bathroom."

"I don't even remember that," Josie said.

"What do you remember?"

This was something they were working on in couples therapy: they were striving to ask each other honest questions, to relearn each other.

"I remember you giving me your gloves when we walked to get a drink after the movie because I'd forgotten mine," she said.

She also remembered a thought she'd had during the movie. But she wasn't ready to tell Frank what it was yet.

They had agreed they would not have sex. Since Frank had moved back into the house the previous week, they'd shared a bed, but they hadn't gone beyond cuddling.

After dinner, Josie changed into her pajamas in the bathroom, feeling a little shy. She and Frank hadn't seen each other undressed in months.

When she came back into the bedroom, Frank was standing by the foot of the bed, holding something in his hand.

She approached and saw what it was: a velvet jewelry box.

"I know you took off your wedding ring," Frank said. His voice was trembling. "And I didn't want you to put that one back on. I wanted us to have new rings. I want us to have a new marriage."

He opened the box to reveal two simple rose-gold bands, one thicker than the other, nestled together in a single slot.

"Is it okay?" Frank asked.

By way of an answer, she reached for his and slid it onto his finger. Then she lifted her hand so that he could mirror the gesture.

She had been so afraid to sleep with her husband again. She'd thought it would take months, that they would redevelop the physical side of their relationship gradually. But when Frank climbed under the covers with her and held her in his arms, what she feared most—that Dana would intrude—never happened. Josie and Frank were utterly alone in the room. He kept looking into her eyes as his hand stroked her hair. It felt to Josie like perhaps the most intimate moment they'd ever shared.

She was the one who leaned in for the first kiss. She was the one who reached for his T-shirt and tugged it off, then guided his hand to her top button. His body and touch felt both familiar and unfamiliar to her.

Afterward, she lay with her head on his chest, his arms encircling her, his steady heartbeat lulling her to sleep.

# Chapter Thirty

*Seventeen years earlier*

On the morning after they met at the party, Frank called Josie at eight o'clock.

The sharp peal of the phone didn't awaken her, even though she hadn't gone to sleep until two in the morning. She'd been lying there, remembering the handstands and milkshakes and Frank's warm lips.

"Is it too early to call?" She'd laughed, because Frank was whispering. "I just wondered if you'd like to go to a movie tonight."

He picked her up at seven. He wore jeans and a dark blue jacket. His hair was a little messy, as if he'd run a hand through it. She'd spent the day cleaning her apartment, doing laundry, and running errands, propelled by a gust of energy that she knew stemmed from her excitement over the night's possibilities.

"Wow," Frank said when he walked into the tiny living area of her one-bedroom. "It even smells good in here."

She'd laughed again and offered him a beer, but they decided to get a drink after the movie instead, because it was starting soon. He'd waited while she locked up, then they'd walked out together into the night. By the time they reached the theater, they were holding hands.

The movie they saw was *Hope Floats*. The film had been out for a few years, but neither of them had caught it the first time around. It was playing at the same theater where Josie would see *La La Land* years later, the one that revived popular movies a few years after their release.

Josie adored Sandra Bullock and had loved nearly every film she'd starred in. Frank bought them a huge tub of popcorn and what he called a "bucket o' Coke" with two straws. The theater wasn't crowded, and they found two seats right in the middle.

The movie opened with Sandra's character going on a talk show, thinking she was about to get a makeover. Instead, she was ambushed by the news that her husband had been having an affair with her best friend.

The snarky talk show host was telling a stunned-looking Sandra that her best friend didn't want to hurt her. "So much for a light comedy," Frank whispered.

Then the camera cut to the young actress who played Sandra's daughter, sitting in the front row of the audience, sobbing behind her thick glasses as she learned her family was imploding.

Frank exhaled loudly.

"How could they do that to her?" he muttered.

"To Sandra?" Josie whispered.

"No," Frank said. "To the kid. Why isn't any-one comforting her?"

And Josie had thought, *I want this guy to be the father of my children.*

# Chapter Thirty-One

*Six months later*

"Don't start dreaming up projects or we'll never get out of here," Josie warned.

"See you in two hours," Frank cracked as he got out of the minivan.

"One extension cord!" Josie called after him. "That's all you're authorized to buy."

She looked in the backseat. Izzy was asleep, her head lolling to the side. Zoe was engrossed in a book.

Then she turned back to watch Frank disappear into the store, a dark-haired guy in a T-shirt and khaki shorts, looking younger than his forty-one years. Indistinguishable from the other fathers and husbands streaming into the Home Depot.

Frank had left the car running because it was so warm outside that they needed the air-conditioning. The radio played softly.

The song "Before He Cheats" by Carrie Underwood came on. Josie instinctively reached to turn the knob to another station.

Reminders were everywhere, still. Frank said they existed for him, too. Some Josie was able to move through. She'd gone into Starbucks for coffee several times in the past month. Others were proving more difficult to navigate.

Frank left his iPhone on the dresser every night now. He never took it into the bathroom, either. Josie checked it whenever she felt the urge; that was part of their new agreement.

Maybe the reminders weren't such a bad thing, Josie thought. They were like the scar she had on her knee from when she'd been a child and had been running too fast, not looking where she was going.

She thought about what had happened that morning, when the girls had piled into their bed. "Family hug!" Frank had said, reaching around to grab Josie, smushing the girls in between them.

She thought about what had happened last night, when Frank's iPhone had buzzed as they'd sat on the couch watching *Modern Family*. Josie had physically jolted. Frank had picked up his phone off the end table and held it out quickly. "It's from my brother. Stu." She'd nodded, but a few seconds later she'd eased out from beneath Frank's arm and had gotten up to refill her mug of tea. She'd needed a moment away from Frank.

"Do you think you'll stay with him?" Karin had asked when they'd gone for a walk a few days earlier.

"Yes," Josie had answered. "As long as . . ."

"As long as he doesn't cheat again?" Karin had filled in when Josie didn't continue.

Josie had nodded, but that wasn't what she had meant. It wasn't that simple. *As long as things stay different,* she'd thought. *As long as we keep on truly knowing each other.*

It was astonishing, how you could become entwined with someone, sharing a bedroom and a life, without truly being intimate.

"I'm bored," Zoe complained. "Where's Daddy?"

"Look." Josie pointed.

Frank was holding up the white looped extension cord, pumping his arm like he was a prizefighter raising a trophy. He was grinning.

"He's coming," Josie said. She found herself smiling back at Frank. "See? He's coming back to us."

# Acknowledgments

Most authors send manuscripts to early readers for critiques before turning the books into their editors. This has traditionally been my practice, too. But *The Ever After* had only one reader from its inception to the final manuscript: Sarah Cantin. Although Sarah has been involved with my books since my debut, this is the first one she has edited. Her strength and sensitivity—both personally and professionally—didn't just improve this novel, they made it possible.

As always, I'm deeply grateful to my wonderful agent, Victoria Sanders, and her team—Bernadette Baker-Baughman and Jessica Spivey.

At Atria Books, I'm thankful for the tireless work of my smart, funny publicist Ariele Fredman, as well as to the lovely Judith Curr, Suzanne Donahue, Lisa Sciambra, Chelsea Cohen, Ann Pryor, Jackie Jou, Albert Tang, Yona Deshommes, and Paul Olsewski. And a special shout-out to Haley Weaver.

My thanks to my wonderfully supportive and loving family: Nana and Johnny; Robert, Saadia, and Sophia; and Ben, Tammi, and Billy.

To my three boys—Jackson, Will, and Dylan—thank you for putting up with a mom who mutters to herself when she writes and occasionally veers abruptly to the side of the road to scribble something in the notebook she keeps tucked in the car's console. You three are my heart.

There's one final person who should be acknowledged here, but I don't know her name. We've never met. Her story was the inspiration for this book.

It began with an overheard conversation in a coffee shop.

Two women, seated at the booth behind mine, were loudly discussing the plight of an acquaintance who had received a text from her husband—a text intended for another woman.

The story that unfurled over the next few minutes was transfixing: There were code names involved, to shield the participants in the affair. Hidden restaurant receipts. Fake business trips. The extent of the seemingly loving husband's subterfuge was stunning. But the most shocking piece—at least to me—was that the wronged wife didn't collapse into grief, or throw her husband's belongings out a window.

Instead, she transformed into a detective.

She became determined to piece together every last detail of the affair, to decipher the extent of her husband's deception.

This book began to bloom in my mind immediately.

In the past, a husband or wife who had reason to suspect infidelity might seek out a private investigator. Today, the same technology that allows cheating spouses to conduct an affair in the shadows—burner phones, social media passwords, dating apps—can be utilized as tools to uncover evidence of the same.

Statistics indicate that an affair occurs in one of every three marriages—and the real number may be higher. In *The Ever After*, after hearing how often infidelity is an issue for her physician's patients, my main character, Josie, thinks to herself, "It really was an epidemic." The line is fictional, but the facts informing it are not.

Writing this book felt markedly different than my previous novels. Perhaps it's because, as a former investigative journalist, I was able to exercise specific narrative muscles I'd long ago retired. It could also be because I—like you—know many people who have suffered the consequences of an affair. Often, they involve the last people you'd suspect. The story behind the unraveling of my characters' marriage is both universal and unique. As are their emotions.

I hope that Josie's story will provide an inside glimpse of this largely secret epidemic and its aftershocks. As for me, I still think about the anonymous woman whose entire world shattered as she glanced down at her phone to read an incoming text from her husband. Maybe they underwent therapy and recommitted to their marriage. Maybe she left. But I hope that whatever fork in the road she chose, it was one that will lead her, eventually, toward a second chance at a happily ever after.

# Topics and Questions for Discussion

1. Josie quickly taps into latent detective abilities in order to discover the full extent of her husband's deception. If you realized a romantic partner had lied to you, would you also try to find out everything that had happened? How difficult do you think it would be to track down all the information you'd want?

2. When Karin confesses her own infidelity to Josie, she says, "It became an affair the moment I answered his text. The moment we created a secret" (p. 147). Do you agree? If so, would you feel differently if it had never escalated to physical contact? What do you think constitutes an affair?

3. How did your opinion of Frank change over the course of the book? Were you able to sympathize with him?

4. When confronted about his emails with Dana, Frank initially says it was "just flirting," which he amends to "only kissing" (pp. 17–18) when pressed on the issue. How important do you feel the specific physical acts that transpired are, as opposed to the betrayal of trust and acts of deception? Why

does Frank think it will be less upsetting if he minimizes how far he went with Dana? Do you think it would be more or less hurtful to Josie if Frank had slept with Dana, but only seen her on one occasion?

5. In the wake of Frank's affair, Josie's instinct is to "make him feel the same sort of agony" (p. 79) that she is experiencing. At times, she expresses the desire to physically hurt him, or to have her own affair simply to even the score. Given the circumstances, was she justified in wanting revenge? In what situations is it okay to wish someone else pain, or to make petty choices?

6. In chapter twenty-one, Josie recalls the memory of when she first realized her parents hid things from her and lied. In the same moment, she experiences a shift in her own relationship to honest communication, recalling how "she'd joined in their game of pretend. She had become a faker, too" (p. 280). What is the significance of this memory for Josie, and how does it relate to her present-day life?

7. Josie asserts that she may be able to reconcile with Frank, on the condition that she could "make sure that this was the only time" (p. 313) he had an affair. At the end of the book, do you feel confident that Frank's affair with Dana was his first and only time cheating on Josie? Why or why not?

8. Amanda theorizes that Frank may have—subconsciously—gotten caught on purpose. Do you believe this was the case? If so, do you think it was because he wanted to confess but didn't know how, as Amanda reasons, or did he have another motivation for sabotaging himself?

9. Josie insists that she doesn't want to fall back into her marriage because "she didn't know how to be without Frank, or out of guilt because of the children" (p. 257). Nevertheless, throughout the novel it is evident that their daughters, Zoe and Izzy, are one of Josie's primary considerations in choosing whether to give Frank a second chance. Do you think staying in a marriage just to protect the children is ever a good idea? Why or why not?

10. Josie is ultimately convinced that Frank never had feelings for Dana. If he *had* cared for Dana, would that change how you understand what he did? If so, in what ways?

11. Through therapy, Frank and Josie both uncover the impact their childhoods and relationships with their families had on their own attitudes and communication styles. Do you think their separation will have a lasting impact on Izzy and Zoe, and if so, what will that impact be?

# Enhance Your Book Club

1. Although Dana is a key character in *The Ever After*, we see only the briefest glimpse of her and her husband, Ron, and never in person. Yet they are dealing with parallel circumstances to Josie and Frank. Write a scene from the perspective of Dana or Ron. In what ways might their experience be distinct from what we saw Josie go through? Has Dana cheated before? Has Ron? What does their marriage look like? Does Ron truly believe the version of events that Dana tells him? How does Dana feel about her affair with Frank? Consider these or any other questions about their side of the story as you write, and share your piece with your reading group.

2. As a result of the variety of definitions of infidelity, it can be challenging for researchers to study or get a sense of how pervasive it is. Nevertheless, it remains a subject many psychologists and sociologists are compelled to learn more about. Take a look online at some articles on the subject from recent years, such as www.business insider.com/science-of-cheating-2017-8. Did

any findings surprise you? Discuss with your group.

3. Consider reading one of Sarah Pekkanen's other novels, such as *The Perfect Neighbors*, *Things You Won't Say*, *Skipping a Beat*, or her cowritten novel, *The Wife Between Us*, for your group's next meeting. You can also connect with Sarah Pekkanen on Facebook and Twitter, and learn more about Sarah's books or invite her to Skype your book club by visiting www.sarahpekkanen.com.

**Center Point Large Print**
600 Brooks Road / PO Box 1
Thorndike, ME 04986-0001 USA

**(207) 568-3717**

**US & Canada:**
**1 800 929-9108**
www.centerpointlargeprint.com